LIKE JAZZ

LIKE JAZZ

by
Heather Blackmore

2013

LIKE JAZZ
© 2013 By Heather Blackmore. All Rights Reserved.

ISBN 13: 978-1-62639-029-4

This Trade Paperback Original Is Published By
Bold Strokes Books, Inc.
P.O. Box 249
Valley Falls, NY 12185

First Edition: December 2013

Credits
Editor: Shelley Thrasher
Production Design: Susan Ramundo
Cover Design By Sheri (graphicartist2020@hotmail.com)

Acknowledgments

Thank you to Len Barot and everyone at Bold Strokes Books for including me in your clan of staff, associates, and writers. It's thrilling and humbling to be counted among you.

I'm indebted to my brilliant editor, Shelley Thrasher, whose suggestions greatly enhanced this novel. Shelley, thank you for your superb guidance and patience. If you didn't need a vacation before, I'm sure by now you need two.

Shelly Lampe and Kathy Chetkovich: I'm grateful for your constructive critiques of early drafts of this work and your encouragement along the way.

I'm pleased to publish this novel in the year the U.S. Supreme Court handed down two landmark rulings for LGBT civil rights. Although there's a long way to go toward equal rights in the U.S. and abroad, I'm elated by these historic victories and thankful to those who've fought and continue to fight for equality.

To the readers of this genre: without your enthusiasm, reviews, feedback, and interest, there would be fewer authors and subcategories. Thank you for your passion and support of the writers in this arena.

Dedication

For my wife, Shelly Lampe

Sometimes I can't believe you said "yes" all those years ago, but I'm so glad you did.

PROLOGUE

Detective Warner. Please come in and close the door."
Commander James Ashby motioned to the chair opposite him in front of his desk. A mountain of a man, he didn't stand as I entered his office, but having met with him a few times previously, I guessed he was at least six-three, 270 pounds, with a sixty-inch barrel of a chest. I sat.

Though it was highly unusual for such a senior officer to dole out cases, I was ready for whatever assignment Ashby was about to throw at me. Twenty-eight, single, and career-focused, I was at the top of my game. No distractions.

I was an expert at uncovering fraud and embezzlement, having developed techniques for detecting financial irregularities during my stint as an SEC examiner. As such, I'd returned to L.A. to participate in a two-year pilot civilian-investigation program of the LAPD, which partnered civilian investigators experienced in white-collar crime with the resources of the nation's third-largest local law-enforcement agency. If it was successful, the department would establish a new unit within the Commercial Crimes Division's fraud section, with me as the frontrunner to lead it. The pilot had already proved effective after only a year, so my promotion was practically assured.

Ashby's bearded face didn't change from the stony expression he'd assumed when I entered. "Status?" he asked in his deep bass voice, referring to my current case.

The owners of a locally headquartered company believed an employee was embezzling, and they didn't want to tip off the perpetrator by calling for an audit. Undercover as a financial analyst, I quickly discovered that the CFO had authorized hundreds of cashier's checks and numerous wire transfers from the company's bank accounts, covering over seven million dollars in personal purchases on her American Express card and making for some serious retail therapy.

Once I uncovered the wire-fraud element, we had to involve the FBI, but by then my investigation was nearly complete. "Special Agent Gutierrez and his team are nearly up to speed and we've already drafted his criminal complaint. I'll be able to roll off by the end of the week," I said, pleased by the ease with which Gutierrez and I had communicated and divvied to win this case.

Ashby nodded, the long sleeves of his blue oxford seeming poised to rip apart, his expression as tight as the material covering his massive biceps. "Good. You'll report to me on a special assignment, investigating the possible embezzlement of funds at a charitable foundation. You'll start Monday, posing as an accountant."

Thankfully, my excitement at the prospect of working directly for the commander stifled the yawn the occupation evoked. Covert work wasn't nearly as glamorous as the movies portrayed it.

"By the end of today," Ashby continued, "you'll receive your résumé by e-mail and will memorize your background and references, which will be unassailable. You'll be provided with the address and name of the person you'll be reporting to. This is my cell number and e-mail address, if you run into any problems." He handed me a business card that looked like a postage stamp in his mammoth fingers. "I've selected you for this assignment because I need someone with your computer skills and finance background. Any questions, Detective?"

The assignment sounded like all the other assignments I'd been given since starting here. Why was the commander involved?

"Yes?" His voice boomed with obvious impatience at my silence.

"Sorry, sir. I was wondering what's special about the assignment and why I'll be reporting to you."

"Because you're reporting to me, the assignment is special," he said irritably. Personable guy.

"Yes, sir. Right, sir." It had been a year, but I still wasn't very adept at the ins and outs of the politics involved up and down the chain of command and all the yes-sirring it required. He continued to survey me as I waited for him to elucidate. He did.

"A personal friend of mine brought this case to my attention, and there may be PR implications to the foundation if this investigation bears fruit. You will exercise the utmost discretion." Again, this was nothing unusual. The job required confidentiality.

Evidently noticing I was still dissatisfied with his explanation, Ashby finally threw me a bone. He seemed to choose his words carefully. "In addition, due to certain…circumstances, my friend is no longer…involved in the matter, and I owe it to him personally to leave no stone unturned. I need my best investigator on this assignment. Is there anything else, Detective?" It was obvious Ashby wasn't used to giving compliments any more than he was accustomed to providing explanations. He wanted to wrap things up.

"No, Commander." I was extraordinarily pleased to have gained his trust and felt honored he thought so highly of my skills.

"Good day, Detective." Ashby picked up a pen and bent his head down to study some papers on his desk. I rose from my chair and departed without bothering to hide my satisfied grin.

I let the words "best investigator" swirl through me, the shot of confidence warming me like a fine scotch. If anyone was stealing from the foundation, I'd expose them and put them behind bars. I'd make Ashby proud. The promotion I'd been working toward would be mine.

I would move on from the bittersweet memories of an L.A. long past.

Without a doubt, no one could prevent me from giving this assignment my undivided attention.

Chapter One

Ten Years Earlier

Finally: sixth period. It was the last class of my first day at my latest school—the second week for the rest of the students—and I couldn't wait for it to be over. Due to my father's frequent military-related relocations, Claiborne High was my fifth high school already, and I was just starting my senior year.

My father was a colonel in the US Army, the rank below brigadier general. Combining a keen intellect with a strong sense of responsibility to the youth our country sent into conflict, he worked within the US Army Training and Doctrine Command to revolutionize joint-services training. As TRADOC's deputy chief of the Interservice Training Office, my father believed that not only did combining military training and education make sound fiscal sense, interservice training saved lives by making sure troops, regardless of their service branch, all spoke the same language and had the same skills so they could work together.

As part of such a transformative team, my father sought to be as agile, creative, and adaptive as the soldiers, airmen, and others he helped train. Meaning that unlike most trainers, my father didn't get assigned to new bases—he volunteered to go wherever and whenever he was needed. His insistence on being as flexible as what he required from his servicemen meant many moves for my mother and me since my parents hated to be separated. The combination of my father reaching the pinnacle of his career, the ever-evolving nature of the threats to our nation, and the proliferation of peacekeeping missions meant that the frequency of our moves increased.

I was able to stay at the same Arizona high school my entire freshman year, including the following summer. As a sophomore in Georgia, I made it through three quarters before we moved. I completed my last quarter of that year and the first quarter of my junior year in Alabama, and spent the remainder of my junior year and following summer in New York. This latest transfer brought us to L.A., where my father continued his work on a joint training collaboration between the army and air force. My new high school was on a semester schedule.

Mr. Wilcox waited until the bell sounded to address the class, providing a brief history of the life of Charles Dickens. As a chorus of groans met his inquiry regarding how many of us had finished the assigned reading, the classroom door opened. A tall, tanned, long-legged girl with high cheekbones, perfectly straight white teeth, pin-cushion lips, and long, wavy auburn hair entered, stopping inside the doorway and smiling brilliantly toward Wilcox. The moment I saw this girl, my stomach did a little cartwheel, leading me to wonder whether I was getting sick.

Interrupted mid-sentence, Wilcox turned to the late arrival. "How nice of you to finally join us, Miss Perkins. I hope the upcoming student assembly will delight us all enough to justify your tardiness resulting from the planning meetings. Perhaps you can further delight your classmates by telling them the main theme of this weekend's reading?"

It kind of weirded me out how Wilcox called his students by their last names. Did the pseudo formalities make him feel superior, or was it his way of getting us used to the idea that we were fast becoming adults?

As if prepared for that exact question, Miss Perkins's smile brightened. She surveyed the classroom before delivering her response. Her smile evaporated as her eyes, having pleasurably roamed the rows of seated students, finally settled on me. Her expression changed from confident showmanship to open curiosity.

"I'd be happy to, Mr. Wilcox, but I wouldn't want our new classmate to feel left out, as she may have missed the assignment. Did I miss introductions?"

Mr. Wilcox followed her gaze to me. "Not at all, Miss Perkins, not at all. I was getting to that. Class, please give a warm welcome to Miss Cassidy Warner, our latest transplant from the East Coast. Miss Warner, welcome to Claiborne High."

My fellow students turned toward the back corner where I sat, and after what seemed to be a prolonged stretch of silence interrupted only by the sound of creaking furniture, Miss Perkins clapped her hands together and raised her voice. "Welcome, Cassidy!" Within moments, the rest of the class was clapping and wooting, giving me their best welcome. I smiled weakly, mortified.

The quieter and larger the classroom, the happier and more inconspicuous I am. This loud, pep-assembly type greeting was the worst welcome imaginable, the best being my unnoticed presence until, say, week six, when some significant assignment or project would undoubtedly be due, requiring my participation. Like a week-old helium balloon, I sagged into the hard wooden chair beneath the small desk, raised my eyes to the clock above the door, and prayed for the final bell of the day to toll prematurely. My eyes drifted lower and landed squarely on Miss Perkins. She was the Bermuda Triangle, drawing me to her with mysterious force.

Mr. Wilcox attempted to extend my misery by shifting his attention from Miss Perkins to me. "Thank you for your help in welcoming Miss Warner. Miss Warner, I believe we were able to provide you with an advance copy of the syllabus, were we not?"

I nodded, swallowing with difficulty and wresting my eyes away from the girl.

"Excellent. Were you able to complete any of the reading required for today?"

I nodded again and looked back to Miss Perkins. My mouth turned into the Sahara, devoid of all moisture. Maybe I should visit the school nurse.

"Splendid. Splendid. Would you care to give us your view of the main theme of *Great Expectations*, then?"

"Excuse me?" I asked. "Me?"

"Yes, you, Miss Warner. Thoughts?"

"Uh...I...sure, I guess." I sat up, feeling the color drain from my cheeks as my new classmates stared at me in expectation, some with goofy grins plastered to their faces. My eyes stopped once again at Miss Perkins, still standing inside the doorway, her head cocked slightly to her left, her arms crossed in front of her waist, her lips curled up slightly at the corners of her mouth, awaiting my response. The Sahara hit high noon.

Did my parched state have something to do with this Miss Perkins? She was clearly popular, given the class's response to her welcoming of me. Moreover, she was impossibly stunning. I'd never laid eyes on such a pretty girl. The simplicity of her outfit (fashionably worn but not tattered jeans; sleeveless, button-down blue blouse to highlight her light-blue eyes; sunglasses resting atop her head that held her hair back; off-white sandals that exposed her painted toenails) accented the classic beauty of her face. The intensely focused but slightly cocky look she bestowed upon me was not something I'd seen among my many high-school mates. But more than that, she seemed to outclass us all with her confident carriage. She was in a league of her own. And she knew it.

I stammered ahead and offered an opinion concerning the importance of conscience and character woven throughout *Great Expectations*, finally finding my verbal footing once I focused my attention away from the Perkins girl.

Mr. Wilcox responded with a nod. "Thank you, Miss Warner, for paying attention to the reading assignment. I can see you'll be a solid addition to our classroom. Mr. Zimmer, let's continue with you. Do you agree with Miss Warner, or do you feel there are other themes as important to Dickens as the ones she identified?"

When the bell finally rang to notify us we could leave for the day, I stayed seated and closed my eyes. I slowly breathed in and out for a few minutes as I listened to my classmates file out the door toward their post-school lives, their excited chatter and laughter slowly fading down the hallway. Usually at ease in the classroom, I continued to consider my health. Was something going on with me physically? Lost in the rhythm of my breathing, I heard a voice above me.

"Hi. I'm Sarah. Cassidy, right?"

My eyes flew open. This Sarah, better known to me as Miss Perkins, stood in front of me, slightly angling her neck to gaze down from two feet above me. I immediately stood, bizarrely thinking I had to take action to avoid any lingering remembrances of her commanding presence above me.

"Yeah, but I prefer Cazz. Like jazz, with a *C*."

Sarah extended her hand. "Well, hello, Cazz with a *C*, welcome to Claiborne. Would you like the grand tour?"

I couldn't connect the dots, so mesmerized by her proximity and the feel of her smooth, warm hand in mine. "Tour?" I gulped, withdrawing my hand.

"Tour. You know, the lay of the land here. Or did someone already point out all our attractions to you?"

Since my previous brief walk-through of the halls and main facilities by the assistant principal had neglected to introduce me to Miss Sarah Perkins, at least one attraction had been left out of my initial tour.

That did it. Something was definitely off—I was suddenly thinking like a boy.

"Ah, tour. I've seen some of it, thank you."

"Glad to hear we're not neglecting you then. We tend to be a bit harsh on our new arrivals. Hopefully we've learned from past mistakes. If you're feeling lost or want someone to talk to, come find me." Sarah took my hand with both of hers. "Anytime." She gave me a huge grin, squeezed my hand slightly, pivoted on those cute sandals, and gracefully exited the classroom.

My eyes never strayed from her departing figure as I dropped back into my seat. Once this strange fact dawned on me, I promised myself to check the nurse's office hours if this unusual daze, this sudden distractedness, didn't improve tomorrow. I was probably coming down with something.

Heading out of the classroom at last, I hung a left down the bank of blue lockers, then right at the stone drinking fountain as I made my way to the library, past the entrance to the senior parking lot. I caught some movement out of the corner of my eye and noticed a couple embracing. I saw the back of a tall, broad-shouldered, crew-cut-haired guy whose head was tilted down and moving languidly back and forth. A pair of hands fidgeted at the back of his neck, teasing the hair above his collar. A girl's body faced toward his, feet clad in the cute off-white sandals I'd just taken stock of. I kept walking as Sarah pulled slightly away from the guy and reached up on her tiptoes to give him a final kiss. I had almost passed out of eyesight when I heard my name.

"Cazz! Cazz, over here."

I turned toward the voice and saw Sarah waving me over. I took a deep breath and walked up to the pretty couple. The tall blond boy with the crew cut grown out slightly longer than that of my dad's army colleagues' had dark-blue eyes, prominent cheekbones, and a strong jaw. He was a good six inches taller than Sarah, who was about my height, which made him at least six-four. Although broad shouldered, he wasn't thick like a linebacker, but he clearly spent many hours in a gym, sporting well-defined biceps and triceps. The combination made for a very handsome boy.

"Cazz, this is Dirk Clemens. Dirk, Cazz Warner. She just transferred here."

Dirk made a display of gradually checking me out from head to toe and back again. "Nice." He drew out the word, and Sarah elbowed him in his abdomen. Dirk chuckled and held out his hand with a welcoming smile chock-full of straight white teeth. "I mean, nice to meet you, Cazz. Where you from?"

I took his hand, returning his firm grip. "All over."

Dirk slightly furrowed his brow without changing his smile, seeming confused by my answer.

I withdrew my hand and clarified slightly. "We move around a lot. Nice to meet you, Dirk." I glanced at Sarah. "Thanks for the intro." I started off toward the library.

"How was the first day?" I heard her ask, and I turned around again.

"Odd."

"Odd?"

"Odd. High school is cliquey and usually no one talks to the new girl. You guys…" I shook my head and shrugged. "It's weird."

Dirk laughed. "That's because this one here's running for student-body president and goes out of her way to know everyone by name so they'll know who to vote for." He playfully poked Sarah's shoulder.

She laughed. "It's called being friendly."

Instead of being offended by her calculated overtures of friendliness, I realized that as much as I hated the attention I'd been paid during the day, her repeated efforts to welcome me made me feel, well, welcome. "Effective strategy," I said, calling out over my shoulder as I walked away. "You've got my vote."

Two days later, in Earth Science, I listened in growing discomfort as our teacher began identifying the recipients of the five top scores on the first test of the semester. It was a refresher, designed to get students reacclimated to Earth Science after a summer-long hiatus, not counting toward our grade. It seemed strangely cruel that the teacher, Mr. Mullens, would call attention to each of the top five students—in terms of how they fared on the test—like they did something wrong. Who wanted to be highlighted for having aced an exam?

Mullens began. "Five: Dawkins, Kip." A couple of catcalls from some girls in the back of class. "Four: Clemens, Dirk." A bunch of hoots from what sounded like football players, with their deep voices and happy amusement at the discomfort of a fellow player. I noted Dirk wasn't only good-looking, but had a brain, too. "Three: Rodgers, Eric." A few groans. Apparently whoever Rodgers was, he was a typical test-acer who wasn't popular with fellow classmates due to consistently high grades and what I guessed was an absence of good looks or athleticism. "Two: Perkins, Sarah." A few "aws" and "whats?" as if there was some miscount of the scores. From the middle rows, I heard Sarah Perkins's voice. "Two? I came in *second?*" As if she couldn't believe what she was hearing. Mullens continued. "Number one and top grade goes to: Warner, Cassidy."

I wanted to die. I should have pretended not to know the answers, but the exam was so easy I owed it to myself to answer as best I could. I slumped in my chair. There were a few murmurs I couldn't make out, and then someone posed a discernible question. "Who's Cassidy Warner?" I put an elbow on the desk, a hand to my forehead to hide my face, and wished for an earthquake (this being L.A.) or something similarly large or frightening that would take everyone's eyes off me. I wanted to disintegrate.

Mr. Mullens called out over the din. "Cassidy, raise your hand so everyone can see you."

Nightmare. Crawling under my desk and disappearing beneath the floor would have been far preferable. Instead, I removed my hand from my brow, raised it slightly over my head, and focused on the ceiling, hoping for an alien spaceship to crash through and beam me up and out of this classroom. I took a few steadying breaths as Mr. Mullens spoke. "Cassidy got a hundred percent on this test and the three bonus questions. If any of you are thinking of taking on a new study partner, I suggest you arm wrestle for her. Well done, Cassidy."

The bell rang, and once again I was relieved to be left alone in the classroom after everyone departed. As I stepped out beyond the door, Sarah, leaning against a picnic table in the quad, called out in a steely voice. "Cazz. Over here." I stopped, dreading confrontation. She stared intently at me and motioned me forward with her hand. That hand comprised long, elegant fingers that would have seemed very inviting in another circumstance, though what that circumstance was, I couldn't say. I walked up to where she waited and stood in front of her.

"What are you trying to do?" she asked.

"Huh?"

"I never come in second."

You just did. "Sorry." I gave her a slight shrug.

She glared at me. "Know that this is the first and last time you will ever beat my score in anything." She delivered each word with such precise diction, a baboon couldn't have misinterpreted her.

I didn't get sucked into these kinds of rivalries or intend to start now. I'd been the new kid far too often to let threats and intimidation tactics faze me. Typically, I'd simply walk away and mutter to myself when out of earshot. But something made me respond to Sarah. Some part of me wanted her to know who I was and for her not to forget it. Before I could contain myself, I shrugged and heard myself say, "Perhaps." It wasn't much, but it was enough.

Sarah's eyes blazed in disbelief and anger. She stormed away toward an awaiting group of girls at the other end of the quad.

God. I loved high school.

CHAPTER TWO

That Friday, back in Wilcox's class, he began by handing out a new assignment. "Time to partner up, people. You'll be working in pairs as you sift through Shakespeare's *Othello*. You have thirty seconds."

Commotion erupted as some students called out across the room to get the attention and agreement of a friend, while others scampered out of their chairs to wherever their friends were sitting. After thirty seconds, Wilcox called time, and I alone was without a partner. "Since there are twenty-six of you, I assume each of you is paired up at this point?" Wilcox asked.

Too embarrassed to speak up, I told myself I'd talk to him after class about flying solo on the project. At that moment, as she had on my first day in Wilcox's class, Sarah Perkins entered, having come from her student-assembly planning meeting, one of the few allowable excuses for tardiness at Claiborne. And like that first day, I had trouble wrenching my eyes from her. She wore cut-offs that showed plenty of leg, and the feminine cut of her pinstripe Dodgers T-shirt tastefully accentuated her shapely chest and trim waist. With those curves, she could easily pass for twenty-two.

"Ah, Miss Perkins. You missed our selection process of pairing up for our *Othello* project. We'll put you in a group of three."

A good-looking boy named Kip Dawkins called out. "Sarah, you can join me and Kevin."

"Wait a second," Wilcox said. "There's an even number of you. Which of you doesn't have a partner?"

Slowly, desperately hoping Wilcox would somehow miss it, I raised my hand.

"Miss Perkins, you and Miss Warner are a team."

"But Mr. Wilcox, why can't I work with Kip and Kevin?"

"Because, Miss Perkins, we're working in pairs. You're with Miss Warner. Please sit down while I go over the details of the project."

Without turning her head, Sarah moved her eyes to me with such a look of annoyance it was as if she were trying to bore a hole through my skull. Keeping her eyes on me, she went to one of the few remaining open desks and sat perfectly erect before turning to Wilcox.

After class, as I gathered my belongings, some of Sarah's friends surrounded her desk and offered condolences on her fate. Remarks like "not fair" and "totally uncool" and "sucks" filled the air as I made my way out the door.

Certain that the pairing would yield us both as much happiness as Othello's marriage, I couldn't help but be amused. It was a first. The perennial new girl, I was used to being matched up with the dregs of the class, the least intelligent students whose "project" grade would rely solely upon my efforts. Now I was partnered with perhaps the brightest of my classmates who was already out to best me. Let her try.

❖

Because Claiborne comprised nearly six hundred students, I had only two classes with Sarah: AP English and AP Earth Science. After sixth period at the beginning of my second week, we had tryouts for the tennis team. My parents both worked, so I spent a lot of time playing sports. Staying late at school made it easier to get home and gave me more time to study, since my mom could pick me up after work. My usuals were tennis, basketball, and softball. I wasn't a star player, but I was respectable because of my good hand-eye coordination, speed, and scrappiness. Sports allowed me to let off some of the steam that built up from our moving around so much, never being able to put down roots or get close to people.

About twenty-five girls in tennis skirts stood around a short redhead who identified herself as the coach. She referred to a clipboard and called out names, each girl responding with "here" or "yep." We were on the fifth of twelve tennis courts, the first four being occupied by other girls, six playing singles and four playing doubles. As the coach described the drills we'd be starting with, I glanced over at the occupied courts and stopped short when I saw Sarah Perkins pound a forehand crosscourt winner against her opponent. She turned around and strode to the baseline.

Her short cream skirt and ankle socks showed off her long, tan legs, and her matching sleeveless V-neck tennis shirt with light-yellow stripes accentuated her collarbone and lean, sun-kissed arms. Like me, she wore her hair in a ponytail that came down to her shoulders. A silver necklace held a charm or medallion that dipped toward the lower V in her V-neck, luring my eyes to her chest. For the first time that day, I noticed when I swallowed. She was stunning. Athletic, too.

With her left hand, she bounced the ball in front of her four times, held it close to her racket, tossed it into the air, sprang up and forward with her body, and struck it hard with her racket. Her motion was at once powerful, yet fluid. The kick serve hit just inside the line and spun out wide off the court. Her opponent couldn't get a racket on it. Ace.

With effort, I turned back to the coach, who was finishing explaining that seven of the girls on courts one through four were already on the team since they were on varsity previously. The others were the prior year's top JV players. From last year's team, only two students—two seniors—had graduated. There were only a couple spots left on varsity, and although JV was wide open, many of us wouldn't make either team. Once we worked on drills, those of us the coach thought had varsity potential would be pitted against one of the varsity players for a set.

My turn. The coach fired off round after round of balls from where she stood next to the ball basket at and across the net, making me run after countless forehands and backhands. Then she hit a drop shot that brought me to the net and struck volley after volley at me. After several minutes, she waved me over.

"Nice work, Cassidy. You have a great backhand, and your instincts at net are impressive."

I didn't respond, but kept my eyes on her. I'm not good with compliments. They make me feel I'm under a microscope, and I'm uncomfortable with the scrutiny.

"I want you to go hit with one of the varsity players." Coach called out across the courts. "Sarah!" Sarah looked up, then jogged over to the fence separating us. "I want you to play a set with Cassidy here."

"Sure, Coach." Sarah glanced at me and quickly tossed her head to the side, indicating that I should join her on court two.

The coach addressed me. "Sarah's one of our top singles players so don't worry about the score. I've got a lot of girls to watch today, but I'll be able to catch some of your play. Just do your best."

I hustled off the court, around the fence and onto court two, and stopped on the opposite side of the net from Sarah, relieved at the court-length distance between us. I felt it would help me concentrate better, though I didn't understand why.

Sarah gazed at me for several moments, as if taking stock, making me uncomfortable under her inspection. Finally, she lightly hit to me the two balls she was holding. "You serve first."

Perfect. My serve was the worst part of my game. Net play, baseline play, return of serve—all fine. My first serve was hard and flat, with zero spin. It would be fine if it actually went in, but it only did so about half the time. My second serve was the epitome of wimpiness. I tapped it in like a third-grader.

I walked to the baseline and watched Sarah across the net, shifting her weight from side to side, anticipating my serve. Sure enough, it slammed into the net. I hit my weak second serve, which landed a good foot inside the service box, and could do little but stand on my heels as Sarah attacked it on the rise, pounding it with devastating effect down the backhand line for a clean winner. Love-fifteen.

From the ad court, I attempted a down-the-line first serve. It was hard and fast, but well wide. On my second serve, I tapped it to her backhand, which she again attacked and drilled for a winner.

"Nice shot," I said. Love-thirty. This was going well.

Sarah walked quickly to the even court without looking at me until she was ready to return. I tossed the ball, bounding into the court as I smashed my racket strings against it, aiming for a serve that would pull her wide to the right, and watched in relief as it fell in. Sarah couldn't get more than her frame on the ball. Fifteen-thirty. Back in the ad court, I decided to go down the line to her forehand. The serve caught the line, and she stretched far for the forehand return, hitting it well wide. Thirty-all. All business, Sarah walked again to the even court, tugging at a few racket strings before raising her eyes to await my serve. This point and the next ended as the first two had, with my second serve coming into play and Sarah taking full advantage, striking each for outright winners. She won the game, and we switched sides.

Return of serve was one of the better aspects of my game. Sarah had a strong serve, but I was able to return each one, forcing us into some long baseline rallies. Serving at deuce, she went wide to my forehand and ran to the net for a serve-and-volley. I returned down the line for a winner. At my ad, she missed her first serve and spun the second serve wide to my backhand. Taking it on the rise, I hit a crosscourt return she could barely get her racket on and won the game.

"Nice," she said, clapping her left hand on the strings of her racket. The set continued with us breaking each other's serve, until she got her tremendous kick serve going and won a service game at love, taking us to 3-5, in her favor. True to form, my first serve failed me, and I lost my service game, giving her the set at 3-6.

We both jogged to the net and shook hands. She had a mist of sweat on her face and neck, making me think of a beverage I wanted to try.

"Nice set," she said, my hand in hers. She wasn't smiling but wasn't frowning, either. She had a look of respect combined with wonder, like she was trying to figure out a puzzle.

"You, too." I smiled. Then for some reason I closed my eyes, smirked, and shook my head, pulling my hand away. I started to head off the court.

"What was that for?"

I turned around. "What was what for?"

"That look. And that head shake."

"Sorry. I didn't realize I did that."

"You did, so spill it."

I sighed. "I'm not good with compliments."

The right side of her mouth curled up slightly, and she tilted her head to the side as she had the first day I saw her in the doorway of Mr. Wilcox's class. "Giving them, or taking them?"

"Either. Both."

"Then you're off the hook, since you're not really giving one if someone has to force it out of you. So 'fess up." Her tone was light, playful.

I faced skyward, unable to say the words directly to her. "I was only asking myself if there was anything you didn't do well." I took a deep breath and exhaled, finally meeting her eyes.

The left side of her mouth joined her right, blossoming into a genuine smile. "Why wouldn't you want to tell me that?"

Embarrassed, I studied my racket and pulled at a couple of the strings before bringing my eyes back to hers. I shrugged. "Anyway, thanks for the set," I said before turning and jogging toward the gate.

Over my shoulder, I heard her call out. "Good luck!"

Coach wasn't ready to make any decisions that day, or at least wasn't ready to announce them if she had, so we eventually went to the locker room to shower and change. As I reached the row where my stuff was, I stopped as if I'd hit a glass wall. A wet-haired Sarah, clad in jeans and a lacy off-white bra, was fishing out her top from her locker and talking to her friend Olivia, who was also changing. I blushed and immediately turned around to head back out the door to wait until the coast was clear, not trusting myself to keep my eyes off Sarah and therefore the color out of my cheeks.

I heard the familiar voice from behind me. "Cazz, hold up."

"One sec," I said weakly before darting to the bank of sinks around the corner, throwing on a cold-water faucet, cupping my hands below the spigot, and splashing several handfuls against my face. Hopefully the color in my face would be mistaken for the cold-water rinse rather than this combination of hot-blooded desire and monumental embarrassment. I turned off the water and stared at my wet face in the mirror. Wide, green eyes blinked back at me in surprise.

This was no coincidence. I was having unchaste thoughts about a girl. And if that wasn't bad enough, not just any girl, but the most popular girl in school, dating the cutest boy in school.

"You okay?" Sarah asked from behind, baring miles of lovely, smooth tanned skin as she held her shirt in her right hand.

I reached for a paper towel and covered my face, nodding. Through it, I mumbled. "Just got something in my eye." I kept my head down and tossed the paper towel into the silver trashcan. As I walked back toward my locker, I freed my dark-brown mane from its elastic band and fanned it around my shoulders in an attempt to cover my face and neck, hoping Sarah would stay behind me until she donned her shirt. I opened my locker and focused all my attention into the tall rectangular metal structure before me.

"How were tryouts? Any news?"

Still staring at my clothes hanging in front of me, I replied. "Not yet. She's going to post the list tomorrow."

"I'm sure you'll make the team. All you need is to work on your serve. Coach taught me mine, so I'm sure she or I can help with yours."

I nodded, facing my locker as if it were doing the talking.

"Lose something?"

My mind. I shook my head. "Just hoping I'm on the list." I quickly flicked my eyes in her direction and back to my locker's contents, exhaling deeply in relief when I processed that she was fully clothed. As I removed my toiletries and towel from my locker, some of my tension lifted once she said she'd catch me later. I heard her retreating footsteps. The aisle was clear. I could finally undress and head for the showers.

Stripped down to my bra and panties, I froze with my hand on the clasp of my bra as I heard Sarah say, "Forgot to ask. When do you want to get together to talk about our *Othello* assignment?" I slowly dropped my hands and stared again into my locker, reaching in as if I'd forgotten something, using every ounce of concentration not to grab the first thing I could get my hands on to cover myself. It would seem incredibly odd for me to suddenly clothe myself moments after I'd undressed to shower, but even though I was wearing the equivalent of a bikini, I felt naked and vulnerable.

Having played on many sports teams, I'd seen and been seen by hundreds of girls throughout the years, never once feeling self-conscious in the locker room or really paying attention to any of the flesh to which I was so often exposed. Until now. Why was I suddenly thinking that I would be anything to Sarah other than just another girl in a long line of girls whose bodies are seen so often they blend into the unmemorable and interchangeable? The same way I had thought—or hadn't thought—of countless others?

"Uh. Lunch tomorrow?" I asked lamely.

"Sure. Let's meet in the quad. We can sit outside so you can get some sun on those white shoulders. Wear a tank top."

The command set my pulse racing. Geez.

The next day, wearing a green tank top under a button-down cream and light-brown plaid shirt, I sat at one of the picnic type tables in the middle of the quad and waited for Sarah. She came around the corner with Dirk, Jasper, and Amy. After spotting me, she said something to them, gave Dirk a quick kiss, and strode over to me with that killer posture of hers my mother would love for me to mimic. She wore tan shorts, burgundy sandals, and a matching burgundy ribbed tank top. The same silver necklace she'd played tennis in lay halfway between her collarbone and the top of her sleeveless shirt, a lure to roaming eyes. I quickly averted mine.

"Hey," she said, removing the sunglasses that were doubling as a hairband and placing them over her eyes. "We're here to get you some sun. Strip." Some of the long hair that had been pushed behind her ears tumbled into her face, and she tossed it back over her shoulders like you'd see in a shampoo commercial.

"I'm fine," I said as I looked down toward her painted toes, embarrassed by my paleness and how attractive I found her.

"You're in L.A. now, so you'd better make the most of it. Besides, you practically blinded me on the court yesterday. You owe it to your fellow students not to force them to wear sunglasses in order to hang out with you." I felt a tug at my sleeve. "Off."

Reluctantly, I unbuttoned and removed my shirt, tossing it onto the table. Sarah looked down at my tank, then up to my face. She smiled and sat next to me on the bench seat with her back against the table, facing the opposite way I sat. Then she stretched out her interminable legs and leaned back on her elbows, her chin parallel to the sky.

"Feels good, doesn't it?" she asked.

Uncomfortable sitting next to her because of the hum her proximity stirred within me, I climbed on top of the table, put my shirt under my head, and, knees bent, lay back facing the sun.

"You're right. It does." I kept my eyes shut, realizing how close my head was to hers and not daring to look at her. I found it difficult to string simple words together coherently when she was so near. The gymnast in my stomach did another cartwheel. I concentrated on our mutual project and managed to ask, "How far are you on the reading?"

"I finished Act Three."

"Nice."

"We have almost two weeks until our presentation's due. Think that's enough time to read it and come up with what we think the major themes are?"

"Sure. Though I can tell you already."

"Plagiarizing study guides doesn't count. We need to have our own ideas and understand them thoroughly. Wilcox smells that half-assed copycat shit a mile away."

"I agree. I've read it before is all."

"You've already read *Othello*?"

"All of Shakespeare, actually. The plays, anyway. Not the sonnets."

Sarah laughed. "I'm sure you have," she said sarcastically.

After several moments of continuing to soak up the wonderful rays, I offered my initial thoughts on the subject. "I think the play is more about Iago than Othello, since he manipulates the other characters and preys on their weaknesses. But if you'd rather stick with the title character, I'd argue that his low self-esteem is his undoing." I heard movement and glanced toward Sarah, who had shifted her body around on the bench to face me. Her eyes flashed angrily.

"You're serious. You have read it."

I nodded.

"You're saying I'm behind already?" she asked with astonishment.

I sat up on my elbows, having already once experienced her wrath at feeling second-best, and shook my head. "No. Not even. If you're already through Act Three, you're way ahead of everyone."

"Everyone except you."

I registered the dismay and anger in her voice. I hopped off the table and faced her. "I'll ask Wilcox to fly solo. Maybe you can work with Kip and Kevin like you wanted." I looked at my feet, took a deep breath, and blew it out. "I…I read a lot. I didn't mean to piss you off." An uncomfortable silence ensued for several moments, until finally I heard her laugh.

"I'm being a bitch, Cazz. I'm sorry." She momentarily touched my forearm. "You didn't do anything to piss me off. I'm just not used to feeling behind." She pushed her sunglasses down to the bridge of her nose so her eyes could meet mine and gave me a devilish smile. "I should be happy I'm working with you instead of against you on this. We have an edge, thanks to you. Forgive me?"

"Yeah, no worries."

She pushed her sunglasses to the back of her nose, covering her eyes. "All of Shakespeare, huh?"

"Only the plays."

"You say that like it's no big deal."

I gave her my best *you're crazy* grimace. "It's not like I can quote from it."

"No?" she asked with a trace of amusement.

I shook my head.

Sarah was quiet for a moment before a smile slowly lit up her face. "Well, that's disappointing," she said in a teasing voice.

"Why's that?" I asked, genuinely curious.

She turned back around on the bench and resumed her earlier sunbathing position, stretching her long legs out before her. Facing skyward, she said nonchalantly, "I can't look forward to being swept off my feet by you comparing me to a summer's day and all that."

Had she just flirted with me? Did girls flirt with each other? Maybe it was a Southern California thing. Or I was simply imagining it. Real or not, it gave me a little thrill, and I went with it. "I'll work on it."

"Do that."

I assumed my recumbent position on the table, then changed the only other line I knew from that poem. "Thou *art* more lovely, but…" I glanced at Sarah, who slid her eyes to mine. "Honestly? Not more temperate."

Swiftly, my shirt was tugged from beneath my head and thrown over my face. "Hey!" I said in mock protest, freeing myself.

"I think I deserved that," she said with a wry grin, before raising her chin toward the sun and closing her eyes.

Taking the hint that our study time was over prematurely, I crossed my arms behind my head and enjoyed the sunshine until the bell rang for fifth period.

That afternoon, I searched the bulletin board outside the locker room to find that my name was one of two selected to join the varsity tennis squad. I was relieved. Coach wanted the team to meet after school five days a week starting tomorrow, to be excused only for illness or student-body political duties.

Over the next two weeks, Sarah and I saw a lot of each other. During practice, we participated in a ton of group drills, though we rarely played against each other. Most of the hours we spent together were in preparation for Wilcox's *Othello* challenge, and as long as she maintained a two-arms' length distance between us, I was able to function relatively normally. She had a good sense of humor, and we laughed a lot. Cattiness wasn't one of her attributes, unlike some popular girls I'd met at other schools. She was down-to-earth and fun to be around. I would miss our time together once the project was over.

And contrary to most of my previous project partners, Sarah was sharp. She backed each piece of plot analysis she performed with several quotes and followed through on every aspect of the assignment we'd divvied to her. More than that, her devil's advocacy of my positions helped me refine our paper and presentation materials into some of my best work to date. Of all my project collaborators, Sarah was the first to demand more from me than I demanded of myself, the first to really earn the term "partner." I finally understood the benefits of having one.

The day we were scheduled to present, we met in the quad before first period. I'd been the first to get there, hopping up on the table and putting my feet on the bench. I read *The Great Gatsby* while I waited. It helped me relax if I didn't feel I was cramming information into my head before a test or presentation. Five minutes later, the table slightly dipped with extra weight, and the outside of Sarah's thigh brushed against mine as she sat next to me.

"Hey. Ready for our big presentation?" She nudged my shoulder like a brother or cousin.

"You're the one doing the speechifying. Are you?"

"If we don't get the best grade on this project, I'll remove my name from Homecoming court," Sarah said confidently. "Assuming I get nominated."

"Ha ha," I replied, knowing how much she was hoping to be voted queen. I didn't bother to respond to her comment about getting nominated since it was a no-brainer.

"I'm serious." She looked at me assuredly, gauging my response. Her face was a foot away from mine, her light-blue eyes mesmerizing, her lips tantalizingly moist. I couldn't speak.

I turned away. "Guess we'll have to win then."

"We will. You going, by the way?"

"Of course. It's my grade on the line, too."

"To Homecoming, silly."

Ugh. The only person I wanted to go to Homecoming with was the girl sitting next to me, and that was wrong for so many reasons. "No," I said definitively.

"No one's asked you, or you've turned down your hordes of admirers?"

"You're so amusing, Perkins." My tone was anything but amused.

"Which is it?"

"Does it matter? I'm not going. It's not my kind of thing," I said, with mounting irritation.

"Your kind of thing being staying up until three AM, reading Shakespeare?"

I held up my book. "Fitzgerald, actually."

"I heard Kip was going to ask you. He didn't?"

"Perkins, lay off. It's not my scene."

"He thinks you're pretty special, you know."

"Well, I'm glad you two have a great time talking about me behind my back." I nearly winced at the alarming clip at which I was regressing into childishness. She couldn't know what buttons she was pushing, but I wasn't proud of my reply.

Sarah jumped off the table, crossed her arms, and glared at me. "What is your fucking problem? Are you annoyed because someone finds you attractive? Or because, God forbid, I—your friend—am asking you something somewhat personal? Or are you pissy because no one's asked you?"

Fuck. None of the above. I was jealous of Dirk and frustrated I couldn't tell Sarah how I felt about her or how uneasy I was with the whole dating subject. "I don't have hordes of admirers, like you, and wish you wouldn't tease me by pretending I do." I returned her glare and crossed my arms defensively, as she had done.

Sarah's eyes burned into me almost as if she stood in the sun and held a magnifying glass to my face. "You're a piece of work, Warner." She dropped her hands and stalked away.

Once Wilcox called our team, Sarah strode to the front of the classroom while I claimed the stool to the left of her podium, at the ready with our flip charts. We didn't acknowledge each other. She presented our material flawlessly and effortlessly, smiling and engaging the class throughout. Dang, I could use such a gift. No doubt about it after that performance: we'd win. And we did. Sarah charmed Wilcox and the rest of the students with her knowledge of *Othello*, natural poise and intellect, and we got the high score. At least we knew who Homecoming Queen would be. The thought gave me comfort, as I hated to think of iron-willed Sarah holding fast to her word and dropping out of contention over a grade on a stupid project with me.

After class, I went to the locker room to change for our team's tennis match against our cross-town rivals. This was our only Friday match of the semester, which seemed to heighten its importance. Relieved yet disappointed not to see Sarah, I made my way to the awaiting bus that would take us to our opponent's tennis courts. I sat in my usual seat in the far-right rear, donned earphones, stared outside, and lost myself in music. The engine roared to life, and soon after the bus lurched forward, the bench seat I occupied dipped slightly as someone sat to my left. I looked over and removed my earphones, unexpectedly finding myself gazing into Sarah's light-blue eyes, which seemed to be searching mine for something, though I didn't know what.

We must have stared at each other for twenty seconds or more. It was weird. Some part of me felt such a strong connection to this girl that I wondered, as I looked at her, whether she could read my thoughts. Whether with her eyes she was somehow reaching into my soul. Whether she could tell she was making me feel like I wanted to tell her things I'd never told anyone. Whether she knew how much it tore up my insides when we argued. Whether she could sense that some part of me physically ached with awe and longing to simply be near her. Of course, mind reading was impossible; yet I was anxious in a way I didn't understand.

"Hey," Sarah finally said.

"Hey." I swallowed hard, quickly returning to the view outside. "Nice job today," I said to the window.

"You, too."

"Glad you won't be dropping out of Homecoming court."

A hand lightly squeezed my left thigh and rested there. "I'm sorry if I made you uncomfortable this morning."

"No worries." I was trying to will away the heat searing my leg. Her touch made me feel I was being branded like cattle, and part of me wanted to be similarly marked by her as hers.

"If you do decide to go to Homecoming, I'd like you and your date to join me and Dirk for the night. We'll be with a bunch of friends, and we've rented a huge limo so it should make for some seriously good times."

"Thanks, but I don't intend to go. Please…" I wanted to finish my statement with authority, but it came out more as a whisper. "Please respect that," I said softly. I continued to stare out the window, and the weight on my thigh lifted.

"I do." After several moments, Sarah headed toward the front of the bus.

She was giving me space, heeding my silent plea to be left alone. Having spent my life on the periphery, it was a message I was used to sending, a shield I was adept at raising. Yet never had I felt so alone as when she walked away.

Chapter Three

A t our rival's tennis club, which was very swanky compared to our modest on-school-premises tennis courts, Coach pulled us into an unoccupied court. "Primrose High is our toughest competition, and I intend for us to give them their best fight. We'll be switching things around from what you're used to. Normally, we try to win sets, but this is going to come down to winning games. If we tie in sets, the squad with the most games will win this meet. Instead of our usual one-two-three singles players going toe-to-toe with our opponents, today I'm putting our top singles players together as doubles teams and moving some of our doubles players to singles. Joanie and Sandra, you're our new number-one doubles team. Sarah and Cassidy, number two. Rachel and Kristin, number three. Jennifer, Barbara, and Olivia, you're our top singles players for the day. Remember, we're fighting for every game. Let's do it."

Sarah and I split our first two matches, barely leading the games column by one, as we lost our first match 5-7 and won our second 6-3. This was our third and final match. We were behind three games to four when Coach told us as we switched sides that ours was the last match in play. Behind her we could see some of our teammates filing into the nearby bleacher seats. Total matches scheduled: eighteen. Seventeen had played, and the games totals favored Primrose by one, excluding our current match. Since the winner had to win by two games, the prevailing doubles team would mean the difference between winning or losing the meet. No pressure.

As I prepared to serve, Sarah joined me at the baseline and tried to pump me up. "You can do this, Cazz. We can beat these chicks." My first serve fell well wide to the forehand side. The girl then pounded my second serve down the line past Sarah's stab volley for a winner. That was indicative of most of the game. Although we got them to deuce, my first serve then failed me twice, and we lost the game due to my weak second serve. 3-5: one game away from losing the match.

This Primrose girl had the weaker serve of the two. Sarah ruthlessly clobbered the return on both serves, as did I. With two of our returns clean winners and the other two so well placed that our opponents' shots didn't clear the net, it was Sarah's turn to serve, 4-5. I felt a slight surge in confidence at the prospect, knowing how hard her serve was to return. Her first serve caught the net and barely exceeded the service line for a fault. Our opponent attacked her second serve, hitting it right at me, forcing me to defend myself with a volley, which luckily landed beyond reach on the sideline. The game's other points ended in similar fashion, and we were soon even at 5-5.

The Primrose girl with the stronger serve caught the outside line, causing Sarah to stretch wide to her forehand. Thinking the girl at net would get the volley, I moved back, hoping to reduce the size of no-man's-land between Sarah and me. The girl at net hit a backhand volley to my feet, and I was able to scoop it up and send it back over her head. Her partner returned the lob with a shallow one, and Sarah rushed forward for the easy overhead smash. Love-fifteen. We high-fived each other.

"Let's go, Cazz. Show 'em what you got." I nodded, and Sarah jogged to her place at net. The next serve went in down the line, and though I barely got my racket on it, the return was deep. The server girl hit a solid forehand up the middle that Sarah anticipated and volleyed at a short angle, past our opponents.

"Way to go, Sarah." Love-thirty. We split the next two points. Fifteen-forty. The server's first serve was well long, and on her second serve, she made the mistake of going to Sarah's forehand.

Sarah took it on the rise for a better angle and nailed a crosscourt winner. 6-5.

Crap. My serve, at the worst possible time. Sarah scooped up a ball with her racket and foot and handed it to me, offering words of support and reassurance. Unfortunately, my first serve wasn't listening. Various points later, although my first serve continued to abandon me, Sarah didn't give up. At thirty-forty, one point from losing the game, she walked over to me before I prepared to serve. "Let's go, Cazz. You can do it. We're going to win this." Serving to the ad court, I nailed it down the line, sending the girl well to the right of a comfortable forehand. The ball hit her racket frame and soared into the fence. Deuce.

Once again, Sarah hustled over to me, trying to pump me up. "Take a little pace off your first serve. If it doesn't go in, do the exact same thing on the second serve. Can you do that?"

"I might double-fault."

"True, but I'd rather lose because we were aggressive than because we played it safe."

"Are you sure?"

"I'm sure. Trust me."

I shifted my grip slightly to the left to add a small spin to my first serve. I tossed the ball and sprang forward into the serve with slightly less power than usual. It sailed long. I looked at Sarah, who nodded. "You can do it," she said firmly. Keeping the same grip, I repeated the process and watched the ball land just inside the line. The Primrose girl stepped into the forehand but couldn't take it on the rise due to the faster pace of the ball. She hit it to Sarah, who lunged left, her stab volley sending over a perfectly placed drop shot. Ad-in.

"Nice!" I called out.

Sarah met me at the baseline. Another high-five. "Same thing, Cazz. Same thing." This time, serving to the ad court, my less formidable first serve landed on the centerline. Our opponent hit a strong forehand deep to my backhand, which I sent down the line to the other girl. She struck a hard but short ball back to me. I raced around it in order to hit a forehand that traveled between our opponents for a winner.

We won.

I hustled to the net next to Sarah, both of us shaking hands with our opponents to congratulate them on a good match. Our teammates cheered and applauded and began filing out of the bleachers to head to the gate leading to our court. Next thing I knew Sarah practically tackled me, engulfing me in a fierce embrace.

I'd never known such joy until that moment. My grin was as wide as our bus. I wanted nothing more than to wrap my arms around Sarah and never let go, but I couldn't bring myself to hug her. My racket in one hand, the other staying limp at my side, I wanted so badly to hold her yet knew I never could, not the way I wanted to.

"Okay, okay, okay." I laughed. "No need to fuss. Geez. All right, already. It's not such a big deal."

She continued holding and rocking me for a few moments. She pulled back, and her eyes beamed with pleasure as she smiled, her hands around my neck, her face inches from mine. Her gaze dipped to my mouth, and her smile disappeared; then she quickly raised her eyes back to mine. My grin vanished, and my mouth went dry. The gymnast in my stomach did a backflip that moved deftly into a somersault. I gazed into her eyes for what seemed like an endless stretch of time. Then, afraid of what was in them or what I feared I might do, I forced myself to turn away.

Sarah released me and took a step back, which gave me the freedom to meet her eyes. "We did it," she said quietly, bringing a smile back to her beautiful mouth. I nodded, pleased and pained by her smile. Pleased to see her happy, pained not to be able to cause it beyond a tennis match or two. She had Dirk for that.

"We did."

Suddenly our joyous teammates surrounded, hugged, patted, and high-fived us, everyone congratulating each other on everyone's contributions to our team victory.

❖

My mother was late in picking me up that evening. It wasn't possible to know when a match would be over, especially away matches, and sometimes I had to wait around until she could come get me. I read under a lamppost as I waited, sitting on a three-foot wall bordering the parking lot. When the brakes of a bicycle startled me, I glanced up to see a front tire a few feet in front of me and Kip Dawkins straddling his bike, smiling at me.

"Hey, Cazz."

"Hi."

"What are you sticking around for?"

"Waiting for my mom. You?"

"Just finished working out. How'd it go against Primrose?"

"We won," I said with a grin.

"Sweet! Good work. I hate those stuck-up pricks."

"I'm sure they say the same thing about us."

"Yeah. Probably." Kip stopped talking and I resumed reading.

"Cazz?"

I looked up.

"You going to Homecoming?" Kip asked.

"Uh, no."

"Want to go?"

Along with Sarah and a few other students, Kip was in both my AP Earth Science and AP English classes. He got consistently good grades, played football and baseball, and was one of the cutest boys in school. And it sounded suspiciously like he was asking me to go to Homecoming with him.

"What?" I asked, lamely.

"Do you want to go to Homecoming with me?"

"Uh...dances aren't really my thing. I'm not...I'm not much of a dancer."

"We don't have to dance if you don't want to. It'll be a huge party with lots of people and good music. Should be fun." He smiled. "What do you say?"

"Kip, I'd hate to be a wet blanket. You should take someone who's into it."

His smile evaporated. "You don't want to go, or you don't want to go with me?"

Both, but I didn't want to hurt his feelings. "If I was going, I'd love to go with you. Honestly, it's just not my kind of thing."

"It's Homecoming. I thought girls lived for this kind of thing."

I chuckled. "Wearing fancy gowns and pretending to be Cinderella?"

His smile returned. "It does sound kind of dorky when you put it that way."

A car pulled into the parking lot and we glanced over. "My mom," I said, rising.

"Tell you what. Think about it over the weekend and let me know Monday. Deal?"

What a sweet boy. I'm sure it's hard enough to ask a girl out, let alone leave the door open after being turned down. "Deal." My mom pulled the car around about ten feet away, and I started toward it.

"Cazz."

I turned back to Kip.

"It wouldn't be right for the prettiest girl at Claiborne to sit home on Homecoming."

I tilted my head and furrowed my eyebrows in confusion. *She isn't. She's going with Dirk and will probably be crowned Queen.*

"So say yes on Monday." He grinned.

I quickly closed the final steps to the passenger door and shut it behind me, securing my escape.

During the ride home, my incipient frustration with Kip's tenacity grew into full-blown annoyance. Until that last bit about the prettiest girl, I actually thought I'd give his proposal some meaningful consideration. After all, going to the Homecoming dance wouldn't kill me. It might even turn out to be somewhat enjoyable, depending on the company and the entertainment. But as with most compliments, his struck me as being insincere. A calculated thing designed to manipulate me. Like many of the recruits I'd met during the numerous events my father took us to or held at our various houses, Kip's compliment was aimed at taking something from me.

The young army recruits wanted sex. Period. And they were very persuasive in trying to get it. In the past three years rotating through school after school, the one constant when it came to my interactions with them was the sheer volume of compliments heaped on me. *You're so pretty. You're so beautiful. Your eyes are incredible.* And so on.

Twice, once at fifteen and once at sixteen, I'd made the mistake of believing the sincerity of the boys wielding those words, wanting so much to feel special. Toward the end of my date with the first boy, he drove us to a scenic point that overlooked the city lights below. He kissed me brutally, shoving his tongue into my mouth and pushing me hard against the door. No tenderness, no gentle words. He grabbed my breast and squeezed until it was painful. I wanted to cry out but didn't want to give him the satisfaction of acknowledging I'd felt his touch. I fought him off and was able to grab hold of the door handle behind me. Since he'd been leaning heavily against me, I fell backward onto the ground as the door opened. He told me to get in, saying he'd take me home, but I refused. I didn't want to go anywhere with him. He got out of the car and forced me against the door.

"Look, you fucking tease, you're going to get in and I'm going to take you home, because if I don't, your father will have my ass in a sling. Now get in the goddamn car, you little bitch, or I'll give you more than you bargained for."

I climbed into the backseat and he took me home.

I fared no better with the second boy. He seemed sweet, telling me I had the prettiest green eyes he'd ever seen. He took me to dinner, followed by an R-rated movie at a small theater. He was twenty, and by then I looked eighteen, so it was easy to get in. Toward the start of the film, he took my hand and held it. About an hour in, during a raunchy sex scene, he put my hand between his legs. As he held it firmly in one of his, I felt something warm, firm yet soft, and couldn't immediately place that I was holding his penis until he forced my hand up and down his shaft. I recoiled and ran into the ladies' room. I cried for a long time, unable to understand what I'd done, how it had happened.

When an employee made her rounds to clean the bathroom, I asked her if there was a rear exit. There was. I darted into the street, saw a tall building that had the name of some hotel, ran to it, and took a cab home.

Although repulsed by the behavior of those boys, I'd been more disgusted with myself for having been so stupid and naïve as to believe their lies. Keeping my distance from people was my surefire method of preventing repeat performances, and aside from those earlier mistakes, I was good at it. In reminding myself that I needed to remain so, my mind inexplicably settled on Sarah's face instead of Kip's, and my resolve momentarily faltered.

CHAPTER FOUR

Saturday morning, the phone rang. "Cazz, it's for you," my mom called to me upstairs. I was reading and not particularly enjoying *Catch-22*; the contradictions were giving me whiplash. I reached for the phone near my bed.

"Hello?"

"Get changed and meet me outside your house in half an hour. We're going to work on that serve of yours," Sarah said. She was one of many seniors at Claiborne with a car. I wasn't, since we moved so much. Even during our *Othello* preparations, we hadn't shared phone numbers, so she must have gotten my home number from the tennis-team roster.

"That's very nice of you, Sarah, but it's not necessary."

Unfazed, Sarah pressed on. "Bring a change of clothes, too. What's your address?" I gave it to her and started getting ready. As I looked in the mirror to put my hair in a ponytail, I noticed I was smiling.

Once we got to the courts, Sarah popped the trunk of her black Jetta and pulled out a cage of balls. "Coach let me borrow it." We warmed up by hitting some rallies, and then she jogged over to my side of the net and met me at the baseline. "Take a few practice serves to loosen up."

I did.

"Show me your normal service grip."

I showed her my hand as it held the base of my racket.

"All right. Now move your grip counterclockwise a quarter of an inch and choke up on the racket."

I did.

"Hold the ball out to where you'd normally hit it."

I held it out as if preparing to serve.

"Now." She stepped behind me and reached around my left shoulder, lightly grabbing my forearm. I stiffened involuntarily. "Instead of hitting it there, you want to toss it closer to here, kind of like eleven o'clock." She pulled my arm up, back, and to the left, then reached around me for my right arm. "Pull your racket back like you're about to serve."

I moved my racket behind me as she'd instructed. She put her right hand around mine, lifted my left arm, and pushed the racket head from just above my head to the top of my reach.

"Pretend you're hitting from six o'clock to twelve o'clock on the ball, like this," she said with her arms around me.

Focused on the tingling heat where she was touching me on my arms, hands and back, I had trouble concentrating on what she was saying. I could feel her breasts against my back, her breath on my neck, and my shoulders tightened slightly upward, as if I was bracing myself for possible injury. It was anything but painful, yet somehow frightening.

"Jesus, Cazz, breathe, will you?" She stepped back and I blew out my breath, unaware I'd been holding it. While I kept my eyes forward, she walked around me and into my field of vision. Without looking at her, I could tell she was studying me.

"You really hate to be touched, don't you?" she asked.

I stared at the net, trying to even my breathing, not wanting to have this conversation. I couldn't tell her what her touch did to me and couldn't admit to the reasons why—except for her—she was right.

"I'm not going to hurt you, Cazz."

"I know." I still couldn't face her.

She continued staring at me for what seemed like forever but was probably a few seconds. "You don't like being touched, and you don't like compliments." She spoke her next words softly, with a tenderness that made me ache. "Somebody really hurt you."

I looked at the soccer field in the distance and silently cursed myself for my weakness as my eyes pooled with tears. *Don't you dare cry right now. Do not fucking cry.*

"Sweetie, I'm so sorry," she said with the same tenderness and compassion. That endearment did me in, and a tear slid down my cheek. I took a staggered breath, my mouth quivering.

"I know you don't want this, but I can't not hug you right now." She closed the gap between us and I shook my head, trying to dissuade her from embracing me, even though part of me wanted her and only her to hold me. She paused, seeming to contemplate whether to abide by my wishes or leave me alone, then threw her arms around my neck. "I can't stand seeing you like this," she said softly. A few moments passed. "I promise I won't hurt you." She was so gentle, so loving, that I couldn't stop the flood of emotion and yielded to my need to cry. She held me tightly, rocked me gently, and whispered words of comfort.

I felt safe in her arms and warmed by her compassion. I felt cared for. It was a feeling so different than any I'd known. But I couldn't trust myself to know the difference between being cared for and being manipulated toward some endgame unknown to me and not in my best interest. Nothing in Sarah's behavior made me think she was anything but genuine, and I couldn't imagine any hidden agenda she should harbor against me. Yet however unfair it was of me not to trust her, I couldn't. Because of my startling realization that I desperately wanted to, I was disappointed in myself for not giving her the chance she deserved.

As my private storm finally passed, my sadness dovetailed into mammoth embarrassment at being so needy. I pulled away and wiped my eyes with the back of my hand. "Can we go?" I asked with averted eyes. She agreed and jogged away to field the balls on the court, allowing me time to pull myself together.

Later, as she finished stowing the ball cage in the trunk, I felt compelled to say something, still feeling exposed and abashed. "Sorry about that, back there. You caught me a little off guard."

She closed the trunk and her eyes registered dismay. She shook her head, looked past my shoulder into the distance, then back to me. Her frown slowly turned into a mischievous grin, as if she were preparing for a duel that only she knew the rules of. "We'll have to work on that then."

I wasn't following. "What?"

"Your guard. Get in."

Aside from the radio blasting alternative rock, we rode in silence as Sarah drove us to the mall. We entered it, slammed with the usual overkill of air-conditioning, and made a beeline for the public restroom where we changed clothes in separate stalls. We threw our tennis clothes and shoes in a tote bag I carried, and after exiting the restroom I followed in step behind Sarah, who seemed intent on a particular destination. The three-foot-tall lettering above the wide store entrance said NORDSTROM. We passed the makeup and perfume counters as we made our way to the escalator and walk-rode up four floors. Formal dresses.

"What's the plan?" I asked.

"You're going to help me shop for my Homecoming dress."

"I'm not much of a shopper."

"Trust me, I'm enough for both of us." She smiled and winked at me. My stomach did a little cartwheel, but I blew out an exasperated breath as if in for a long bout of torture.

Sarah methodically picked through rack after rack of dresses, seeming to opt more for the long, traditional gown than the short sexy type. In her wake, I'd occasionally pick out a horrid dress merely to get a rise out of her. One particularly awful number was a short black thing with a white leaf print. I wasn't sure whether the designer was irreverent or clueless, but the leaves were shaped like those of a marijuana plant. I pulled it off the rack and pushed it toward her.

"Perfect," I said.

She glimpsed it and snickered before raising her eyebrows in question.

"Very high society."

Sarah barked a laugh that caused a couple patrons to glance up from their shopping.

Four gowns were resting over her arm by the time she stopped at a rack that held cocktail dresses. Rifling through the options, she shoved hanger against hanger until she saw one she liked. After she pulled out her selection, she looked at me then back at the dress. She waved me closer. "Here, try this one on. Don't peek at the price tag. We're trying, not buying."

I eyed the one-shoulder black dress with the sweetheart neckline on the fitted bodice. Crisscross ruching would wrap around the wearer until bottoming out at the hem of the dress, mid-thigh. "Why? I'm not going to Homecoming, and even if I was, this certainly isn't a Homecoming dress."

"I'm testing out a theory," she said vaguely.

"I would never wear something like this."

"Humor me." She continued holding out the dress to me, and I reluctantly relented, taking it from her. She pointed with her chin. "The fitting room's over there. I'm not quite through here, so come find me when you're done."

In the fitting room, stripped down to my bra and panties, I held out the dress, trying to divine Sarah's purpose in my wearing it. "Ugh." I slid the tight-fitting garment over my body and looked in the mirror.

It was a perfect fit.

I turned around several times, examining myself from the front, sides, and over my shoulder to my back. Though I'd never wear such a thing in public, I had to admit it wasn't a bad look. I had enough leg and height to get away with the modest length, enough cleavage to fill out the bust material, enough definition in my arms to get away with the sleeveless aspect of the left shoulder, and just enough hip to accentuate my flat stomach. The dress lent me an almost seductive air.

I became hugely self-conscious that I'd cause a stir if I left the fitting room—the kind that often made me the object of my father's recruits—and decided I didn't want the attention. It had been my experience that the less notice I received, the better. I grabbed the lowest part of the dress and was starting to remove it, when I heard Sarah.

"Cazz? I'm waiting. Where are you? Are you coming out?"

I froze, the skirt of the dress at my hips. I called out. "It's not my style. I'm taking it off."

"You'll do no such thing. Get a grip and come out here."

Fuck. I shimmied the dress back in place. "Fine," I growled, "but I'm not leaving the fitting-room area." There was a hexagon-shaped section at the center of the fitting rooms with benches and 270-degree mirrors to allow for the kind of show-and-tell I was thinking of, where I wouldn't have to leave the women-only sanctuary.

She coaxed me. "No one's here but me."

I undid the lock, opened the door, and stopped within the confines of the common area where Sarah stood to the side. At the sight of me, her eyes widened, her breath caught, and her lips parted slightly as she took me in from head to toe and back. After taking a moment to shake herself free from whatever thought was plaguing her at that moment, she held out her right palm and dipped her head, indicating that I should move into the center of the mirrored space. I did.

"Stop slouching and stand up straight."

I took a deep breath and assumed a fake smile as I copped a whole lot of attitude, squared my shoulders, stuck out my chest, and twirled around the way I imagined a fashion model would. I gestured with my hands that she should behold the outfit from top to bottom. "Better?" I asked sarcastically.

A slow smile played across her face and I assumed she was approving of my ability to follow direction. "Well? What do you think?" she asked.

"What do I *think*?" I mocked her. "I think I look ridiculous. Am I done?"

"You think you look *ridiculous*? You can't be serious."

"Maybe not ridiculous. Just…" I shrugged, closed my eyes, and shook my head.

At that moment, two attractive thirty-something blondes entered the fitting-room area, each with armfuls of clothes to try on. I opened my eyes at the sound of their footsteps, and as they passed the show-and-tell section, they both stopped and surveyed me. "Wow," one of them said. "Hot damn," said the other. "That dress is incredible on you," said the first. "Whatever it costs," said the second, "buy it. You look hot." "Truly," said the first, nodding in agreement. "Truly," she repeated. They both turned and headed down one of the short halls to their fitting rooms.

I studied the ceiling.

"You're excused."

I turned my eyes to Sarah, wondering if I'd correctly recognized the smug tone in her voice. She had a wicked, self-righteous grin on her face, as if she'd won round one of whatever duel we were squaring off to fight. I darted into my fitting room and, locking the door behind me, heard her voice through the wooden slats. "Wait for me right here. I'm going to want your opinion." Greatly relieved to have my own jeans and polo shirt back on, I sat on one of the two benches in the common area.

A few minutes later, Sarah entered the mirrored hexagon room where I waited. God. Could she be any more beautiful? She wore a strapless, white stretch-taffeta dress with a high waist and a slim skirt with a flared hem at the ankle. Even with bare feet, she walked tall, keeping her back and neck straight, her bearing regal but unpretentious. I felt slightly light-headed and my mouth went dry. A sharp pang, like hunger, arose in my abdomen, though I'd eaten only a few hours earlier.

"Not bad," she said, twirling around to assess herself from various angles. She flicked her eyes in my direction and gave me a tantalizing smile. "Cazz, stop staring and close your mouth."

Helplessly, I obeyed.

"Well?"

"Not bad," I agreed, barely managing to choke out the words and thinking it was the biggest understatement of my life to that point.

"This one's a *maybe*," she said, heading back to the fitting room. The next three dresses were equally stunning on Sarah. The first was a black strapless stretch satin with a layered ruffle bodice and long, slim skirt. Succeeding this was a white, charmeuse strapless with a looped bodice and a flared skirt. Last up was an agave-colored satin, floor-length V-neck with an asymmetrical skirt. The draped bodice hugged her curves so well she looked poured into it. Something about the greenish hue perfectly offset her auburn hair, and the thirty-degree angle at which the sleeves tilted away from her collarbone spawned visions of gently pushing those sleeves off her shoulders in search of underlying treasure. She was mesmerizing. I turned away and studied the exit.

A moment later, she was standing with her back in front of me. "Unzip me."

The quiet demand made my pulse race. I stood. My mouth was mere inches from her neck, and as she lifted her hair to give me better access to the zipper, I caught her delicate, jasmine fragrance, which enticed me to lean closer. My eyes wandered over her neck and shoulders, and I had the sudden urge to replace my eyes with my mouth. Sarah's skin was flawless and exquisite, and, inexplicably, I wanted to taste it. Yet as soon as the carnal thought surfaced, I resolved to eradicate it. No matter how enticing she was, I was her friend, nothing more. Not wishing to make an unwanted advance or take advantage of the situation, I reined in my atypical licentiousness and silently complied.

I reached up with my left hand to hold the top of the fabric. Though I tried not to touch her, as I grabbed the zipper with my right hand, the fingertips of my left accidentally brushed the skin below her neck. As my fingers grazed her, she shivered. I did grant myself a margin of leeway, pretending to give careful consideration to the delicate fabric by taking my time to lower the zipper down her back, allowing myself a few moments to soak in her closeness. I held the left side of the dress so it wouldn't fall off her shoulder. After I finished, her right hand reached up to hold the dress on and she placed her left hand gently over mine to take over. She turned her chin in my direction, whispered "Thanks," and headed back toward her fitting room.

Being so close to Sarah and—for God's sake—undressing her, had been equal parts delightful, overwhelming, and unnerving. I was glad to have some time to pull myself together.

Done with her fashion show, Sarah reentered the hexagon wearing her street clothes and hung the dresses on the return racks.

"I don't suppose you have a favorite?" she asked.

I swallowed hard and shook my head.

"Could you be any less helpful?" she teased me.

"I told you I'm not much of a shopper."

"You have eyes, don't you?"

Eyes and hands and lusts and fantasies and other feelings I shouldn't, yes.

"Let's go. I want frozen yogurt," she said as she seamlessly zigzagged through the displays toward the escalator.

Seated across from each other at a plastic circular table in the food court, spooning frozen yogurt into our mouths, Sarah eyed me inquisitively.

"What did you think of those two women who saw you in that black dress?"

"What about them?"

"What did you think about what they said? About how you looked?"

"They were being polite."

"You think they were disingenuous?"

"I wouldn't say disingenuous, exactly. Just…like I said, polite."

"How do *you* think you looked, now that we've removed 'ridiculous' from the available adjectives?"

I shrugged. "Serviceable, I guess."

"Not horrible?"

"No."

"Pretty?" Sarah asked, as if fishing for something.

I shifted on the plastic bench and my foot involuntarily began tapping the ground in a nervous tic. "I wouldn't get carried away."

"But you agree you looked good," she said, more of a statement than a question.

"I agree that people wouldn't necessarily run screaming from the building if they happened to see me. Okay?"

She stared at me and bit her bottom lip, seeming to want to say more. She scooped a spoonful of yogurt into her mouth before continuing. "Okay. I'll drop it, but only if you tell me which dress I should buy."

"Why don't you ask Dirk?" It came out with more bite than I'd intended.

Her eyes narrowed. "I'm asking you," she said flatly. After several seconds of silence, she added, "Please."

I dodged. "I'm sure you're a much better judge of this sort of thing."

"I'd like your opinion."

I gazed into my yogurt cup and stirred the contents with my spoon. "You can't go wrong with any of them." She didn't respond. I continued stirring. Finally, I took a deep breath and looked at her. "The agave one."

She arched her ever-expressive left eyebrow. "Why?"

My yogurt became interesting again, and I shifted my weight, crossing my legs under the table. "Because…" I shrugged and met her eyes. "It's magnetic. Dangerous." Her right eyebrow joined its counterpart. "If…I mean…that is, if you like that sort of thing," I stammered. She tilted her head, waiting for me to continue. "If you want Dirk to be physically unable to keep his hands off you, that's your dress. Hell, anyone. Geez, I could barely keep my hands to myself, and I'm not even a guy." *Please, God, tell me I didn't just say that.*

"Oh, really?" she asked, as the corner of her mouth curled up slightly.

"Crap, I didn't mean *I* couldn't. I meant, you know, generally speaking. It's…you looked…" I swallowed with difficulty. "Um, alluring, I guess."

Sarah sat up even straighter than usual, her eyes searching mine as if she were trying to read my mind. Suddenly wondering once again if she could, and not wanting her to be able to, I jumped up abruptly, wishing to escape.

"You finished? I should get home."

Sarah stood slowly and held out her hand to me. Bewildered, I stared at it, unable to comprehend what she wanted me to do. She reached forward, pulled my wrist toward her, gently withdrew the yogurt cup from my hand, gave me a teasing smile, and walked our cups over to the trash can. I grabbed the tote bag and followed her out.

Once Sarah parked in front of my house, I pulled her tennis clothes and shoes out of the tote bag and placed them on the backseat. I reached for the door handle, holding my things in my other hand, and turned toward her.

"Thanks for today," I said as I opened the door. After I placed one foot in the street, I felt her hand on my upper left arm.

"Why wouldn't you tell me Kip asked you to Homecoming?"

I spun my head around. "How could you possibly know that already?"

She killed the engine. "Dirk and Kip are best friends. Of course I'd know. So why not tell me?"

I closed the door and sat back before answering. "Because I'm not going. And I'm not a gossip. It wouldn't be fair to Kip if I said anything."

She furrowed her brow. "Why wouldn't you go? Kip's one of the most sought-after boys in school. He's sweet, thoughtful, and he happens to be a friend. I want to know why you're not going."

"Are you always this nosy?"

She gave me an artificial smile. "Yes. So get over it and tell me."

I focused on the glove compartment. "I don't like being teased about how I look."

"He teased you? *Kip*? That can't be right. Kip's like, the nicest guy I know. What did he say?"

"You wouldn't understand."

"Try me."

"You'll think it's stupid."

"Are you going to tell me?"

"Are you going to tell him what I say? Or Dirk?"

"You think I'd do that?" Sarah sounded genuinely taken aback.

"I don't know you well enough to know."

"Ouch." She stared out her window.

Several uncomfortably silent moments passed, all of which found me feeling like an ass. "I'm sorry. You didn't deserve that. No, I don't think you'd say anything to either of them. It just sounds stupid, even to me. I'm frustrated with myself, not you, and I don't mean to take it out on you. Okay?"

She glanced at me, her eyes full of hurt, then grabbed the steering wheel and started the car.

"Fuck." I reached for the keys and killed the engine again, taking the keys and shifting my body to face her. "Sarah, please."

She looked at me again, her hurt starting to fade as she read my sincerity.

I powered through to get this over with.

"All Kip said was, basically, something…" I took a deep breath and exhaled. "Something like not wanting the prettiest girl in school to sit home on Homecoming night. That's all he said, okay? And I'm sure he meant me, and I'm sure if I were a normal person, if I were anyone else on the planet even, it would have seemed super sweet. But I'm such a fuck-up, and I've heard it all before so many times from guys that treat me like a piece of meat, that only want a conquest or a piece of ass or whatever, that I wouldn't be able to tell a sincere compliment from one designed to get me into bed. I haven't the slightest clue how to tell the difference, and my track record so far is abysmal.

"I don't mean to hurt your friend's feelings, so if you tell me he's a great guy, I'll trust you. But there's no way I can go to Homecoming with him or anyone else if I have to hear one single word about how pretty I am or how beautiful or whatever, because all it does is put me on the defensive and make me recall past mistakes and wonder whether I'm making another one. All right? I've never told anyone that before and I don't intend to tell anyone again. I'm just trying to convey to you that however unfair it is of me to keep potentially well-meaning people at arm's length, and however irrational it might seem, I have my reasons. Now will you please, *please* just accept that I'm totally fucked up and do your friend Kip a favor by keeping him the *hell* away from me?"

I was so wound up that my voice was louder than I intended, straddling the fence between anger and pain. Sarah's eyes held so much emotion I couldn't make heads or tails of, and her silence wasn't reassuring. Feeling too exposed, I inserted the key back into the ignition and opened the passenger door again.

"See you Monday," I said.

I felt her reach out for me like she had earlier and thought maybe I heard my name, but I needed to be alone. Racket and tote bag in hand, I closed the door behind me, hopped up the porch steps to my front door, and quickly pushed my way into the refuge of home.

Chapter Five

O n Monday, after Wilcox's class, I decided to try to get a moment alone with Kip. As much as I wasn't looking forward to it, I owed him a timely response since he'd been nice as well as accommodating. I stood two steps above the quad and watched as he conversed with Sarah, Dirk, Jasper, and Amy. Still raw from our Saturday conversation in front of my house, not to mention my unraveling on the tennis court that morning, I didn't want to talk to Sarah. That stopped me from walking over and interrupting in order to get a word with Kip. After several minutes, since it didn't seem like the group conversation would end any time soon, I headed to the locker room to dress for practice.

Relieved not to run into Sarah, I bounded down to the courts and sought out my usual doubles partner, Kristin. We made small talk with some of the other players for a while as we awaited Coach's instructions for the afternoon. As we chitchatted, I glanced around to see Coach and Sarah at the base of the parking lot behind court twelve. Sarah had the ball cage with her, presumably returning it, and she and Coach were conversing. Coach nodded at something Sarah said, and then they both walked along the fence between the courts and the parking lot, until they reached the rest of us on court one. Coach handed out the drills and partners for the day, sending pairs and foursomes of girls to various courts, until only Sarah and I remained.

Because I was the fourth-best singles player and the meets were typically played in teams of three singles players and three doubles teams, I usually played and practiced doubles with Kristin. Coach occasionally changed things around so some of the doubles players could play singles and vice versa, but it was fairly rare for Sarah and me to practice together.

Coach studied me. "How's that ankle?" she asked.

"Ankle?"

Sarah jumped in. "I told Coach how you twisted your ankle on Saturday after we'd started working on your serve."

"Oh. Right." I wasn't very adept at lying, so I turned to face Coach and told the truth. "It's feeling pretty solid, honestly. Good as new."

"You're sure?"

"I'm sure, Coach. No worries." I flicked my eyes over to Sarah, who wore a sly grin.

"Glad to hear it. Take it up where you left off. Cazz, I want you to focus on learning the kick serve from Sarah. Sarah, work on your return of serve with Cazz. Court eight."

Sarah grabbed the ball cage and we walked along the outside of the fence toward court eight. Still feeling raw from my admissions over the weekend, I didn't hide my irritation.

"Sarah, what the—"

"Before you start in on me, I knew you'd probably be angry for the ruse, but I wanted to talk to you and you've avoided me all day." She glanced at me as we continued to the court. "Tell me I'm wrong."

I couldn't argue; I had been avoiding her. I didn't respond.

"I thought so."

We got to our court and stopped at the baseline. Sarah set up the cage between us, then looked at me. "Listen," she said. "I know Saturday was a pretty big deal for you, and I'm guessing you're feeling vulnerable right now."

I shifted my gaze to the soccer field, letting my eyes settle on a boy juggling a soccer ball with his knees, head, and feet.

"I'm sure I'm the last person you want to be practicing with today, but Cazz, you got out of the car before you gave me a chance to respond. I wanted to tell you that Saturday meant a lot to me. I'm glad you told me what you did, and I know how hard that was for you. I promise I'll never use it against you, and I'll never tell anyone about any of it. I feel like you gave me a gift, and it meant more to me than you can know. So thank you for telling me and letting me in as much as you did. And now, I'm going to drop the subject so you can focus on your serve, and I'm going to stay at least four feet away from you while we go over this again, so you won't be uncomfortable. Or at least less uncomfortable, since I wouldn't exactly call you the touchy-feely type." Sarah said this last bit in a lightly teasing tone, trying to get a reaction from me.

I pulled my eyes from soccer boy and looked at her. "No, not exactly," I said with a half smirk.

She raised both eyebrows. "So, are we good, or do I have to embarrass you into submission by giving you a huge hug in front of all our teammates and not letting go until I get you to promise to stop avoiding me?" She gave me a wicked grin. She really had my number. And she'd do it, too.

"Aren't you funny?" I grabbed a ball from the cage. "So. Ball toss at eleven o'clock, racket head moving across the ball from six o'clock to twelve o'clock. What else?"

Practice that afternoon felt strange, but in a good way. I felt an odd kind of peacefulness. Restfulness. Liberation. For the first time in my life, I felt that someone really *got* me, understood me, accepted me for who I was. Hell, liked me despite it.

On the court, Sarah was unparalleled. She made for a tough opponent: strategic, quick, tough, and determined. She exhibited impressive coaching skills when helping me with my serve, displaying patience, humor, knowledge, and intelligence, pushing hard but not too hard. Having been her doubles partner in a tight match, I found her to be nurturing, self-confident, tenacious, and gritty. She was all of this and more off court, whether a resourceful and analytical study partner who followed through and demanded excellence, or a fun, kind, giving, and loyal friend to those she cared about. And of course, on or off court, I couldn't help but be struck by her physical beauty.

Slow on the uptake, I realized that afternoon for the first time what a beautiful person she was on the inside. She'd held me when I needed to be held and backed off when I needed space. How she knew when to do one instead of the other was a mystery. But I felt grateful for it, for her. More than grateful, I felt somehow expanded, like I was a fuller version of myself when I was with her. Through the very simple act of sharing herself with me, she made me feel like I was a better person than I was—richer in spirit, more complete. What's more, instead of feeling undeserving of her, I was buoyed by her. She lifted me up to a place that made me sense we were both special, worthy, and deserving of happiness.

After practice, I went to the library for an hour before heading back to the parking lot to wait for my mother. Mom was notorious for telling me "five minutes" when she really meant twenty, but if I wasn't where I was supposed to be on the rare times she actually did come in five minutes, I'd catch hell.

As I made my way to my usual perch on the short wall, Kip was straddling his bicycle, speaking to another boy who was sitting in a car in the senior lot, talking to Kip through the rolled-down window. I decided to walk over. I stopped about twenty yards from where they conversed, and after another minute or so, the driver and Kip exchanged a fancy dude handshake and the driver sped off.

"Kip!" I called. He turned to me and his face lit up with a bright smile. He hopped off his bike as we approached each other.

"Hey, you," he said. "I was hoping I'd run into you today, but I figured you'd be long home by now. You waiting for a ride?"

"Yeah."

"You should get some wheels."

Not wanting to get into the gory details of my family's moving history and why a car was not in my immediate future, I went with a simple reply. "Yeah, I should. Hey, I wanted to talk to you about this Homecoming thing."

"Great." His earnest response wasn't helping.

"I really don't think I'm up for it. I know you mean well and you think it'll be fun, but it's hard for me to get excited about it."

His smile evaporated.

"Trust me, I'm not one of those girls who says no because she's hoping for a better offer. I think your offer is great, and if I were going, I'd love to go with you."

He searched my eyes for the truth. "You're serious."

"Yeah."

"But it's not because of me?"

"Definitely not."

He smiled slightly. "Then let's bail on the dance and go out instead. You and me. On a date."

I gasped in disbelief. "Kip! No! It's your Homecoming! This is your fourth year at Claiborne and it's your time to celebrate. I practically just got here. I don't have that kind of history with this place or with any of you guys. You're super-awesome and a ton of girls want to go with you. You need to go to Homecoming."

"Forget about Homecoming. Say yes and go out with me."

I sighed heavily and practically whined his name. "Ki-ip."

"Ca-azz," he teased me, sing-songing my name as I'd done with his. "Well?" He grinned.

"God, you're a royal pain in the ass." I shook my head with a smile, finding him annoyingly endearing. "Fine. You win. I'll go to Homecoming with you."

❖

Practice ran long for Kristin and me on Wednesday, since Coach had us playing a doubles match against our best singles players, Joanie and Sandra, to work on their volleying. Kristin and I were on fire, playing much better than usual, forcing them to elevate their game. We lost, as expected, but had some long rallies with fast volleys, and we all enjoyed the caliber of play. As the four of us filed into the locker room, a few of the other girls were drifting out. Some had already gone home. Sarah was walking out as we entered, and as we noticed each other, she reached for my upper arm and stopped me.

"Hey. Got a minute?"

I nodded and she pulled me outside the locker-room door.

"What are you doing the Saturday after Homecoming?"

Happy at the thought Sarah's question might mean I'd be doing something with her, I didn't hide my enthusiasm.

"I don't know. What am I doing?"

"My dad's foundation is having its semi-annual L.A. fund-raiser, and I was hoping you might come."

"What kind of fund-raiser?"

"A black-tie affair with a five-course dinner, top-notch entertainment, and a silent auction. It should raise over a million dollars."

This had to be a joke. I played along by giving her an apologetic look and shrug. "Sorry, I left my purse at home."

Keeping her eyes on mine, she dropped her chin, affecting exasperation. "Not as a donor, obviously."

"You're not kidding."

"I know it sounds kind of major, but they're usually pretty fun."

"I don't have anything to wear to that kind of thing."

"Don't worry about that. The Foundation will cover it."

I eyed her in disbelief.

"I'll explain later, but it's a nonissue," she said.

"Is Dirk going?"

She shook her head. "I'd be the only one you'd know."

This was starting to sound better. "Assuming I'm adequately dressed, it's not going to annoy anyone that some high-school girl is hanging out with the rich-and-famous?"

Sarah's eyes shifted to the locker-room entrance, then back to me, and a look of concern shadowed her face.

"Listen, Cazz. Full disclosure. It's selfish of me to even ask you to this event because it may be well outside your comfort zone. The truth of the matter, and something I want you to consider very carefully before agreeing to come, is that many of these donors are wealthy, powerful, often famous men. Married men, sometimes attending with their wives, sometimes not. They're harmless, but they tend to be a little more…hmm…I guess…let's say, philanthropic, with pretty, young girls around. They'll be far from annoyed by your presence." I couldn't follow what she was trying to tell me and must have looked perplexed. "To be blunt, you'll be eye candy."

I was momentarily confused. A small part of me was wondering whether Sarah had asked me to attend this function solely because it might possibly be advantageous to her father's organization, but the other, larger part of me was staunchly defending her, telling myself she was being forthright, trying to give me the honest lay of the land so I could decide for myself whether to accept her invitation.

My internal struggle must have been playing out on my face because she crossed her arms, glared at me, and shook her head.

"No, I didn't ask you to come because I think you'll be good for business."

I believed her. Though I couldn't seem to prevent my inherent—or learned—suspiciousness from creeping into my thoughts, I trusted Sarah. If I was going to get hurt, it would be beyond measure, because in less than a month, Sarah had single-handedly torn down the walls I'd instinctively spent years building around myself.

I decided to mess with her and pretended to be offended. I mirrored her posture by crossing my arms. "I see. You think I'll be bad for business." I bit back the smile that was threatening to show itself and gave her a cool stare.

Sarah appeared flustered and uncrossed her arms to gesture with her hands. "What? No! No. I didn't mean you wouldn't be good for business, I meant—" Realization dawned on her as she noticed the teasing smile blossoming on my face.

"You little shit." She gave me a light shove. "I'm glad you can joke about this, but don't kid yourself." She provided yet another warning. "Seriously. You're bound to receive a lot of attention in the form of compliments and prolonged handshakes. Are you up for that?"

"If we're going to be at a swanky place surrounded by hundreds of people, I think I can handle it. But I appreciate you looking after me, Sarah. I really do."

"So you'll come?"

"I'd be happy to. Thanks for inviting me."

She awarded me with a delighted smile. "I'm so glad. Details to follow." She wagged her eyebrows flirtatiously, then walked away.

If I'd been able to focus on anything aside from the prospect of having an almost-date with Sarah, the idea of hobnobbing with the jet set would have unsettled me. As it was, probably a full minute elapsed after her departure before I could recall why I was standing alone outside the locker room. Sarah had chosen *me*, and instead of letting doubts seep into my consciousness, I reveled in the choosing.

CHAPTER SIX

Once Sarah found out I'd agreed to go to Homecoming with Kip, she insisted we join her, Dirk, and some other seniors in the massive SUV limo they'd rented. In the week and a half that followed before the big night, I saw a lot of Sarah, as I kept being invited to hang out with her and her other friends from Homecoming court. The nominees had been announced as a kickoff to over a week of Homecoming-related events, including daily dress-up themes (e.g. superhero, nerd, and pajama day), leading up to Saturday afternoon's football game, half-time coronation, and evening dance.

Most of these girls seemed to require an endless amount of shopping and preparation and to have a similarly boundless desire for gossip about who was going with whom, who turned down whom, what so-and-so was wearing, and so on. Sarah occasionally partook of these gossip sessions but never in a spiteful way. She seemed to be having fun with it all. I kept more or less to myself, but enjoyed being able to hang out with some of the more popular girls at Claiborne. I especially relished being in Sarah's company, even though I missed having time alone with her.

The night before the big dance, Sarah invited me over to her house, ostensibly for "final preparations," whatever that meant. It turned out she wanted to spend time away from the company of others for a change, since there'd be no shortage of them the night of the dance, had been no shortage of them in the days leading up to it, and she knew I was relatively low maintenance.

Sarah's parents were out at a dinner gathering, and after my mom dropped me off, Sarah showed me around for the grand tour. Her house was large but not ostentatious. It was warm and inviting, and spoke of wealth and taste. Her father was some well-known philanthropist who traveled a good deal and knew many famous people. Whenever Sarah talked about him, she was childlike in her regard, looking up to him like a saint or hero. She told me all her best qualities were from her father, and that her comfort and poise in social settings was due to his influence. She dearly loved her mother, Linda, but seemed to have a special bond with her father, Luke. He taught her how to make people feel at ease, how to exude warmth and friendliness, essentially how to charm anyone in any circumstance. She wanted to follow in his footsteps, which meant going to work for the nonprofit he'd founded and built. College was first, perhaps even an advanced degree, but Sarah had her heart set on working side by side with the man she most loved and admired.

After the house tour, we started the evening by chilling out in the family room watching a cheesy romantic comedy. Once the breezy ninety minutes was up, Sarah led me upstairs to her room, which I'd glimpsed during the tour and was seeing up close for the first time. It was large and well-appointed, elegantly patterned in various shades of gold, red, and brown. Sarah turned on some music. She sat on the floor, rifling through her CDs, while I sat perched on her bed and we talked about our favorite bands. Conversation eventually turned to the following night.

"How are you going to deal with it if Kip asks you to dance?" Sarah asked.

"I already told him I'm not much of a dancer."

"I'm sure he'll want to slow dance with you. You don't have to be good to do that."

"Can we move on to the next subject, please?" I didn't want to be talking about slow dancing with Kip with the only person I wanted to hold that closely.

"No, we can't. Have you slow danced before?"

"I've watched people do it. It's simple."

"Yes, but very intimate. You need to be prepared for what might be in store for you tomorrow. Kip's a pretty affectionate guy, and he likes you. So unless you tell him not to, I'm sure he'll be very affectionate with you. How are you going to deal with him when he gets in your personal space?"

"I'll figure it out if and when the time comes."

Sarah finished manipulating the stereo and a ballad came on. "You need to know going into it what you'll be comfortable with. Are you going to let him slow dance with you?" She wouldn't let it go.

"I don't suppose it'll kill me."

"Knowing you, it might. Show me you can do it."

She gracefully stood and walked over to the bed, leaving meager dance-floor space between us. "Dance with me."

"No," I said in a tone meant to convey she was insane.

She held out her hand and wiggled her fingers in invitation. "I mean it. Show me you can take it."

"Perkins. No." My voice was stern and deliberate.

Sarah put her hands on her hips. "Don't 'Perkins' me. If you can't do this with me, someone you know and trust, then how the hell do you expect to be able to do it tomorrow? You need to get over your fear of being held or you're going to be miserable."

"I'm not afraid of being held." *Not by you.*

"All right, my mistake. I meant your *discomfort* at being held."

"I don't want to do this with you."

"You'd rather do it with Kip?"

"I'd rather not do it at all."

"Exactly my point. But you're going to have to, so you should try to get a little comfortable with it now, where it's safe and quiet and no one else is around."

"I'm sure it'll be fine," I said through gritted teeth.

"Great. Show me." Sarah gave me the "come-hither" gesture with her fingers again.

I nearly growled. "Sarah."

"Come here." She took my hand and pulled me off the bed, standing me in front of her. "If he slow dances with you, you're going to place your arms around his neck, like this." She took my right hand and draped my arm over her shoulder, following suit with the left. "And he's going to put his arms around your waist, like this." She slid her arms around my waist.

My face was suddenly inches from hers and blood surged to my cheeks. I turned my head to avoid her eyes. I could smell that faint jasmine perfume she occasionally wore, and inhaling her scent made me want to give myself over to her completely. I kept myself in check and pulled my arms away from her neck, but she held me firmly by my waist.

"Sarah, I can't do this." I was frightened she'd be able to feel my racing pulse and glean its meaning.

"I know." She reached again for my right hand and placed it back over her shoulder. "Which is why you should practice. Focus on breathing." She moved my left arm back into position as well. Our heads were just above and past each other's shoulders in the dancing embrace, our cheeks touching. Her breath tickled the skin on my neck, which sent shivers through me. Her breasts pressed against mine and our hips melded to each other, the heat of her hands around my waist scorching the skin through my shirt.

My body was on fire and I was having trouble concentrating. "You don't understand," I whispered, my voice losing an octave since my last protestation. "I can't do this."

Her right hand moved to my chin, turning my face to hers. "You can," she said quietly, gazing into my eyes.

"Sarah, please." I was reduced to nearly inaudible begging. I watched her watching me, searching me from one eye to the other, until I couldn't take the longing anymore.

I tightened my arms and drew her to me, bringing my mouth to hers and kissing her gently. Her head pulled back a little and the hand around my waist stiffened, but somehow, I ignored it. If I'd realized she wasn't responding, I would have broken the kiss immediately, but the softness of her lips and sweetness of her mouth created a craving in my abdomen that momentarily shuttered my doubts and willfully ignored hers. I tugged her to me with slightly more force, my mouth tenderly roaming the soft landscape of her lips. As my tongue lightly traced her upper lip, I heard her breath catch. I opened my eyes at the sound, my mouth still on hers, and saw wide eyes looking back at me. Unable to read any of the emotions there, I finally broke the kiss.

Still entranced and moving in slow motion, I gradually became aware that I'd probably irretrievably fucked up our friendship. Panic set in as I finally made that connection. After I pulled farther back, the deer-in-headlights expression on Sarah's face shifted into realization, then further into determination.

Sarah tugged me forward and brought our mouths together again. She tightened her arms around my waist and pressed against me. When she parted my lips with her tongue, I brought mine forward to meet hers, and the sensation was so exquisite, so electrifying, that we both whimpered. As our tongues continued to dance together, I found myself amazed to learn how much surface area of lips and tongues deserved to be so studiously examined. As I explored her mouth with mine, I felt I could linger along that welcoming, wondrous, soft warmth for days, discovering one breakthrough after another in the delicious details that were Sarah. Each moment our mouths were connected was a treasure, and I drowned in the pleasure of discovery.

After several marvelous minutes, Sarah drew away from me, though our bodies remained connected. I opened my eyes and watched hers flutter open. My mouth hung open, and I quickly closed it. We stared at each other, only our breaths breaking the silence. I was stunned and confused. Whatever emotions she'd awakened within me had knocked me off kilter and left me baffled. Where I usually would have fortified my defenses and leapt from her embrace into the safety of isolation, I wanted only to be closer to her, wanted to remove barriers, wanted to feel the warmth of her body against mine.

She had completely captivated me, and I desired nothing more than to remain in her arms forever. I felt helpless, lost in the sea of light-blue eyes that sought answers in mine, for I had none to give. I'd never experienced such longing before, never craved such closeness, never felt anything so wonderful. I moved my gaze to her mouth, as if I could find knowledge there. Explanations. But the only thing I found was an intensifying of the ache I'd already felt when she pulled away, the yearning to hold and be held by her.

Her lips parted slightly and her chest rose and fell with deep breaths. I flicked my eyes back to hers. Though I was incapacitated by the fear that kissing her again might push her away, desire smoldered within me, and I willed away the distance between us. As if reading my thoughts, Sarah trained her eyes to my mouth, threw her arms around my neck, and threaded her fingers in my hair. She crushed her lips to mine, and I responded in kind, as if I could devour her. I splayed my hands across her back, pulling her closer and melding her body into mine. She moaned as I deepened the kiss, and the sound stoked within me a craving I'd never known. Brazen need replaced the sweetness of the previous kiss, and my blood ran hot from the friction we were creating with our bodies.

Reality or common sense or something finally took hold of Sarah, who, while still kissing me, walked us several steps backward and gave me a gentle push that broke our embrace and left me sitting at the edge of the bed. I was breathing heavily and trying to concentrate on steadying myself.

She gazed down at me for a few moments, furrowed her brows, shook her head, and started pacing.

"Shit," she said.

It wasn't the first word out of her mouth that I was hoping for, though I wasn't sure exactly what that was. She ran both hands through her hair before hugging herself pensively and continued pacing.

I didn't know what to say, couldn't begin to process what had just happened between us, so I stayed silent. I couldn't add anything except words of astonishment.

"Shit," she repeated. She ceased her strides and stood looking at me from across the room. "I'm taking you home."

I watched her for several seconds, contemplating a response—something, anything, to say—but words failed me. I peered down at my hands and nodded. I felt ashamed. Not so much because I knew what we'd just done was wrong, but because I hadn't wanted to stop.

Her feet came into view, and I glanced up as she stepped between my legs and gazed down at me.

"Cazz. I have no idea what to say to you right now, so I'm not going to say anything." She bent down, cupped my face in her hands, and gave me the gentlest of kisses. Then she removed her lips and regarded me with astonishing tenderness. After several moments, she walked to the door. "Come on."

I followed her downstairs, and she drove me home, into the longest, most confusing night of my life.

CHAPTER SEVEN

Before the amazing turn of events of the previous night, I'd already had low expectations heading into Homecoming, knowing I'd be sharing a limousine with Sarah and Dirk, the picture-perfect couple. I didn't usually dwell on how great they seemed together, possibly because I honestly liked Dirk, or possibly because I didn't view myself as a rival. But after sharing mesmerizing kisses with his girlfriend, the last thing I wanted was to have to watch Dirk and Sarah cuddling up together the entire night.

Turns out that with my low expectations, I'd set too high a bar.

Outwardly, I doubted anyone noticed how traumatic the evening was for me. I was, after all, a nomad, unable due to circumstance to forge long-term bonds and therefore used to playing the stoic with practiced indifference. Inwardly, I felt out of place, alone and confused.

The night before, I'd been too wound up to fall asleep at a reasonable hour. I'd replayed everything over and over and over until it felt so raw I could bleed from it, as if it were a strange scab I kept picking at. I replayed the dance Sarah led; the kiss I initiated; her responding hesitation, followed by her determination and desire; her mouth on mine; her scent; her body pressed tightly against me; the warmth of her breath; her gentleness when breaking apart; her silence during the drive to take me home.

What did it mean, any of it? Was I a horrible creature who took advantage of the kindness of a friend to get what I wanted? What was it I wanted? What was I to her? Friend? Suitor? Would she ever talk to me again? Would she be so embarrassed or guilt-ridden by what we'd done that she'd end our friendship? Would she blame me? Be angry with me? Disgusted by me?

I didn't know what Sarah thought about me. I didn't know what it meant for me what I thought about Sarah. All I knew was it was Sarah's mouth I wanted on mine, Sarah's scent I wanted to inhale, Sarah's smile I wanted to stoke, Sarah's body I wanted wrapped around mine. Yet even if I could never touch her again the way I had last night, I'd be happy if I could simply be with her, talk with her, laugh with her, soak up the sun that was her. She made my heart soar.

She could also make it come crashing back down, if my trust was misplaced. But none of the uncertainty mattered. Only one thing mattered.

There was only Sarah.

I wasn't sure if I should have been freaking out or what it meant to my future, but that simple truth finally carried me into sleep.

Tonight, however, here we were at Homecoming.

From the start, it seemed I was destined to remain on the periphery of Sarah's—I mean, Queen Sarah's—enchanted evening. She'd been crowned at the football game, as had Dirk. The only alone time I was able to get with her lasted all of about ninety seconds, right after we'd arrived at the dance. Of the five couples sharing the packed limo, Sarah and Dirk were the last to file out, behind Kip and me. The other three who'd ridden with us didn't hesitate to make their way into the dance. Dirk and Kip asked for a minute and stepped away from us to have a few words, something about planning the smoking of some Cuban cigars. During this tiny moment, I had the Queen to myself.

She was in the agave dress, and I quickly looked away to minimize the flush rising to my cheeks at the sight of her, unflanked, having emerged from the previously packed limo and standing up to her full height (more, in her heels). Sarah, whom I hadn't seen since the night before when she dropped me off at my house without saying a word. Sarah, who filled my waking thoughts and restless night. Sarah, in this phenomenal dress exuding high-octane sensuality and magnetism. She turned to me with a boys-will-be-boys eye roll as Dirk and Kip made their secretive plans.

I regarded her nervously, a million thoughts churning through my mind. What did I say to her? Should I compliment her? Compliments weren't really my thing, but I was okay with stating the obvious. And the obvious was that Sarah was gorgeous. Should I tell her how pretty she was or would that sound lecherous? Were we still friends? Was she regretting having invited Kip and me along? Did she hate me?

God, I wouldn't be able to handle that.

Sarah didn't take her eyes off mine, the cinema that was my face giving her ample entertainment as I cycled through my worries. Of all my concerns, one kept bubbling to the surface: fear. I was so afraid of losing her, so afraid of what she'd become to me, my chin started quivering and my eyes pooled. I was never more obvious or vulnerable with another human being and couldn't comprehend what it was about her that brought out this annoyingly desperate side of me. We continued to regard each other in silence, with me doing my darnedest to keep my tears from tumbling over. I was pathetic and frustrated with myself.

Sarah's expression turned from amused and questioning to concerned and tender. She lightly grasped my forearm.

"Hey," she said quietly. "We're here to have a good time tonight, remember?"

I nodded and focused on the ground.

"You don't seem like you're having such a good time."

I looked up at her and wondered if I should acknowledge the truth in that statement. Then I figured my eyes had already answered for me. I shook my head.

"What can I do to make it better?"

My relief was so great I let out something halfway between a sob and a laugh. I couldn't help but give her a half-hearted smile. Sarah was making me feel better by letting me know she still cared about me. But my relief was fleeting—Sarah was a kind person and would probably be asking the same thing of anyone who appeared the least bit upset.

I quickly chastised myself for that ungenerous thought. Here she was, trying to lift my spirits, literally and figuratively reaching out to me, and I immediately responded by making it out to be a bad thing, like she didn't really care about me. I certainly wasn't deserving of her warmth or concern if that was going to be my reaction to this girl who had consistently been there for me when I needed her.

We couldn't get into anything too personal, given that our dates were expected back at any moment. I put my hand on top of hers where she was still holding my forearm.

"Forgive me." As soon as I said it, I knew it could be taken to mean different things. I meant it as something between "forgive my moodiness" to "forgive my emotional reaction," but now that the words were out, it could mean I was asking for her to overlook my actions from last night. Was that subconsciously what I meant?

Sarah narrowed her eyes and cocked her head to the side, a puzzled look on her face. As she was about to respond, Dirk called out. "You ladies ready to rumba?" He clapped and rubbed his hands together enthusiastically as he and Kip sauntered toward us with big smiles.

I let go of my hand on Sarah's and she removed hers, then held my gaze for another moment before turning to Dirk. Following an exaggerated bow, he extended his hand to her. "Shall we, m' lady?"

She beamed up at him and curtseyed. "We shall."

With that, my brief connection to Sarah the night of Homecoming vanished.

❖

By Monday, I was aching for some one-on-one time with Sarah. We had a lot to talk about. Rather, I had a lot of unanswered questions. We hadn't spoken to each other since the Homecoming dance, which meant we'd been unable to debrief on our evening together at her house. As much as I preferred to avoid conflict, by Monday morning, having slept only a handful of hours during the past three nights combined, I was such an exhausted mess I felt willing to confront Sarah just to get some clarity and move on.

Well, not move on, exactly, but at least get an understanding of where we stood. No matter what happened, I would never be able to move on from Sarah.

Our assigned seating in English and Earth Science meant we wouldn't have any time to converse during our shared classes, so we wouldn't be able to connect until snack, lunch, or after school. We never saw each other during snack because our classes beforehand were at opposite ends of school. Sarah usually shared lunch in the quad with half a dozen friends, so that was out. And after school, we had tennis. My only opportunity would be right after sixth period before either of us had to show up for tennis shortly thereafter.

As I entered the quad, Sarah and Olivia slid into opposite bench seats at one of the picnic tables. Olivia was on the tennis team, Homecoming court, and had been part of the limo clan. They each pulled a textbook out of their backpacks and started conversing. An uneasy calm settled over me and I decided it was now or never. I strode purposefully over to them. Sarah was the first to notice me. The trepidation in her eyes as I approached made me wonder if she was afraid I'd tell Olivia—and others—about our night in her bedroom. Or maybe she was anxious about hurting my feelings and ending our friendship. Or perhaps she was afraid of what she felt for me.

That last thought was so hair-brained I couldn't believe I'd conjured it. For God's sake, this was the same girl whose adorable and adoring boyfriend had been crowned Homecoming King and was majorly crushed on by nearly all unattached—and some attached—females at Claiborne. Feared what she felt for me! Give me a break.

I tried for nonchalance as I approached. "Good afternoon, Princess," I said to Olivia during a lull in their conversation, watching Sarah watching me. As Olivia looked up, I offered a wobbly curtsy.

"Good afternoon, my loyal subject," Olivia responded good-naturedly.

I nodded and turned to Sarah, offering the same curtsy. "Your Highness."

Sarah rolled her eyes in Olivia's direction, pretending to be bored, but delivered a smile.

"Chemistry?" I nodded toward their textbooks, knowing they were in that class together.

"Ugh. I'm at a complete loss as to how she understands any of it," Olivia said, tilting her head in Sarah's direction. "She's helping me cram before our match. You don't need her too, do you?"

If you only knew. I bit back the honest reply and couldn't help but be amused by Olivia's unwittingly loaded question. I gave Sarah a mischievous smile and watched as she arched her left eyebrow. Though curious, she also seemed wary. Thankfully, Olivia read my playful look as relating to schoolwork and she answered her own question.

"Never mind. Of course you don't, seeing as you two are neck-and-neck for the top smarty-pants award."

Given my apprehension of two minutes ago, I didn't know why Olivia's commentary struck such a funny bone, but I bit my lip as I delivered another frisky smile, inwardly laughing at the absurdity of the situation. Yes, I could imagine being neck-and-neck with Sarah. In fact, I suddenly envisioned just that, and it gave me a little rush of delight. I glanced at Sarah, who was now studying me with concern, probably wondering what had gotten into me.

"Don't you look like the cat that ate the canary. Do tell." Olivia wagged her eyebrows at me.

I shook myself out of my reverie and got back to the business at hand. I needed to know if Sarah and I were still friends. As wonderful as it was, daydreaming about her wouldn't give me an answer.

"No, no, no," I said. "Don't be silly. I promise not to steal your study partner." I shifted my eyes to Sarah. "But I was hoping I could borrow you for a minute?"

"If this is about Kip, you better not be holding out on us, girl," Olivia warned playfully.

"Nice girls don't kiss and tell," I replied with a wink, trying to silently communicate to Sarah to relax, to convey that I didn't intend to share our secret.

"If I wasn't freaking out about this midterm, you'd be so busted right now. Get out of my face before I slam this shut and tickle it out of you," Olivia said with a mock threat, closing the textbook around where her fingers marked the current page.

Sarah turned to Olivia with a shrug and stood. "Be right back."

We walked into an empty corridor and each leaned a shoulder against a locker, facing the other. Sarah crossed her arms and spoke in a stony voice.

"What *did* happen with you and Kip?"

I looked at her like she was from Mars. "What does that matter?"

She took a moment before responding. "It matters."

"Nothing. Nothing happened with me and Kip. I don't care about that. I care about—"

"Did he kiss you?"

"For God's sake, Sarah, I don't care about that. I care about us. I care about where things stand between us." I thought it would be harder for me to say that, but she was making me angry. My exasperation made it sound as though I didn't care about us at all.

"What's that supposed to mean?"

Why was she playing dumb? Did she somehow forget what we did at her house three nights ago? Was it so unimportant that it failed to register? So run-of-the-mill? So unexciting and ordinary? Suddenly my gumption to have this conversation wavered. Just because I hadn't been sleeping because of it didn't mean she wasn't sleeping like a baby. Maybe kissing girls was something she did. Often. I dialed it back a notch and took a deep breath.

"With study groups and midterms and our tennis schedule this week, we're not going to have any time together, and I…and I guess I just wanted…some. Time with you. To maybe have a conversation."

"Are you saying you're not coming on Saturday?"

Saturday? Oh, right. The fund-raiser. "Do you still want me to?"

"There you are," I heard Dirk say from behind Sarah. "Olivia said I'd find you here." God, this guy really had crummy timing.

Ignore him and answer the question! Not that it'd make me feel any better. Sarah was so friendly and practiced at the art of socializing, she'd never renege on an invitation, even if she desperately wanted to.

Sarah turned her back to me so she was facing him as he approached.

"Hey," she said.

"Hiya, sweets," he said as he gave her a quick kiss on the lips. He peered past Sarah to me. "Hey, good lookin'," he said with a smile as he casually rested his arm across Sarah's shoulders.

"Your Majesty." I gave him my unpracticed, off-center curtsy.

"You coming over tomorrow?" Dirk asked Sarah. Before she could respond, he enlightened me. "Precalc study group. You're invited if you want to help your underachieving classmates." He grinned, having alluded to my being in Calculus. Dirk's grades were top-notch and he was in two AP courses. He was no slouch in the classroom or on the football field. I didn't want to contemplate other ways in which his performance wasn't lacking.

"You're in Calculus, too," I told Sarah, wondering why she'd be in that study group.

"I got suckered into helping the underachievers." She playfully poked Dirk in his side.

My, aren't they cute?

"Lucky you," I said, offering Dirk a weak smile. I glanced at Sarah before taking my leave. "See you in the locker room."

So much for quality time.

CHAPTER EIGHT

Midterms week was hell and not because of the course load. I was coming out of my skin. Each school day passed at the speed of quicksand, slowly swallowing me, allowing me no respite. If Sarah and I were okay, couldn't she simply say that? She was so good at reading me—couldn't she see how miserable I was in this limbo? Couldn't she give me a smile and a wink? Or put me out of my misery by telling me to go to hell? Why was she making me feel so unhinged?

The few times we shared looks that week, it was like she was silently questioning me. And since that was what I was doing to her, we were stalemated. It was awful. Part of me longed for the days when I didn't let anyone get close enough to hurt me. Another part knew this girl had irrevocably changed me, and that if our friendship was over and memories of her were all I'd be able to take with me into the future, I would do it all over again.

It didn't help that days passed without the details she'd promised would arrive before Saturday's fund-raiser. Friday afternoon, with still no word from Sarah and no understanding of what I was to wear the next night, I began to wonder if I'd imagined the invitation. After my mom picked me up from school and we got home, a nondescript package sat waiting for me from a return address I didn't recognize. It was a sizable cardboard box, which held a large black apparel box, a small apparel box, and a shoebox. A handwritten card with my name on it was attached to the largest of the boxes. I opened and read the card.

A car will be by at 6:30 PM to pick you up. If the shoes don't fit, call my father's assistant, Carol, at (323) 555-1100, and another pair will be couriered to you.
Looking forward.
—S

I pulled off the top to the largest box first, pushed red tissue paper aside, removed the black fabric beneath, then stood as I held it up by its shoulders. I recognized the dress immediately as it fell open and stopped before hitting the floor. It was the elegant, sleek number Sarah had me try on at Nordstrom. I'd been right: I'd never wear something *like* it. I'd wear the very thing itself.

Inside the smaller apparel box lay a beautiful black cashmere wrap. The shoebox contained a pair of diamond-embossed patent Ferragamos on a slingback pump finished with a grosgrain bow. The entire outfit screamed of a sophistication and class I didn't possess, and I hadn't a clue as to how I'd pull off such a look. I also didn't have the time, money, or transportation to search for alternatives. As I took in the thoughtful ensemble, I wondered if Sarah and I might get through this after all.

A black Mercedes sedan pulled up in front of my house at exactly 6:30 PM on Saturday. The driver opened the rear door and waited. Aside from greeting me with a polite "Good evening, Miss Warner" and telling me his name, he drove me in silence to the Grand Biltmore Hotel in Downtown L.A. The uniformed doorman who opened my door upon arrival directed me to the elevator bank and told me to proceed to the Paragon restaurant, located on the top floor.

As I exited the elevator, my jaw nearly fell open. The restaurant was elegantly decorated with A-line fabric backdrops of fuchsia, brown, and ivory panels. Large floral bouquets and columns of tasteful balloons reigned throughout. Near the entrance were exquisitely designed pyramids of appetizers on small round tables. Waiters and waitresses in fancy uniforms wandered between the tables and guests holding silver trays of champagne, wine, and more appetizers. Beyond this section lay dining tables that each had three ivory balloons rising from the center, small centerpiece bouquets, and crystal tea-light candleholders. The guests, primarily over fifty years old, were richly attired, the men in tuxedos and the women in variously colored gowns and dresses. I was far and away the youngest of the hundreds of people I could see.

After taking a few steps, I stopped and searched my surroundings, hoping for a glimpse of Sarah. Amid the sea of predominately black-and-white attire, without the benefit of knowing the color of her outfit or standing atop a table, staircase, or ladder, I couldn't locate her. Several unsuccessful scans of the room later, I started to make my way into the crowd to continue my search when a thirty-something man stopped me midstride.

"Excuse me," he said as he grabbed my forearm. I settled my gaze at his hand on my arm, and then looked pointedly at him. He didn't take the hint, merely moving the hand from my forearm to the back of my elbow. "I didn't think this shindig would be particularly enjoyable, but you, my dear, have made my attendance very worthwhile." He grinned and held out his hand, finally removing his claim to my arm. "Preston Butterfield. Of the Scarsdale Butterfields." He said this as if I'd be impressed, but it only made me think of an upscale candy, perhaps something I'd find on tonight's dessert menu. And like a candy, Preston seemed covered in a sticky sweetness I didn't want to get on myself. Nothing about him seemed genuine. "And you, besides gorgeous, are?"

I took his hand and donned a polite smile. "Cassidy Warner." I didn't want the shortened version of my name to be forever tainted by his saying of it. He turned my hand over and made a display of kissing my knuckles, which seemed like a move an overconfident person makes when mistakenly believing he's suave. As he straightened himself, he pulled my hand toward him and gathered it in both of his while he softly caressed the back of my wrist.

"Cassidy, it's my great pleasure to meet you. May I take your entrance as a sign that you're flying solo at this event?"

Preston was making me feel claustrophobic and in need of a shower. I supposed some girls would find him attractive enough, with his dimpled chin, strong jaw, light-brown eyes, and dirty-blond hair. Yet I felt I'd walked onto a movie set with the male lead accidentally saying his lines to me instead of to his female co-star. He sounded as authentic as a politician. I nearly turned around to see if a teleprompter lurked behind me.

"I'm, uh, I'm meeting someone, actually." I removed my hand from his and took the opportunity to peer past his shoulder into the crowd behind him. Where was Sarah?

"Ah, well, we're all meeting someone tonight, aren't we? That's part of the point of such a gathering, after all. You and I have just met, for example, and I'm so glad we have. Tell me, Cassidy—one sec." Preston spied a waiter passing by with a tray of filled champagne glasses. "Excuse me, sir?" Preston called out to him. The waiter stopped in front of Preston, who grabbed two glasses from the tray. He thanked the waiter, who nodded and continued on his way.

Preston held out a glass of champagne to me. "For you, my dear."

"No, thank you." It would be just my luck to have the police storm the place at that very moment and ruin the entire event because they inadvertently served alcohol to a minor. That would be a great start to meeting Sarah's father and patching things up with her.

"Please." Preston pressed. He was aptly named.

I shook my head and crossed my arms in front of my waist to thwart any attempt by him at forcing a glass into my hand. "I don't drink."

"Of course. My apologies." Preston bowed his head slightly and placed the drinks on a nearby table.

To avoid further interaction, I took the opportunity of his finally being out of my personal space to make my move. As he re-approached, I nodded and pivoted away from him.

"It was very nice to meet you, Mr. Butterfield, but if you'll excuse me, I—"

Instead of allowing me to slip by, Preston grabbed my hand. He placed his arm around my waist and steered me away from the dining tables toward one of the balconies overlooking the city.

"Please, Cassidy. Call me Preston. I'd be honored if you would allow me to be your escort this evening, at least until you find your date."

I stopped allowing myself to be pushed toward the window. He wasn't making it easy. I had to literally twist my body to move out of his grip in order to stop our momentum.

"Preston, that's very kind of you, but I really do need to find my friend. She's expecting me." I'm sure the smile I'd plastered on my face appeared as fake as it felt.

He didn't seem to notice. Rather, his face lit up at the pronoun. He placed his hands in front of him, palms up and toward me, in a gesture of mock defeat. "Tell you what." He dropped his hands. "Describe her to me, and we'll search for her together."

The idea of describing Sarah to this asshole held no appeal. Even the thought of him seeing her made me slightly nauseous. If he purported to be this interested in me, he'd surely need the handkerchief from his tuxedo jacket pocket to capture the drool he'd manufacture upon seeing Sarah in whatever dress she was wearing tonight.

"I'm sure I'll find her, but thank you."

Preston slid his arm around my waist and once again tried to steer me forward. "Nonsense. It's the least I can do."

No. The least you could do is keep your damned hands to yourself.

I stopped our forward progress. "No. Thank you." There was an unfamiliar edge to my voice. I pushed his arm off me. I wasn't smiling even fake smiles anymore.

I heard a man bellow from a few yards away. "Ah, there you are, Preston!" Preston and I turned to face the newcomer. In step behind the approaching, extremely handsome, dark-haired man was Sarah. The man grabbed Preston's hand in a firm, double-handed shake and forced Preston's attention to him. "Your father swore you were milling about. Come, we were just talking about you."

As my good-looking savior physically pushed Preston into the crowd, behind Preston's back he surreptitiously gestured the cut-off sign at his neck while rolling his eyes at me, finally waving to me in a manner that said he'd ensure I'd be safe from Preston hereafter. As they departed, Sarah slid up next to me and purposefully led me into the ladies' room. We entered a makeup and lounge area that was separated from the stalls and sinks.

"Are you all right?" Sarah turned me around and eyed me with concern.

I was not all right. I was in a mild state of shock. Seeing Sarah brought about a wave of relief and anger. She'd purposefully put me in a position she knew I'd be uncomfortable with, yet she'd not only forewarned me about the possibility of a Preston-like encounter, she'd saved me from it. Well, she and that man who'd whisked Preston away. I didn't know whether to yell at her or hug her.

To further befuddle me, she looked like a million dollars in a floor-length, black halter dress. Her bare shoulders, exposed collarbone, and toned arms all conspired to diminish my brainpower. How could I be expected to keep my wits about me when she was impossibly stunning, radiating poise and elegance no teenager should possess? Instead of declining the champagne, maybe I should have downed it for courage. Preston's too. Along with the other glasses on the tray.

"Cazz?" Sarah sounded worried.

I stared at her, a thousand thoughts racing through my head like items written out on an imaginary Wheel of Fortune that was spinning and spinning, clicking and clicking, until finally landing on one: escape. I shook my head and quickly walked to the elevator. After pushing the down arrow I waited, trying to mind-control the doors to open. Sarah followed close behind me, and instead of waiting with me, she grabbed my hand and tried to lead me to the stairs.

I shook her off. "I need to get some air," I said hoarsely. Actually, I needed to find my driver and be taken home. I turned back to the elevator, unable to look at Sarah.

She stopped me with a hand on my shoulder.

"Come with me." She grabbed my hand again and we headed back to the door to the stairs. She flung it open, walked us down one flight, and opened the door to the 49th floor. It was devoid of activity and she led us to a balcony identical to the one upstairs Preston had steered me toward. We were alone.

"Why am I here?" I said aloud, mostly to myself. Why had Sarah invited me to this event?

Sarah mistook my question as wondering why we were on this floor. "There's no good place upstairs with any privacy. I'm sorry I didn't see you before Butterfinger put his paws all over you. As soon as I saw he'd cornered you, I grabbed my dad and got him to run interference so I could get you away from him."

"Butterfield," I grumbled.

"Butterfield, Butterfinger." Sarah rolled her eyes. "Jerk. His parents are friends of my dad's and this is the first—and last—time he was invited. He's here from New York on business or something. After the shameless way he greeted me, I told Dad not to stray too far from the entrance until you got here." She sighed. "Most people here are good folks, Cazz. Some can be a little too friendly and a little too forward sometimes, especially after a few drinks, but they usually understand 'no.' Very few are downright creepy. I didn't sign you up for this, and I'm sorry."

"No worries." My canned response lacked a sincerity we both could feel. Neither of us spoke for several moments. My jumbled feelings weren't finding any greater clarity during the silence, though my anger was dissipating. "Thanks for rescuing me." It seemed the polite thing to add, but even it sounded mechanical, devoid of actual gratitude. Several more moments passed. Until last weekend, our silences were usually comfortable, easy stretches. Not so anymore.

"Are you upset with me?" Sarah finally asked.

I shrugged. "Not really."

"Not really? That means you are."

"It doesn't matter."

Sarah crossed her arms. "It matters to me."

"Why do you care?" I sounded like a six-year-old.

Sarah cocked her head to the side and stared at me for several long moments. Then she nearly imperceptibly shook her head and looked out the window.

"You didn't seem to care earlier this week," I said, remembering how I couldn't seem to get even five minutes alone with her.

"Well, don't stop now. Tell me what that means."

"I don't know." It was the truth. I couldn't make sense of anything at that moment. "I can't…I can't figure you out, I guess.

I don't know what you want from me. I don't know why I'm here. Why *am* I here?"

"Why do you think I asked you to come?"

"I asked you first." Ever the six-year-old.

"Fair enough. I promise to answer your question, but you have to answer mine first. Why do you think I asked you to this event?"

"I don't know."

"That's not an answer."

"To help your father." What a chickenshit I was.

"If you really thought that, you wouldn't be here. But I'll rephrase. What's the reason you were *hoping* I'd asked you here?"

"I wasn't hoping anything."

"Jesus, Cazz. Stop with the self-protectiveness already. Do you think I'm having this God damn conversation taped?"

"I don't know what to think."

"You know what? Fine…Fine. Let me guess. You're thinking I asked you here so I could…Jesus, I don't even know how to bullshit this. I don't know how to make my brain go where yours goes. But fine, I'll try. You're probably thinking something crazy like…like I asked you here so I could…so I could purposefully make you feel uncomfortable. Because that's so fun for me. I have so little real enjoyment in my life and so much free time on my hands that I feel the need to prey on select girls in my school, treat them to a nice evening out, and then get my kicks by watching them squirm while some creep hits on them. Does that really make any sense to you? Because it sure as hell doesn't make any sense to me!"

Sarah winced at the volume to which her voice had risen. She took a breath before continuing in a much more subdued tone. "I'm going to ask you one more time. You're the most infuriating person in the world, but at least you're honest. So I want an honest answer. What was the reason you were hoping I'd asked you here tonight? And, damn it, tell me the truth."

I couldn't believe Sarah was backing me into a corner like this. I was so anxious about saying the wrong thing and scaring her away, my brain was going to hemorrhage. My emotions were getting the best of me and moisture was beginning to pool in my eyes. My hands started to shake. I wanted to be anywhere but standing here next to her, facing this question. Could I lie? I closed my eyes and focused on my breathing. When I opened them, I looked out the window instead of at Sarah as I spoke.

"I was hoping you wanted to spend time with me. That we could hang out together, just the two of us. Obviously, amid a bunch of other people, but still. That's all." I responded truthfully. It took all my willpower not to caveat my reply by saying it was no big deal or adding a casual "whatever."

Sarah closed her eyes briefly and exhaled a sigh of relief. "Exactly. That's exactly what I wanted, too."

"You did?"

Sarah smiled. Then she halfheartedly chuckled. "Yes, you numskull. I wanted us to hang out. Like adults, for once. The schmoozing part of the evening isn't too long. Then I thought we could have dinner, go dancing, pretend we're going to buy some of the silent-auction items…that kind of stuff. Plus…well, plus I wanted you to get a sense of what my dad does, because it's what I want to do after college. Tonight we'll hear from some of the people the foundation has helped and learn about various projects this event will help fund. It's pretty cool. I mean, you know, for that sort of thing."

I'd never seen it before, but Sarah was nervous. She seemed almost as nervous as I'd felt a minute earlier.

"You're not upset with me?" I couldn't stop myself from asking.

She shook her head. "I'm a little upset that you're so hard on yourself, and that you always think the worst, but given your penchant for moving cross-country every other month, I'm trying my best to understand it."

"Thanks, but that's not exactly what I meant." She had to know I was talking about our kiss. Kisses.

She gave me one of her trademark winning smiles. I had to concentrate to keep my knees from buckling from the force of her radiance. Instead of responding, Sarah took my hand, raised our arms until they were parallel to the ground, and held me at arm's length to survey my ensemble.

"I see the package arrived."

I indicated myself with my free hand. "Your foundation's going to need a lot more donors if it keeps wasting money like this."

She laughed. "In that outfit, I guarantee a minimum ten-X return in the form of contributions."

I smiled and decided to try out my newly practiced response. After Sarah's warning that I could expect some attention this evening, I'd spent some time talking to myself in the mirror, trying to get used to flattery and responding courteously.

"Thank you."

"Wow, a thank you? We're making progress."

Possibly true, but it was time to change the subject to something other than me. "I hope I get to actually meet your father tonight, since I only got the flyby. Was he, like, twelve, when he had you?"

"Thirty-four."

"Get real. That man is not in his fifties." Sarah didn't respond, but gave me a look that said she knew of what she spoke. "No way."

"Way."

"Geez. With genes like that, no wonder you look like a super-model." At that moment, I wouldn't have been able to say whether blood was rising to my cheeks or draining from them. I only knew that it seemed to be darting anywhere except to my brain. Sarah raised her left eyebrow, and the right side of her mouth curled up. I tried to act casual. "Tonight, I mean. In that dress, I mean. Never mind."

Taking pity on me in my discomfort, Sarah tilted her head toward the elevator. "Come on. I want to show you something." Her light-blue eyes sparkled and I didn't hesitate to follow.

We went back upstairs. Behind the elevators on the 50th floor was a door over which a sign read, SKYDECK. Sarah pushed it open and we walked the length of a hallway to the corner of the building, where there was another, smaller elevator bank. She pushed the up arrow. Next to the control panel was a sign that read, DO NOT ENTER THIS ELEVATOR IF YOU ARE AFRAID OF HEIGHTS. A host of small print said something about unconditionally releasing the hotel of liability if you accessed the top floor. The metal doors slid to the side and we entered. Sarah pushed the up arrow again. The tiny elevator jerked slightly and rose. Similar to those of certain subways, the doors opposite those we entered opened a few moments later, and we stepped out into what looked like the observation deck from some sci-fi flick.

Thank God I wasn't afraid of heights. We were surrounded top to bottom in an all-glass enclosure. Extremely thick glass, I surely hoped, since there was nothing but darkness and twinkling lights underneath me. No obvious floor. It was disconcerting, yet beautiful. If Sarah hadn't exited first, I wasn't sure I'd have been able to step out. The L.A. city lights glittered all around us in an astonishing 270-degree view. I never knew such a thing existed.

I stepped slowly to the corner of the small glass lookout, taking in the beauty of the night from the most wide-ranging vista. A three-quarter moon stood watch over the cloudless sky. Though there were too many city lights to allow us to see any stars, the sight was almost as breathtaking as the girl standing next to me.

"Why isn't anyone up here? This is amazing," I said.

Sarah shrugged. "You saw the view from the restaurant. I think people forget it's even better up here."

I kept staring out at the lights in the distance and below us. "I've never seen anything like this."

"I thought you might like it."

I couldn't contain my awe. "It's magical." After several minutes reveling in the panorama, I turned to find Sarah watching me, not paying attention to the incredible spectacle below.

"What?" I asked.

"You're such a contradiction, Cazz. You're impossibly difficult to get to know, yet you make it so easy to want to try."

My lips parted in surprise. When I couldn't think of a response, I closed my mouth.

"I suppose it's not fair of me to keep you up here for the evening when I've got to make the rounds for my father. We should go mingle before dinner starts."

I didn't want our time together to end, so I tried to delay our return by pretending I wasn't done taking in the city lights.

"Do you like coming to these events?" I asked.

"I do. I enjoy helping my dad, and I believe in his organization. It's neat to see him in this element, working the crowd. He's a mastermind at fund-raising."

"Yeah, I imagine. In the five seconds I saw him, he seemed very captivating. I see where you get it from." I wasn't sure what was with me tonight. I seemed to be opening my mouth and inserting my foot every few seconds.

She smiled. "You've been taking notes." I blushed. "He likes having Mom and me at these events because he believes people are more comfortable giving money to a family man. It's a relationship that gets built over time. Many of the people you see here tonight will still be prominent donors in ten or even twenty years. It's about establishing trust. These people trust my dad. They know he'll safeguard their donations and put them to good use, making sure people who need it most are going to get the help they need." She spoke of her father like he was a prince, or Robin Hood.

"You seem to be good at that yourself."

She lifted her eyebrows. "At what?"

"Getting people to trust you."

She gave me a playful grin. "I do love a challenge." The conversation swerved into personal territory.

"Is that what I am?"

I hadn't meant anything in particular by my question. I hadn't been taken aback by her suggestion that I was a puzzle she was trying to piece together. Aside from being concerned that we still had a relationship, I hadn't wondered whether or how to define it. There had been no brooding over what it meant for my sexuality or my place in society. I knew only that wherever Sarah was, I wanted to be. Beyond that, I wasn't sure what I felt. Lost and found, all at once. I couldn't make sense of my feelings, understand why my entire being was mesmerized and possessed by her, or why I felt at peace in the very rightness of it. With Sarah, I didn't think of the past or the future. I simply thought of her, of spending time with her, of being with her.

Her eyes widened briefly, then narrowed, and her smile lost some wattage as she grew contemplative. With her eyes on me, she took her time before responding.

"I don't know how to categorize you." She seemed hesitant, as if wondering whether to continue. Seconds later, she crossed to me in three steps, leaned her left thigh against me, and placed her left hand on my hip as if to steady me. She reached up to the single strap on my right shoulder and, using the back of the first two fingers of her right hand, ever so slowly traced a line under my strap, along my skin. The seductive trail ran from just beneath the tip of my shoulder to the dip in my dress's sweetheart neckline, continuing along a path toward my other arm.

Her caress was deliberate. Sensual. Magnificent. My whole body trembled at the contact, and my breath caught. Her face was inches from mine, and her eyes followed the path her fingers outlined. I couldn't breathe and couldn't stop shivering, though with the heat of her touch, I was far from cold. It was a slow, delicious torture to feel her fingers unhurriedly gliding along my skin beneath the upper curve of the dress above my breast. When she finished, she removed her hand and searched my eyes. Mine hadn't left hers since she began her travels, and I stared at her as I exhaled.

"See what I mean?" she asked softly.

I could barely nod, rendered immobile by her caress.

"This thing between us," she said quietly. "I don't know what it is."

I shook my head slightly to convey my agreement and bewilderment at what she could do to me with the slightest touch. She raised her right hand and placed it gently on my cheek as she kept her left hand on my hip. She looked into my eyes, shifting between them, examining me. She smiled and brushed my cheek with her thumb. Then she removed her hands and took a step back. I suddenly felt a strange void at being apart from her.

"I need to attend to our guests. Join me?"

The last thing I wanted was to leave this private haven and lose Sarah to a crowd of lustful old men, but I could empathize with them. Bewitched, I nodded, and we reentered the small elevator.

Chapter Nine

M y mother delivered the bombshell the next day. "I'm so sorry, honey," she said, after telling me we were moving again. "This is the first time I've seen you happy in so long. You know I wish there were another way."

I'd be allowed one more week at Claiborne. That was it. I'd been so wrapped up in my new life I hadn't noticed my father's extended absence over the past week, a sure sign he was already committed to a new base and scouting for a neighborhood his wife and daughter could call their own. Up next: Fort Hood, Texas.

I think my mom tried to explain the reasons for the extraordinarily short stay, but I didn't listen. It didn't matter.

I was numb. I didn't know how to respond—couldn't respond—to the idea that I'd be torn away from Sarah, would never see her again. To say I was devastated would be the very definition of understatement. I was dismantled. Tears sped down my cheeks. I ran to my bedroom, threw on a T-shirt and a pair of old shorts, and dashed out the front door with my racket and a can of balls. Our rental was nearly an hour's brisk walk from the high school, but I made it in a third of the time, as I part walked, mostly ran, to one of the backboards behind the courts. In an uncontained fury, I smashed ball after ball against it, praying for one to land somewhere that could alter the outcome of this horrible unfairness. After exhausting myself of anger, I collapsed to the ground with my back against the backboard and sobbed.

"Cazz?" I heard a familiar voice call out. "Cazz, are you okay?" I glanced up to see Kip set down his bicycle on the half court and walk quickly toward me. I wiped my tears away with the back of my hands.

"Hey." He knelt in front of me. "You okay?"

I couldn't muster a verbal response. I shook my head slightly. I was distressingly far from okay. I buried my face in my hands.

"Hey." This time he drew out the word soothingly. He moved closer, taking me gently into his arms and rocking me lightly back and forth as he spoke softly. "It's okay. It's going to be okay." Though it was going to be anything but, I appreciated his compassion and concern. Kip was a gem, no doubt about it.

After several minutes, finally able to muster some composure, I wiped my eyes and nose with my sleeve and spoke. "Thanks."

He pulled away from me and smiled, trying to offer solace. "Anything." After some hesitation, he finally asked, "It's that bad?"

I looked away and nodded, willing away the latest tears.

"I'm sorry," he said.

I nodded again.

❖

Monday afternoon, after Wilcox's class and before practice, I heard a familiar voice call my name as I walked through the quad toward the tennis courts. Sarah.

"Hey," she said, joining me stride for stride.

"Hey." I kept my eyes forward. No way could I face her.

"I saw Kip."

I nodded, not needing more.

"Can you talk about it?"

I shook my head. The thought of only being able to see Sarah for five more days—four after today—forever—shattered my semblance of control. I choked up, trying desperately not to cry.

A few yards before we got to the locker room, I felt a hand on my upper arm, pulling me to a stop. Sarah tugged gently until I finally met her gaze. The concern in her eyes brought tears to mine.

I couldn't speak. I quickly turned away and wiped my eyes with my knuckle.

"Okay." She didn't press. She stayed by my side until we were in the locker room, where she moved to a separate corridor to let me change in peace. A match was scheduled for Wednesday that week, but I couldn't be part of it. I wouldn't be able to concentrate, which wouldn't be fair to my teammates.

Before practice got underway, I found Coach and asked for a minute alone. I told her my situation and begged for her confidence, saying I wasn't quite ready to say good-bye to my teammates. She said she understood and told me how much she appreciated having me on her team. I asked to be excused from playing in the match.

"Are you sure?"

I nodded.

"Will you talk to Kristin, so she knows what's going on with you?"

I considered the request, unsure. I owed it to Kristin to tell her the truth, but I owed the same and more to Sarah, whom I couldn't face. I nodded. I would tell Kristin during practice.

❖

I was a basket case that week. I couldn't function. I couldn't make sense of this turn of events. After Monday's practice, I didn't return to Claiborne. My teachers agreed to give my mother my upcoming assignments and midterm exams, which I'd aced. I asked my mom to take messages if anyone called for me. Part of me wondered what happened at Wednesday's tennis match, and whether we won. Another part knew that world was irrevocably closed to me now.

Thursday afternoon, I heard pounding at the front door of my parent's rental, followed by Sarah's voice.

"Cazz!" She knocked hard. "Cassidy Warner, I know you're in there!" She knocked harder. "God damn it, Cazz, open the God damn door and come out here!" After several more minutes of pounding and shouting, she left.

I wanted so badly to go to the door and talk to her. See her. Touch her. Hold her. But that was all in the past now.

First thing Saturday morning, the moving truck backed into the driveway. By late afternoon, everything was packed into it, and the familiar sight of an empty house completely devoid of furniture or warmth surrounded me. Nothing left to prove we'd ever lived here. Moments after the truck pulled away, my mother and I gathered our remaining belongings and headed out to her car. After she got in, I surveyed my street one last time.

Two houses down, on the side street leading away from ours, a black Jetta was parked. I couldn't tear my eyes away from it. Seconds later, Sarah opened the driver's side door. She stood on the pavement, regarding me, hand atop the doorframe, forearm on the roof.

To the untrained eye, we were separated by yards, but to me, the distance measured in light-years. I was now as close to Sarah as I would ever be—the chasm that would grow with each passing minute, my future.

We stared at each other. I took a deep breath and finally climbed into the passenger seat of my mom's car. I didn't look up as we passed Sarah's Jetta, and I left the sanctuary of Claiborne High forever.

Chapter Ten

Present Day

I was pumped, and not just because I was already on my third cup of coffee. Commander Ashby had personally selected me for this assignment. *Bring it on.*

Monday morning at nine o'clock sharp, dressed in a beige skirt suit with a sleeveless, button-front, point-collared blouse, I arrived at the address given to me and found myself outside the offices of something called the Kindle Hope Foundation. I recognized the name, but couldn't place how I'd heard of it. As instructed via e-mail, I asked for Gregory Morrison, the associate director of the organization. Carol, the receptionist, asked me to wait in the comfortable, well-appointed lobby.

Although I spotted a stack of available magazines titled *Philanthropy* and another titled *Need* that I could have fanned through, I opted to spend my time silently rehearsing my background—my purported professional experience as dictated to me by Ashby's team. As I walked myself through my fake job experiences for the hundredth time, a captionless photograph hanging in the reception area caught my attention. It was a post-weight-loss picture of former President Clinton shaking hands with a handsome, dark-haired man who looked vaguely familiar. Both men beamed toward the unseen photographer.

Curious, I was considering asking Carol about the man in the picture when I heard a door open somewhere down the hallway. A smartly dressed man with salt-and-pepper hair and a ready smile approached and extended his hand toward me as if we were old friends.

"Cassidy Warner? I'm Greg Morrison. Good to meet you."

I took his hand and gave him my best confident smile, hoping it exuded "hire me" vibes, though Ashby had made it sound as though my job was a done deal.

"Nice to meet you, too."

The positions weren't assured to the first investigator assigned since we often had to go through appropriate HR channels to get hired, but things were stacked heavily in our favor given that a board member was typically either the whistleblower or involved by one.

Behind the scenes, the pilot program partnered with Maddox Staffing International, a well-known staffing firm specializing in accounting and finance. The firm gave permission to the LAPD to use its name solely for investigative purposes but was otherwise uninvolved. The board member who contacted us would be provided with MSI business cards, which he or she would then pass along to HR as part of a strong recommendation to work with the staffing firm. The phone numbers and e-mail addresses purportedly of MSI personnel were actually those of LAPD personnel who would send over a trumped-up résumé of a pilot-program investigator.

Given that our backgrounds were written to coincide with exactly what the company supposedly needed from a candidate and the fact that it was usually a board member applying pressure, it was fairly common for the initial investigator to get a same-day offer. We offered our services as a temp-to-perm solution, which gave our prospective employers time to "try before you buy," reducing their perceived risk and expediting their hiring decisions. Plus, since the city paid us, the wages we received as "employees" were city property, which obviated the need for us to properly negotiate our salaries.

Morrison led me to his office and closed the door. "Please, have a seat, Cassidy." He gestured to the two plush chairs facing his desk, and he took the seat behind it. "I'm afraid we've had a bit of a misunderstanding where you're concerned," he said apologetically. "Our managing director opened this job requisition without fully consulting me, and we simply don't have a position available." Morrison immediately stood in front of his chair and offered a regretful frown, unwittingly winning some sort of Guinness Book record for the fastest job interview never to take place. "I'm sorry to have wasted your time."

I was stunned. This kind of thing didn't happen. The managing director or board member or whoever had contacted Commander Ashby would never have taken things this far and then simply changed his or her mind. Our investigators got in the door because someone of authority concluded that an institution they cared about was being so criminally compromised that inaction was no longer viable. People don't like to be duped.

I tried to sound even-keeled but felt a rising panic. "There must be some mistake." I gave him a halfhearted smile.

Morrison nodded. "Indeed, the mistake is ours—we should have been proactive enough to call and cancel. Things were a bit hectic around here last week, and unfortunately it fell through the cracks, I'm afraid. I hope you can accept my apology."

I was so astonished by the sudden turn of events it took me a moment to process that I was coming out 0-for-2: no accounting job and no way to save face with Commander Ashby. I hadn't been informed who Ashby's friend was, so I didn't even have a way to name-drop in an effort to delay or ideally avoid my imminent departure. As I stood, trying to come up with some sort of rebuttal, a knock on Morrison's door prompted him to call out.

"Come in!"

I turned my head toward the door and heard the click of the handle. The door opened. It took me a millisecond to recognize the striking woman who walked into Morrison's office: Sarah Perkins.

Holy Christ.

Sarah. My Sarah.

She entered with the fluidity and grace of a gazelle, her self-assured gait instantly recognizable. She'd lost the slight roundness of face she'd had as a teenager—which, as a teen myself, surrounded by other teens, I hadn't noticed at the time—and, as impossible as it seemed, was even more beautiful now. Her auburn hair maintained that slight wave that gave it body, and, a little shorter now, it still fell loose past her shoulders. She was wearing a black, single-button, boot-cut pantsuit, black heels, and a traditional blue button-down long-sleeve blouse that accentuated the light blue of her eyes. She looked sharp and svelte, poised and together. *Tremendous.*

With sickening clarity, I suddenly realized exactly who the other man in the lobby photograph was: Luke Perkins, Sarah's father. I wondered if Luke was Ashby's "personal friend."

I fought to maintain my quickly unraveling composure. It was difficult to breathe normally. I couldn't believe any of the things I was confronting at that moment: losing out on a job that was essentially a sure thing, facing the disappointment of Commander Ashby—who could decide to use this as a sort of demerit against me when it came time to evaluate my performance for the directorship promotion—and realizing I'd failed to perform a simple step that would have better prepared me for this morning. In an unforgivably amateur move, I hadn't taken the time to check online to ascertain the name of the Foundation that would match the address Ashby had given me. I'd have discovered its managing director and placed him and this organization immediately.

But most of all I couldn't fathom running into the one person who had once meant more to me than sunlight. The one person to whom I had never said, *couldn't* ever say, good-bye. Not with my heart.

Sarah stared at me for several moments. She narrowed her eyes for an instant before tilting her head as if trying to assess what manner of life form I was. She turned to Morrison, who beat her to the punch.

"Sarah, what are you doing here? I didn't expect you in the office so soon after…I mean, I thought you planned to take as much time as you needed."

"I did. I was off last week and now I'm back."

"Sarah—"

"Carol mentioned you had a guest. I was hoping to be next in line to meet our newcomer." Her eyes stayed on Morrison.

"No need. I was just apologizing to our interviewee that we've had a bit of a miscommunication relating to the position she's here for. She was just leaving." Morrison stepped around his desk and motioned that I was to depart. "Again, I'm so sorry for this," he said as he reached me.

"Greg. Wait a sec. What miscommunication?" Sarah asked.

Morrison stopped and regarded her. "Sarah, please. I'll only be a moment and we can discuss it." He indicated to me to once again move toward the door. I was a human yo-yo.

"Assuming her references check out, we do, in fact, have a position for her. Daddy was clear on that."

Morrison stopped once more. "Sarah." He said her name in a tone that implied she was a simple creature who had trouble understanding basic concepts.

"Greg." Her voice was low, defiant, challenging. They assessed each other for an uncomfortable amount of time before he finally smiled and turned to me.

"Come, Miss Warner, please." Morrison took my elbow and steered me back toward the guest chair I'd vacated moments earlier.

Sarah's voice stopped me a few feet later. "I apologize for the strange welcome you've received." I turned around. "Hi. Sarah Perkins." *Maiden name?* She stepped toward me and stuck out her hand to greet me.

"Cassidy Warner," I said, taking her offered hand. It was as strong and warm and soft as I remembered. Unsure as to whether we were going to acknowledge having once known each other, and frankly unsure whether she had any recollection of me whatsoever,

I decided to follow her lead. I didn't want to say "nice to meet you," because it felt like a lie, and noticed she hadn't said it.

"You have a résumé and references?" she asked, releasing my hand.

Morrison spoke up. "I have them here."

Sarah walked over to his desk and took the proffered papers. She scanned the résumé and separate reference list. "You don't mind if I follow up on these, do you, Greg?"

"Be my guest."

"Great. I'll leave you to your orientation. Unless you hear otherwise, assume these will pass muster." She departed without a glance in my direction. Her casual yet authoritative use of "orientation" instead of "interview" wasn't lost on Morrison.

After the awkwardness of his initial greeting faded, Morrison was accommodating and kind. He gave me an overview of the organization, showed me where the accounting records were kept, assigned me log-in credentials for the accounting and donor-tracking software programs, provided me with read-only access to the foundation's bank accounts, and gave me some basic tasks to occupy my first day. I was happy for the work, happy for any distraction that would help keep my mind off the fact that Sarah—*my* Sarah—was quite possibly mere yards down the hall from me, though I hadn't seen her since our brief introduction.

At six o'clock, Morrison knocked on the doorframe. "Time to pack up, Cassidy. We don't want to overwork you on your first day." He smiled, took a couple steps forward, and waited for me as I shut down my computer and grabbed my belongings. "I trust you've found everything in order?"

"Very much so."

At that moment, Sarah stopped in front of my office door, her attention on me. "Sorry I wasn't able to join you for lunch." She shifted her eyes to Morrison. "Where did you and the team end up taking Cassidy today?"

Morrison's eyes grew wide as he realized his oversight. "Oh, isn't that embarrassing? I completely forgot to take you out for a welcome lunch, Cassidy! We'll make up for it tomorrow, I promise. Please forgive my horrid manners." He smiled apologetically.

"What about drinks?" Sarah asked from the doorway.

Morrison shook his head. "Can't tonight. Honestly, we'll make good tomorrow."

Sarah gave me a curious smile. "Cassidy? Any interest in an adult beverage to commemorate your first day? My treat."

Morrison looked at Sarah. "Bar Nineteen Twelve?" he asked.

"Absolutely."

He turned to me. "I'm jealous. If you haven't been, you'll enjoy it," he said.

Sarah prompted me. "Well?"

I contemplated the offer. Part of me was desperate to go out with Sarah, and part of me was thinking I shouldn't be fraternizing with any of the Foundation's employees because of my investigation.

"That's very nice of you, but I wouldn't want to keep you from anything. Lunch tomorrow will be more than enough welcome, thank you."

"Nonsense. Follow me in your car so we don't have to come all the way back here. Unless you have other plans?"

After a moment's hesitation, I consented. I followed them to the parking lot behind the Foundation's offices and watched Sarah gracefully slide into the driver's seat of a peridot Lexus LS sedan. I got into my blue Toyota Corolla. I refocused on Sarah's Lexus after she pulled in front of me and turned right out of the lot. Twenty-five minutes later, after crawling in traffic along Sunset Boulevard, we pulled into valet parking. I followed Sarah into the bar and sat to her left in a brown leather chair, a glass-top table in front of us.

We each picked up one of the small drink menus from the tabletop. I ostensibly perused it, but my thoughts were solely on Sarah and what to say. I wondered if she felt similarly perplexed, since we were careful not to look at each other. As we waited for someone to take our drink order, Sarah was the first to speak.

"Small world," she said, with a knowing smile.

She does remember me. "It is."

"Are you going by Cassidy now?"

"Depends. My friends call me Cazz." She studied me, as if expecting something further. "I would hope that includes you," I said, feeling an odd mixture of comfort and caution take hold of me. She raised her left eyebrow, and I hedged. "But if you're more comfortable with Cassidy, that's fine, too."

She mulled that over for a while. "Well," she said finally, piercing my eyes with her blue ones, "my *friends* usually say good-bye when they're leaving. Or moving. And usually keep in touch afterward."

I held her gaze for a few moments until I had to look down toward the table, nearly swooning from the sudden rush of a long-buried, painful memory. Closing my eyes, I tried to push down the tide of emotion burgeoning within me. I swallowed hard, shocked at how raw the recollection of moving away from L.A. made me feel, astonished that an event from so long ago could take on a sense of urgency *now*. In addition to feeling awash in my old grief, I felt a strong need to apologize. And something else I was unprepared for: wetness pooling in my eyes. Aside from a natural response to a few tearjerker films, I hadn't cried in years. I raised my eyes to Sarah's and spoke in an unsteady voice.

"I wasn't a good friend to you," I said.

Her face lost its challenging veneer and softened.

More quietly, I continued. "I regret not being able to say good-bye." I paused, wondering why I needed to explain, but pressed on. "I couldn't…I couldn't stand the thought of losing you." I quickly amended that comment so it didn't sound as desperate to her as it did to me. "Your friendship, I mean. And I was too…too immature to deal with it. I'm sorry for that. I…I should have been a better friend."

Wiping at a tear welling up in the corner of my eye, I offered a small laugh and shook my head. "This is embarrassing." I stood. "Back in a minute," I said over my shoulder as I went to the ladies' room.

Grateful no other women were in the restroom, I wet some paper towels with cold water and dabbed them against my face. I stared at myself in the mirror. *Where is this coming from? What is your problem? Get a fucking grip.* I took a few deep breaths and laughed out loud. *Fuck.*

As I walked back through the bar, Sarah watched me. When I sat back in my chair, I noticed a drink on the table in front of each of us.

I smiled sheepishly. "I have no idea where that came from."

She continued to study me. "How do you do that?"

"Make a total idiot of myself?" I replied, trying to lighten the mood. "Lots of practice," I said with a halfhearted laugh.

Her serious expression didn't change. "No. I mean, how do you always manage to get under my skin with your devastating honesty? Jesus Christ, Cazz. I haven't seen you in ten years, and it takes all of five minutes for you to completely disarm me. It's maddening." The exhalation that streamed upward from her lower lip caused a few strands of hair above her eyes to billow.

It took me several moments to analyze her comment before I could respond. The notion that something I could do could actually affect Sarah, let alone disarm her, was not a little gratifying, given her ability to seep into my every pore since I'd seen her that morning.

"If it's helpful, I could say the same thing," I said.

She raised her left brow—that telling feature I'd always found so perfectly Sarah—in annoyance. "It isn't." She gazed at me for several seconds, and eventually a smile slowly played across her lips. "Well, maybe a little."

We simultaneously leaned forward to grab our respective drinks, sat back holding our beverages, faced one another, and took a few moments to adjust to each other through the lens of a decade.

I remembered wondering during high school whether anyone could be more beautiful than seventeen-year-old Sarah. Now I knew. Yes. The answer was literally staring me in the face: Sarah at twenty-eight. She was *Vanity Fair* pretty—she made me want to touch her to see if she was real or digitally enhanced. I had a feeling my comfort in her presence would disintegrate if we were to sit any closer to each other, and, for my assignment's sake, felt grateful for what little distance was between us. Not only had my emotions already gone haywire within minutes of being alone with her, she was short-circuiting the strength of calm I'd begun to take pride in during my career. Her uncanny ability to knock me off my game seemed immune to the passage of time.

I sampled my mystery beverage that had mint leaves floating in it. "Mmm. What is this?"

"Pear Vodka Mojito."

"Tasty."

"You still go by Warner." She didn't skip a beat. Normally I would feel she was being forward, jumping in like that in no time, but given the roller-coaster ride our brief conversation had already taken, it almost seemed natural.

I decided to be coy. "You still go by Perkins."

She gave me a playful smile. "Are you asking if I'm married?" she asked, knowing full well she'd initiated the subject.

"Yes."

"No, and I have no desire to be."

I puzzled at her response.

"You?" she asked.

"Unmarried, though I wouldn't say I've ruled it out."

She shrugged in a "suit yourself" gesture, as if to say marriage was overrated and it would be my loss for trying it.

"How long have you been back in L.A.?" she asked.

"You read my résumé." Ashby's staff made sure the positions I'd held per my fabricated experience dovetailed with my actual geographical locations to make it easier for me to recall in normal conversation by being closer to the truth. *So much for my devastating honesty.* Sarah gave me that deliciously mischievous smile again. Damn, I missed that smile.

"A year then?"

I nodded.

"So at least that part's true."

"What's that supposed to mean?" Her statement caught me off guard.

She promptly ignored my question. "And you graduated from Columbia?"

I nodded.

"So that part's true."

I was suddenly glad Ashby's people had left out my J.D. from Georgetown.

"And you've been in various *finance* roles since that time?"

I preferred to avoid outright lies, if I could help it. I played innocent. "Didn't you check my references?"

"Absolutely. They were marvelous. Impeccable. One might even say, scripted." She was still smiling that smile. I decided to counter her playfulness—or was it suspiciousness—with a bit of feigned cockiness.

"Be fair. There are only so many adjectives one can use for how great I am."

"I look forward to being impressed by your skill set."

Blood flowed to my cheeks, warming them faster than the vodka, though I assured myself she meant no underlying flirtatiousness. I wished to swing the subject away from me.

"What's your role there, at the Foundation?"

"It's twofold, really. My favorite part is grant-making. I spend most of my time researching organizations to see whether our missions are in sync. I spend time fund-raising as well, but I do it because it's necessary, and I'm good at it." Sarah paused and appeared to contemplate something before continuing. "Unfortunately, I suppose now I'll have to focus even more of my time fund-raising."

"Why?"

"Because I have to take over for my father."

"Why?" I asked again.

"You haven't heard?"

"Heard what?"

"He was…" Sarah swallowed with difficulty. "He was killed in a car accident just over a week ago." Her voice had fallen to a whisper that cracked at the word "killed."

My mouth dropped open. *"What?"*

I stared at Sarah like she'd said something very important in Latin, because it wasn't conceivable I could have properly understood what she said. A pall fell across her face, followed by a panoply of emotions I couldn't begin to make out, with the exception of unmistakable grief. I quickly covered my mouth with my hand and stared at her in horror. A glimmer of water welled in her eyes, which she tried to hide by quickly turning away from me. I immediately squatted in front of her, and put my hand on hers.

"My God, Sarah, I am so sorry."

She wouldn't look at me and was trying hard to keep it together to avoid causing a scene. I glanced around the bar, searching for something aside from the ladies' room that could offer some privacy. Spying a door to the terrace, I noticed it was blessedly empty. I stood and grabbed Sarah's hand, tugging her out of her chair and forcing her to follow me. I yanked her through the doorway outside and pulled her into my arms. She moved back a step, shook her head, covered her face with both hands, and started to cry. Undeterred, I embraced her again and held on tightly. After a moment, she yielded and leaned into me; her crying turned to chest-heaving sobs that wrenched my heart out.

I couldn't stand being so powerless. I knew how much Sarah loved her father and couldn't fathom what she was going through. She was hurting, and I could do nothing to diminish her sorrow. After several minutes, her body finally stopped convulsing in my arms, and her staggered intakes of breath eventually transformed into regular, nearly inaudible breathing. She stepped back and whispered into a tissue she'd pulled from her pocket.

"It's hard," she said.

I nodded.

"I miss him so much." She still whispered.

I nodded again. She sniffled, blew her nose, drew out another tissue, and wiped her eyes with it. She was so vulnerable and so beautiful; I ached with a need to protect her.

She gave me a weak smile. "Some reunion this has been," she said.

I gave her a half smile and some more space. "Do you want to head home?"

She shook her head.

"Do you want to finish that drink?"

She nodded.

"You sure?"

She nodded again. "Better to keep busy."

I waited for her to signal she was ready to head back to our table. She took a deep breath, brushed past me, and opened the door that led back to the bar. I followed.

We spent the next couple hours getting reacquainted over drinks and appetizers. My desire to be a distraction for Sarah easily outweighed my wish to maintain a healthy distance between me and anyone associated with my investigation. I wasn't about to tell Ashby how the job stacked up against Sarah tonight. She caught me up on the lives of a few kids I'd known at Claiborne, I gave her the skinny on finishing high school in lovely Killeen, Texas (adjacent to Fort Hood), and we swapped some college stories.

I didn't want to lie to her about my career so I kept reining the conversation in around undergrad, only glossing over post-Columbia days at the ten-thousand-foot level. Aside from the earlier personal nugget that neither of us was married, we steered clear of asking about each other's dating lives, though I was terribly curious. The only other thing she mentioned about her father was that he was killed in a hit-and-run accident. Given how small the Foundation's staff was, I wondered if that wasn't too much of a coincidence—someone had contacted Ashby regarding possible embezzlement, and the managing director of the same establishment was recently killed.

Once we finished the finger food and our second round of drinks, we decided to call it a night. It saddened me that I couldn't come clean about why I was at the Foundation and who my real employer was. I was being dishonest, which in turn made me feel I was putting a barrier between us.

Just these few hours in Sarah's company gave me a sense of place, a sense of belonging that had escaped me for too long. She was filling a void in my life I hadn't realized existed, and the thanks I offered in return were various shades of deceit. I was suddenly ashamed of the job I'd always been proud of until today. It was one of the most significant differences between my work with the SEC and my work with the LAPD. With an SEC investigation, although also of a highly confidential nature, I didn't have to concoct a backstory. My education and experience spoke for themselves.

Now, however, my background was fabricated each time to mesh perfectly with whatever finance-department job opening my new prospective employer needed filled, and all my professional references (being other LAPD personnel) would confirm the story. As much as my investigations with the LAPD required such ruses, it didn't make it sit easier with me to have to hold myself out as something or someone I wasn't.

When we walked outside and handed our stubs to the valets, we stood nearly shoulder-to-shoulder and turned our heads toward each other. Sarah broke the comfortable silence.

"I'm so glad our paths have crossed again, Cazz. I think I've missed you."

I smiled shyly, secretly drowning in the sweetness of her comment. I tipped my head up and back to indicate the entrance we'd stepped through a moment earlier.

"Thanks for the fancy welcome. This was delightful."

She turned fully toward me and smiled. "It was."

The valet pulled up her car. The combination of joy at seeing her again, compassion for her grief, and warmth at being in her presence moved me to advance toward her and gather her in my arms. After a momentary stiffness from surprise, she returned my embrace. When we broke apart, she raised her telltale left eyebrow in disbelief while the right corner of her mouth teased up.

"Twice in one night. Since when did you become so affectionate?" she asked.

"I'm not. Not usually." It was the truth.

She squeezed my hand. "It's nice." She rummaged through her purse as she walked to the open car door, gave the valet some money, and slipped into the driver's seat. Moments later, she was gone.

As the other valet pulled my Corolla forward, my mind flashed to my confident musings of mere days ago: that no one could divert my attention from this assignment. I shook my head and gave the valet a few dollars before climbing into my car. As I put the car in drive, I offered a crooked smile to the universe. *No one, that is, except Sarah Perkins.*

CHAPTER ELEVEN

Tuesday morning, Morrison assigned me to handle all the checks that had arrived over the past week. I had to endorse and scan them, print the bank deposit slip, and enter the data into the donor tracking system that synced with the accounting software. The latter effort was a mind-numbing task avoidable with optical character-recognition software, and I intended to suggest acquiring this time-saving upgrade to Morrison.

Apparently many of the donors were using their wallets as sympathy cards, as the memo field on some of the checks had sweet comments such as "Miss you, Luke!" or "In honor of Luke P." People didn't seem to realize that unless they were paying a bill and using that field to note the invoice number so someone like me could properly apply the payment on their account, no one ever used these comments; no matter what they wrote, only some lowly clerk would ever see it. I made a mental note to tell Sarah that people were missing her father.

The Foundation also received many donations via wire and electronic funds transfer, so I set about manually entering the incoming wire and EFT information into the donor tracking system and ensuring the accounting software accurately reflected the transactions. Once it was properly updated, another employee would handle sending the written acknowledgments regarding whether goods or services (such as the cost of fund-raiser dinners) were provided in exchange for monetary gifts.

By the end of the day, I'd been a productive accountant and was comfortable with the systems and processes the Foundation utilized. That comfort would allow me to interact with Morrison and keep up my front. Tomorrow I'd have to start using my investigative skills to track down whether anything was amiss financially.

Toward the end of the day, Sarah, who had been out all day in various meetings, popped her head into the office I'd been assigned.

"What are you doing first thing tomorrow?" she asked.

"Coming here."

"I mean before that."

"Spin class, probably. Six thirty."

Sarah tilted her head. "You still play tennis?"

"Not in years."

"Are you up for trying something new?"

I cocked an eyebrow. "Such as?"

"Meet me at the Pinnacle Sports and Fitness Club on Wilshire at six thirty. Wear gym clothes, and bring your work attire."

I'd heard of the Pinnacle and doubted I had the pedigree or bank-account balance that would gain me access. "I'm not a member."

Sarah looked at me as if my comment was asinine, then gave me a winning smile. "Tell them you're with me, silly." She instantly vacated the doorway.

The next morning, having no idea what was in store for me, I decided to hedge by wearing layers and going for comfort. I sported a white-trimmed navy jog bra with matching shorts in case I was going to be running. Over that I wore a tight-fitting light-gray workout tank top made of a stretchy material that felt wonderfully soft against my skin. I covered all that with a navy fleece pullover and my least-ratty sweat pants.

When I arrived at Pinnacle at six twenty-five, I told one of the three clerks at the front desk that I was with Sarah Perkins. The girl nearest to me immediately rose and offered a welcoming smile. "Please, right this way," she said. I followed her into the women's locker room. It was more like a spa prep area, complete with a closet section filled with plush white cotton robes. She pointed to an open locker from which a plastic wrist coil key ring dangled, allowing me to lock my personal items. She then motioned for me to follow her through another door and showed me a small waiting area with magazines, lemon water, and tea.

"You're welcome to wait in here for Miss Perkins. She's usually here no later than six thirty, so she should be here any moment." She turned and closed the door. I glanced around and wondered if this was a waiting room for massage appointments. Lavender scented the air and relaxing new-age music wafted quietly through the ceiling speakers. Pinnacle membership was definitely above my pay grade. Moments later, the door opened and Sarah walked in.

How anyone could look so good this early without makeup seemed both unfair and impossible. Her hair was pulled back in a ponytail; she wore a light-green V-neck tank top with pink accent stripes, matching shorts, and running shoes. The stretch of sinewy, tan leg she showed between her ankle socks and shorts was as long as the Nile. She gave me a wide smile.

"Good morning." Her cheerful voice reminded me she was a morning person. I stood and her eyes narrowed as she appraised my outfit.

"Morning," I responded, in my not-a-morning-person voice.

"Didn't you get a locker?"

"I did, but since I'm not sure what's in store for me, I didn't know what I'd need to wear. Or not wear."

Her eyebrow rose at that last comment and she gave me her mischievous smile. "Follow me."

We returned to the locker room, where she removed a racquet from a large red duffle bag. "Racquetball. Ever played?" She held up the racquet.

"No, never."

"Good, then I have a slight chance of beating you." She grinned and pointed to my sweats and fleece. "You won't be needing those or that."

I sat on the bench between the lockers and gently tugged my sweat pants over my shoes. I stood and pulled my fleece over my head, then hung both items in my locker.

"Will this work?" I asked.

Her eyes traveled unhurriedly down my body to my shoes and back up to my shoulders. "With those arms, you must do more than spin class."

I felt a mix of pleasure at the recognition of my routines and discomfort at feeling on display. "I get bored if I do cardio every day, so I do some weight training now and again. But you should talk. You're the one who looks like you're shooting an infomercial for some insanely effective fitness machine." Though I was merely stating the obvious, Sarah's eyes gleamed with delight.

"Schmoozing donors at L.A.'s finest restaurants is part of the job, and I like to eat. It's either stay active or balloon to a size twenty." She handed me a racquet. "Let's go."

I desperately over-swung during the first game. Tennis training was helpful for hand-eye coordination, but I found myself trying to hit hard groundstrokes with fully extended arms instead of flicking my wrists and aiming for good angles. For a fairly jerky kind of game, racquetball as Sarah played it was almost elegant. She swung through the ball efficiently, and her racquet position always seemed properly placed.

The second game was a little less lopsided as I concentrated on trying to follow what Sarah was telling me: lead with the elbow, snap the wrist, follow through. I still over-hit everything but flailed about slightly less. I was breaking quite a sweat, surprised at how much exertion went into hitting a little blue ball within a small, confined rectangular space.

After the second game, we crouched through the bite-size door built into the court wall, drank from the nearby water fountain, and toweled off our faces. I was breathing heavily compared to Sarah, who gave me her assessment.

"I'm impressed. Usually it takes longer for tennis players to get the hang of the wrist action involved. You're doing great."

I laughed. "If I'm doing great, I'd hate to think of how awful the not-great players are."

"Trust me, your ability to retrieve nearly everything makes you a tough opponent."

After a minute or two, my breathing finally returned to normal. "All right. I'm done taking it easy on you. Ready for your beating?"

Sarah squared her shoulders, took a step toward me, and met my challenging glare with a playful cockiness. "I'm shivering with fear."

I stepped forward and stood nearly toe-to-toe with her. "Bring it."

As if a lighting designer was staging a production starring Sarah and me, the only thing that seemed suddenly illuminated was her face and upper body; I noticed nothing else. A current of electricity shot between us. Our eyes shifted back and forth as if we were both searching the other for the party responsible for flipping whatever switch had just been thrown. After several moments passed, Sarah swallowed audibly.

"I intend to," she said. Then she stepped back and motioned for me to enter the court. It took me a few seconds to register that I was supposed to move, and a few more to get my shaky legs to walk toward the door since all I'd wanted to do was step forward and kiss her. *Jesus. Not this again.*

Feeling a bone-deep weariness from the strenuous workout and my third straight loss, I seconded Sarah's invitation to head to the locker rooms and clean up. Thankfully her locker was around the corner from mine, so I didn't have to pry my eyes from her or pretend not to notice her when she undressed. We both seemed to shower and dress on the same schedule, since she appeared at the shared multi-sink area that housed the personal and hair-care products right after I grabbed one of the hair dryers. I was wearing a black pantsuit with a lavender oxford shirt, while she wore a periwinkle skirt suit with a pale-yellow blouse.

While I dried my hair, I occasionally stole glances at her as she dried hers. She could have been in a hair-color commercial, though the reddish tint in hers was natural. Her auburn hair was shiny, silky, and radiated a softness that begged to be stroked. Its natural wave made it look like she curled the length that fell over her shoulders. She set aside the dryer, then leaned in toward the mirrored wall in front of the sinks and began to apply mascara.

After finishing with her right eye, she stopped and looked at me through the mirror. "What?"

Only then did I realize I'd been staring. I quickly turned back to the mirror and started to arrange my hair so I could snap in a hair claw.

"Cazz." Her voice held a smidgen of annoyance, trying to prompt a reply.

I flicked my eyes through the mirror in her direction. "Sorry. Just intrigued by your transformation." I had to work to keep my voice steady. She was astonishingly pretty, and the way she'd slightly parted her lovely lips and exposed just a hint of tongue when concentrating on her eye makeup was fantasy material.

"Transformation?"

"You're a far cry from looking like the take-no-prisoners opponent crusher you were a half hour ago."

"I am?" She began to apply mascara to her left eye. "Then what do I look like?"

"Like you could have breakfast with the president."

She finished with her mascara, straightened, and turned to view me directly. "More demure?" She was clearly amused.

I finished inserting my hair claw and faced her with a smile. "Less assertive."

"I find it has more to do with attitude than outfit."

"Possibly."

Her expression became focused—almost cocky—as she held my gaze. After a few contemplative moments, she strutted over and stood directly in front of me, the toes of our pumps nearly touching. I noticed my breath for the first time since our final racquetball game. Her face moving to within inches of mine, she reached past my ear and pulled the claw from my hair, sending my dark tresses tumbling to my shoulders. She held one end of the plastic clip in her teeth and kept her eyes on me as she combed back her hair with her fingers in several strokes.

She placed the claw in her hair, which lifted some of it off her enticing neck. "Have dinner with me Saturday."

As with my breath earlier, I noticed for the first time today that I swallowed. Unable to take my eyes off hers, I gave a weak response. "Okay."

She smiled, looked back to the mirror, made slight adjustments to the way her hair was arranged, and turned to me.

"Like I said. Attitude," she said. She spun around and spoke over her shoulder. "Follow me in your car. I'll introduce you to my favorite bagel place."

Thankfully the destination was merely breakfast, not some remote location involving BASE jumping or the equivalent, since I would have followed her anywhere for any—or no—reason.

Having Sarah single me out for one-on-one time felt just as wonderful as it had a decade ago.

Damn the woman and her "attitude." I was spellbound and she knew it.

CHAPTER TWELVE

Iwas lucky the desk in the office I was given faced the doorway, which meant my computer screen wasn't visible to anyone who peered in. They would have to stand behind me to see what I was up to, and by then I could easily use my keyboard to ALT-TAB away from a software application or close any open windows on my screen.

I launched the accounting software and ran an income statement. Given the small office space the Foundation occupied, I was shocked to see the staggering amount of donor contributions and special-event revenue it received. The Statement of Activities (an income statement, a.k.a. P&L for a nonprofit) showed prior year support and revenue of nearly twelve million dollars, excluding investment income of almost two million. Grant expenses totaled roughly nine million, and general and administrative expenses came in at close to three million.

I ran a Statement of Financial Position (balance sheet). The Foundation had a combination of cash and investments exceeding forty-four million dollars. I couldn't believe how much money this place brought in and spent, and how much more it had on hand to continue executing its mission. Luke Perkins had built an impressive charity.

While Morrison was at lunch, I searched the file cabinets for the audited financial statements. When I found them, I sent the latest report through the multi-function copier/scanner and typed my personal e-mail address into the menu so I'd have a PDF version waiting for me to review from home tonight. Once the scan had been sent, I scrolled through the options on the copier until I found the screen that logs all activity. I cleared the cache to wipe out the log.

Having returned the report to the file cabinet, I switched windows to display the P&L again and clicked into the general and administrative expenses to see what cost three million last year. The small staff and building lease couldn't account for much in the way of salaries or rent—unless it was very generous with its salaries, which was possible given how much the Foundation brought in with so few personnel. The Foundation must be utilizing an outside payroll-processing service since the records were synced by pay date but excluded information by payee. The information came through lump sum, so I could see how much cash went to the IRS, California Franchise Tax Board, and the employees in total, but couldn't determine how much was paid to each employee individually.

The annual bite with employer taxes was about one point five million, which meant that the twelve staffers averaged about a hundred fifteen thousand annually. These were historical and thus would include Luke Perkins, who clearly would have earned sizably more. The Carols of the office would make far less. Didn't matter. These numbers told me nothing strange was going on with payroll.

The employee benefit plans must be of the premium variety with the numbers I was seeing, but generous did not mean untoward, and they meshed with the hefty club and membership expenses I found. Given the irregular hours Sarah—and I imagined Luke—kept in order to take donors to fancy clubs like I'd been to this morning, as well as dinners and weekend events, a little extra something for the employees in the benefits department appeared reasonable. Rent for this floor was pricey, but not extraordinary. All the other usual expenses seemed, well, usual.

The big unknown was in the form of consulting expenses, which tallied a whopping six hundred thousand. I clicked into the account to view the detail. Aside from some miscellaneous one-off projects, the Foundation was paying on the order of forty-five thousand a month to a firm called Mastick Consulting Inc. Since the investment income was already reported net of investment management fees, I couldn't fathom what services this Mastick company must be rendering. I clicked into a few of the bills and further into the bill payments that tied to the check register of the main bank account. The payments were made electronically by wire. Usually a recurring payment of this nature to a US company would be sent via ACH (automated clearing house) to avoid unnecessary wire-transfer fees.

I walked over to the filing cabinet that held accounts payable and searched for the M folder. The first Mastick invoice read like this: Consulting Services—August. And unlike all invoices on the planet, there was no remittance address to which to send payment. Not helpful. I scanned more of the invoices and found the same generic description and same absence of address. I needed to track down the governing consulting agreement to find out what services Mastick provided to the Foundation. By the time Morrison returned from lunch, I'd finished my tasks for the day and asked for more to do.

When I got home that night, I dropped my purse and Chinese takeout onto the kitchen counter before changing into my favorite tattered blue Columbia sweats and a T-shirt. Veggie chow mein in hand, I booted up my laptop, intent on reviewing the audited financials I'd e-mailed to myself. After entering my login credentials, I settled into my faux leather recliner and savored a bite of broccoli.

It had been a good day. I closed my eyes, relaxed further into the chair, and smiled. *Of course it was a good day. It started with Sarah.* Images of her played through my head: looking sharp in her black pantsuit on Monday and sporty in her workout clothes this morning, mesmerizing me when she treated herself to my hair claw and asked me to dinner, the grief and vulnerability in her eyes in the wake of telling me of her father's passing.

My cell phone rang, startling me out of my reverie. I placed the take-out container on the coffee table, headed to the kitchen, and fumbled for the phone in my purse. I didn't recognize the number, but since this was one of those prepaid smartphones issued to me before every job, I never updated the contacts with names or numbers. I knew by heart the numbers I needed, and that was enough.

"Hello?"

"Do you want a rematch, or have you given up already?" Sarah asked cheekily.

"How did you get my number?"

"Am I not allowed to call you?"

"No, it's not that. I'm just kind of anal about who I give my number to." I winced at how ridiculous I sounded.

"It's on your résumé," she said coolly.

"Oh. Right." I hadn't created my fake résumé so I'd forgotten the personal details Ashby's team would have certainly included. I'd memorized my entire career according to that document, and even made up some stories about what it was like to work at those phony establishments in case someone questioned me, but I'd overlooked something as simple as my phone number. My professional aplomb seemed to fade around Sarah.

"Sorry," I said. Silence. I managed to recognize I was annoyed with myself, not Sarah, and appreciated that she'd called. Before I could think about what it might sound like, I said, "I was just thinking about you." It was true, but I don't know if I would have said it had I not been trying to dig myself out of a hole.

"Mm-hmm." She didn't believe me.

"I was thinking I've never had such an enjoyable time getting walloped before. Though, as pleasurable as it was, I don't intend to repeat my performance."

"Meaning you are giving up?"

"Meaning, watch out. I don't like to lose."

"I remember that about you. Six thirty again?"

"Sure, but Friday's better. I don't do the early morning thing as well as you. I'm good for three a week, tops. I'm sleeping in tomorrow."

"Well, it does work for you."

"What does?" I'd somehow lost a thread of the conversation.

"Getting your beauty rest. It obviously pays off. Friday it is." She hung up.

I clicked the button to end the call, picked up my dinner, and dropped lazily into my recliner. Grinning into my chow mein, I savored the feeling of hearing Sarah's voice in my ear and knowing I was on her mind. It had gone from a good day to a great one, starting and ending with Sarah.

❖

The next couple days rounded out a busy first week at the Foundation. The audit report was interesting in two ways, but lacked details I'd have to track down by other means. The first thing I noticed was the Investments footnote that said the Foundation owned land as well as the more typical publicly traded equities, fixed-income securities, and mutual funds I'd expected. In fact, the Foundation owned nearly four-and-a-half million in land as part of its investments. Where was this land it owned, and why? It made up about ten percent of total investment holdings excluding cash equivalents, which seemed like a lot of property. Especially since it was clearly not tied to the ownership of the office building where it leased its floor, which would have been included in the Property and Equipment footnote had it been used in operations.

Also, the accounting firm of Broderick LLC that had performed the audit and provided the report didn't have a website. Not only was it lacking a basic landing page, but I also couldn't find any reference to the firm. Where were their offices? Furthermore, the company wasn't listed as a CPA licensee with the California State Board of Accountancy. That didn't seem possible, but there might be a perfectly reasonable explanation. Worse, I came up empty when I performed a business search of Broderick in the California Secretary of State's website. Since the SOS records included out-of-state businesses operating within the state, such as corporations owned by California shareholders but incorporated in Delaware because of various benefits of doing so, it appeared Broderick was operating in California without having properly registered to do business here.

I searched for the remittance address from one of Broderick's invoices in our Accounts Payable files and was stumped as to why, as with Mastick, there wasn't one. Unlike Mastick, however, payments to Broderick were made by check. If I could locate a cleared check, I should be able to trace the general vicinity of the firm by noting the processing bank's city and state.

❖

Friday morning, Sarah beat me during our first racquetball game, but not by a mile as she'd done on Wednesday. During the second game, I even held a small lead for most of the game, though she ended up winning fifteen to thirteen. I was a much more formidable opponent and made her strive for her victories. We were both catching our breath when we stepped out of the court through the door that seemed only slightly bigger than a mini fridge. After sipping from the drinking fountain, I leaned against the wall and slid down until I sat with my legs stretched out in front of me. I wiped my face with a towel and hung it around my neck.

"Third time's the charm." I exhaled deeply. "Next game, I'll be able to take you."

"It's good to hold out hope, no matter how remote the chances." She gave me a teasing smile as she sat down next to me, both our upper backs against the cool wall. I tried not to be riveted by the tantalizing stretch of toned, tan leg suddenly at my side.

"What's the plan for tomorrow night?" I asked.

"I'll make dinner. You'll bring wine. That work?"

"You cook?"

"Not often, but I have a couple favorites."

"White or red?"

"Whatever you prefer."

"What time?" I got to my feet and stood in front of her.

"Seven?" She looked up at me.

I extended my hand. "Sounds good." She placed one hand in mine, moving her legs back to make it easier for me to pull her up. "One thing though," I said as she popped up and stood before me.

I removed my hand from hers and grimaced slightly, never having gotten comfortable telling people of my dietary restrictions when they've offered to prepare a meal for me.

Sarah raised a quizzical brow.

"I'm vegetarian," I said.

"What was it you used to say? No worries." She winked and returned to the court.

The potentially awkward moment instantly vanished, reminding me of the grace with which Sarah had been maneuvering through all manner of social situations since her youth. Moreover, she infused me with joyful amazement that she'd remembered such an old saying of mine—one I'd long since forgotten. I didn't want to read too much into it, but it felt good all the same.

As easy as she'd made that for me, however, her charity didn't extend to racquetball, and I followed her inside to get schooled on another of her many skills.

CHAPTER THIRTEEN

Saturday night, I pulled into Sarah's driveway at five after seven feeling uncharacteristically giddy, as if I were a preteen girl getting to meet the lead singer of her favorite boy band. It wasn't a date—logically, I knew that—but I was having difficulty containing my enthusiasm for this simple evening out with a friend. Rather, a former friend. Aside from the stark emotion we'd shared the night of our reunion at the bar, we hadn't engaged in much conversation of a personal nature in the ensuing days. With Sarah's frequent excursions to visit current and prospective donors, I rarely glimpsed her at the office, and our early morning racquetball battles didn't leave much room for talk.

Yet while Sarah had been back in my life barely a week, considering the amount of time I'd already spent thinking of her, it felt longer. Something about her besides her physical beauty drew me to her, something that seemed almost as if it had always been there. I hoped tonight would give me better insight into what that was and who Sarah had become. And as much as I wanted to believe I could calmly and coolly conduct myself in her presence tonight, I was almost euphoric as I ascended the steps to her front door, wine bottle in hand. It would take considerable effort to rein in the exhilaration I was feeling.

As soon as she opened the door, Sarah beamed at me, making me feel inordinately welcome even before saying as much with her voice.

"I'm so glad you're here."

It was difficult to look away from that smile, but when I did, I found her outfit wasn't helping my composure. She was wearing safari capris and a pale-yellow cami tank top that, combined with the loose French braid that gathered her hair off her shoulders, left miles of her flawless tanned skin on display. It was a simple outfit and, complemented by her smile, made for a delightful package. Even her feet were delectable with their cotton-candy-tone toenails.

I swallowed audibly. "Thanks for inviting me." Having barely managed to utter the words, I handed her the bottle to distract myself from staring.

"Come in." She stepped aside to allow me to enter. "My uncle owns this house, but I'm lucky enough to live here."

I stopped inside the entryway and added my shoes to the small pile of hers. Ahead of me were floor-to-ceiling windows that put a substantial portion of the L.A. basin in view.

The city lights transfixed me. "Wow." My eloquence this evening was astounding. I stepped forward and stood close to the glass, admiring the twinkling city below. "I'd never leave, if this were mine."

"You get used to it, sad to say."

I turned to her and wondered, as I took in her undeniable beauty, whether the same could ever be said by whoever is, was, or would be lucky enough to awaken to Sarah each morning. The L.A. panorama was remarkable, but could anyone ever get used to seeing such a lovely sight beside them in bed? *Whoa. Down, Cazz.* I shook my head out of my reverie and tried to focus on the conversation.

"It beats what I see from my apartment, at any rate," I said, unable to conceal my smile as I worked fruitlessly to push away thoughts of what it might be like to wake up next to Sarah.

"What's so amusing?" Sarah said, catching me.

"Uh…nothing. Sorry. Just…happy to be here."

She gave me a curious look but let me off the hook. "Shall I open this?" She held up the Zinfandel I'd brought.

"Please." I nearly choked on the word as I failed to will away thoughts of her skin against mine.

"Follow me to the kitchen. I've got some stuff to take care of. We'll take the house tour when we're done with dinner. For now, forgive me, but I've got to put you to work."

Grateful for the opportunity to remove my eyes from Sarah's body since I couldn't very well explain my focus on her instead of the city below, I followed her, enjoying the delightful aroma emanating from the kitchen. Almost as soon as we entered it, Sarah put a wooden spoon in my hand and directed me to a pot on the stove. She told me that stirring rubbed the starch off arborio rice, which helped the starch dissolve in the stock. My work was creating the sauciness that would give our risotto its flavor and satisfying texture.

While I continued to stir the contents of the pot, Sarah flitted in and out of the kitchen to set the dining-room table, uncork and pour the wine, place some mixed greens and veggies onto salad plates, and carry them to the table. I was half pleased that she seemed to be going out of her way to make me comfortable and half bothered that it needed to be any kind of production, since I would have been willing to eat Pop-Tarts or dry toast to hang out with her.

Once the risotto had absorbed the liquid, Sarah directed me to turn off the burner. At her instruction, I stirred in some butter and Parmesan cheese to complete the dish. She grabbed two plates from a cabinet and spooned a mound of risotto onto each, then lifted a glass top from a large saucepan on the stove, puffs of steam rising from within. From a drawer of utensils, she removed a set of tongs, grasped some asparagus from the pot, and placed portions on both plates.

"Could you bring the wineglasses?" she asked as she took a plate in each hand and entered the dining room. I followed with our beverages.

Once we sat and placed our napkins in our laps, Sarah lifted her glass to me.

"A toast."

I raised mine to hers in reply.

"To old friends," she said.

"To old friends." We clinked glasses and each took a sip. "Thanks for inviting me over, Sarah. This looks fantastic."

"*You* look fantastic," she said while swirling the wine in her goblet. She'd tilted her head as she said it and wore an expression that seemed laced with challenge.

I set my glass down and assessed her. I couldn't read her expression. Either she was setting me up for something or testing me, but I'd worked hard at overcoming my issues with compliments and wasn't inclined to fall back to my old habits.

"Thank you," I said simply.

She smiled broadly, apparently pleased I didn't make an issue of her comment. "Glad you could join me." She lifted her fork and stabbed at some salad. "There are things I've been dying to ask you," she said, waving her fork at me before taking a bite.

"Such as?" I picked up my fork and pierced some salad.

Sarah launched in. "How did you get over your discomfort at being touched and complimented?"

I chuckled, amused. "Guess we're done with small talk already?"

She grinned and nodded. "If you don't mind."

"I wouldn't say I'm over it. Just…more accepting."

"How?" She took a bite of risotto.

I wasn't sure I wanted to go down the path of the entirety of my modest love life with Sarah. "I met someone who kind of made a project out of me. Someone…" I bobbed my head right and left, searching for the right words. "Someone patient and loving."

She appeared thoughtful and interested. "A lover?"

I nodded.

"And are the two of you still…" She raised an eyebrow that finished her sentence.

I shook my head.

"Tell me." Sarah encouraged me gently, taking a sip of wine.

I set down my fork and glanced up at the ceiling, wondering where and how to begin. "We met through mutual friends when I was a junior at Columbia. We hit it off immediately and she fell for me pretty hard."

"She?"

I nodded and studied her for a sign to continue, some indication she wouldn't freak out or be uncomfortable.

"And?" She took another bite of risotto.

"And...we dated for about a year. She—Alex—was hugely affectionate and kind of...wore me down over time, I guess. She'd grab my hand out of my pocket and hold it in hers, she'd put her arm around me or link elbows when we'd walk, and she'd smile triumphantly when I'd sulk or groan about it. Then she'd further push my buttons by saying something complimentary, like, 'You're so cute when you crinkle your eyebrows at me like that' or 'I love how you get so serious when I hold your hand in public' or 'You can hide those pretty white teeth all you want, but I know they're in there.' It would drive me crazy." I rolled my eyes, reliving the exasperation.

Sarah smiled. "I imagine."

"I didn't really have much choice but to kind of deal with it."

"So what happened?" She sliced off a section of asparagus.

"To us?"

She nodded.

I briefly bit the inside of my lower lip. "I couldn't give her what she needed. What she deserved." Recalling my failure, I focused on my napkin. "I wanted to return her feelings, to fall in love with her as she'd done with me. I mean, she was such a great person. Smart, kind, cute, loving...Everything you could ever want, really. I don't know what was wrong with me, but..." Meeting Sarah's gaze, I shook my head and lifted my wineglass. "I wasn't in love with her." I sipped my Zinfandel.

"You were honest with her about how you felt?"

I set my glass down. "Yeah, of course. From the beginning. It wouldn't have lasted as long as it did, but she kept hoping my feelings would change. Thought I was worth waiting for." I half-shrugged in embarrassment.

"The silly girl." She gave me a smirk that told me she was teasing.

Sarah acted as if she wanted to ask something further but would twist her fork amid the mound of risotto on her plate, look at me, raise an eyebrow, then drop her eyes and repeat the process.

After watching her do this three times, I was curious. "What are you thinking?"

"Have you ever been in love?" Sarah blurted out the question before taking a bite.

"Are you going to grill me all night?" I didn't want to answer.

She finished chewing and swallowed. "Sorry." She wiped her lips with her napkin. "I'm being impolite. But you've piqued my curiosity, Cazz." She shrugged. "You called me nosy once. Guess it still applies."

I picked up my wineglass and watched the red flash in the light as I swirled its contents. "Once," I said truthfully, keeping my eyes on the liquid. "A long time ago." I set my glass down without taking a sip and peered at Sarah. "You?"

She eyed me coolly and her mood darkened. She sat back in her chair and focused on her plate. "Twice." Based on the cloud that suddenly hung over her features, whatever happened with number two couldn't have been good. Or was it number one?

"Does that include Dirk?"

After several moments, she lifted her eyes to me and a smile lightened her mood. "No," she said with a secretive look.

I didn't know what that look meant, but I was surprised Dirk hadn't made the cut. They'd seemed pretty together when I knew them.

Sarah picked up her fork and stabbed at her salad. "Don't tell me third time's the charm, because I don't intend to make that mistake again." She took a bite.

"Yikes."

"Yikes is right," she said after swallowing. "I think maybe we've switched places, Cazz. Now I'm the one who doesn't trust so easily." Sarah dropped her gaze back to her plate and cut a thin piece of asparagus into smaller pieces.

I was eager to ask her to clarify her remark, since I'd never thought of Sarah as overly trusting nor had I thought of her as cynical. But as curious as I was, I didn't want to press her into revealing any part of herself that would make her feel uncomfortable—defensive or vulnerable—around me. I wanted to soak up our nearness, hold onto the decade-old bond she alluded to when she mentioned we'd switched places, cling to the kinship those old memories invoked. It pleased me she'd acknowledged our history because it meant she'd been contemplating a past—an affiliation—we shared.

Yet without further prompting, she looked up at me and continued her line of thought. "Single guys, even women, see me in fancy restaurants, elegant ballrooms, and exclusive country clubs, wearing stylish clothes, approaching all manner of extremely wealthy guests with friendliness and ease, and they see a mirage. They're lured to the idea of me, of some trophy or stepping-stone they think I can be for them because of how I live and who's in my network. They're not interested in knowing me, really knowing me, and I've stopped wanting to know them. I allow myself occasional distractions when I want them, always on my terms, and it's satisfying enough and uncomplicated."

"Distractions?" I didn't like the direction this conversation seemed headed.

"Distractions. One-night stands. Casual sex. Whatever you want to call it."

"That seems like an extreme reaction to getting hurt," I said, making the obvious leap that someone had deeply wounded her.

She deflected the comment. "Does my shallowness offend your sensibilities?"

"I would never think of you as shallow."

"Guess you have a lot to learn about me then."

I wanted the opportunity to take lessons, if that was the case. I contemplated how to respond.

"You don't strike me as a 'distractions' kind of woman," Sarah said, scooping some risotto, cocking her head to the side, and studying me as she chewed.

"I'm not." I had a sudden loss of conviction, second-guessing myself in light of Sarah's revelation and wondering if I could turn on a dime.

"Guess you won't be staying the night then?" Sarah posed the question with a provocative set to her slightly open, lovely mouth, resting her tongue against the inside of her upper teeth.

My gaze dropped inadvertently to those magnificent lips. I was being challenged, only I wasn't sure if she was testing me on my ability to read between the lines or my ability to engage her with some clever riposte. Unfortunately for my wit, I was overcome by the thought—however impossible—of staying the night. Of putting my mouth along every delicious curve and in every delightful crevice Sarah's body offered. Of being one of her *distractions*. My cheeks grew hot and my stomach trembled at the prospect. I met her eyes and blinked. She let me linger in my flustered state, watching my reaction with obvious pleasure, the cat that had cornered the mouse.

After an endless stretch of silence, I finally managed to swallow before offering a bland response. "Guess not."

"Besides, I care about you, which ruins everything." Her voice held a tinge of regret, and her smile morphed into a slight frown.

Her flirtatiousness abruptly halted after that, and I sensed in her a desire to keep me physically and emotionally out of reach. Conversation turned to current events, movies we'd seen, and other impersonal subjects. After dessert, I offered to scrape the plates and put the dishes in the dishwasher, but Sarah refused. She continued to be polite, but became more reserved, less openly friendly the way she'd been throughout dinner. When I said I should go, she didn't try to delay me and walked me to the door.

After stepping onto the front porch, I turned around. "Sarah, I'm not sure if I said something to upset you, but if I did, I'm sorry."

She held the door and gave me a sad smile. "You didn't do anything to upset me, Cazz. You were wonderful company."

It was driving me crazy not knowing what switch had been thrown, or how to flip it back, because she was clearly erecting a wall between us no matter the polite veneer she was putting on. I decided to play ignorant, pretending not to notice the physical distance she'd been placing between us since dessert. I stepped forward and drew her to me in a tight embrace. I felt and heard her gasp in surprise and noticed she didn't return my hug. Undaunted, I held her and spoke softly into her ear.

"Thanks for tonight. Dinner was delicious and it was great to see you."

She sighed, her body relaxed slightly, and finally her arms wrapped themselves around my shoulders. I let myself linger, taking in the scent of her hair and the warmth of her neck.

Holding Sarah felt so right. The only time someone felt so right in my arms was ten years ago. I'd only known her for a few months then, and only for a week now. Yet the odd sense of belonging was quickly dovetailing with arousal. Under the influence of her scent and the heat of her body against mine, I was overcome with a desire to push her inside and take her right on the floor. She wasn't helping things, as the fingers of one hand lightly played with the hair at the back of my neck while she tightened her hold on me with the other. She seemed to be allowing herself a similar reconnection to me that I was feeling toward her. It felt…amazing. Perfect. Impossible. I stifled a moan.

Summoning all my willpower, I pulled away and held her upper arms, physically holding myself back from her. We stared at each other. I couldn't speak for her, but lust was raging through every cell in my body, and my breathing was more pronounced even though we hadn't even kissed. When her eyes dipped to my mouth and her lips parted just enough to reveal the tip of her tongue, I had all the evidence I needed that I wasn't alone in wanting more. She swayed almost imperceptibly toward me before closing her mouth and slowly raising her eyes to mine.

I removed my hands from her, cleared my throat, and smiled sheepishly. "Good night, Sarah," I said, shoving my hands in my pockets to keep from reaching out to her again. I turned around and started walking to my car.

"'Night, Cazz," I heard Sarah say before she closed the door.

I longed to hear her whisper those and other soft words in a more intimate setting. But as much as I dreaded leaving, staying wasn't an option, even if I'd been welcome. If I had to choose between having Sarah in my arms for only one night versus clinging to the faintest of possibilities of one day having more, hope would triumph.

CHAPTER FOURTEEN

The following week, I continued in my dual capacity as accountant and investigator. The accounting piece was easy; I'd supplemented my undergraduate scholarships with similar part-time work. It was the investigation that was giving me trouble. I couldn't find the governing consulting agreement between the Foundation and Mastick Consulting anywhere in the filing cabinets or on the server. I wasn't faring any better at tracking down its owners. After searching the Secretary of State websites for nearly two-dozen states, I finally located a Mastick Consulting in Nevada. Rather, it was a Nevada corporation—I still didn't know where the business was physically located. But it was strange to find no record of such a company in California given that it was supposedly providing significant services to the Foundation. And wouldn't actual consultants render those consulting services in person?

The fact that the firm was incorporated in Nevada made it difficult for me to trace its owners. Nevada had privacy laws allowing companies that provided incorporating services to out-of-state organizations to appoint a "designee" for all the offices of the corporation such as president or secretary, such that this random designee—completely unaffiliated with the out-of-state organization—would hold all the offices of public record. Meanwhile, the true owners of the corporation maintained operational control and ownership with complete anonymity. Unless I had a court order, the chances that I could identify the owners of Mastick using any information available to me in Nevada were nil.

I did make headway on another aspect of Mastick, however. During a casual conversation in the break room when Carol and I were eating lunch, I asked about other faces at the Foundation. Carol was ostensibly the receptionist, but she functioned more like an office manager and executive assistant. I'd met the dozen or so employees during my time there, all of whom had multiple roles and expertise regarding the intricacies of its operations. Such variety of knowledge and access made collusion—an inherently difficult scheme to detect that accounted for only two-fifths of all fraud yet five times the financial losses—a very real prospect at the Foundation.

I told her how impressed I was that such a small staff seemed to get so much done. This buttered her up nicely and gave me adequate cover for my questions.

"Doesn't anyone else help? You know, consultants or firms that work on specific projects? I mean, the fund-raising events alone have to take a lot of planning." I didn't want to identify Mastick by name because I didn't want Carol to think I was concerned about anything or feel I was snooping.

Carol nodded and forked something that resembled pasta in the plastic tray in front of her. "Oh, sure, we might get a temp now and then to help with data entry or filing or something, and we occasionally work with outside event planners to help us keep events fresh and interesting, but really, what you see is what you get. The staffers around here do it all. We're all very committed to the Foundation. Most of us have been here over ten years."

"You don't have little elves helping you in the wee hours?"

Carol chuckled. "No. No elves. No other staff. No consultants. Although some of us do work late. Luke was especially a workhorse on the entertainment front. He seemed to have one more gear than the rest of us." Her expression turned contemplative and somber. "It's too bad you didn't get a chance to meet him." Her respect for Luke and sadness at his passing were genuine.

I didn't need to let on that I'd met him briefly in high school, when Sarah and I had attended the fund-raiser together. "He seemed like a remarkable man, from what I've heard."

"He was. He really was. A down-to-earth, truly decent person. Made you feel like you were the only one in the room when he talked to you. At least you've had a chance to meet Sarah. She's exactly like him. Same tireless work ethic. Makes you feel special when she talks to you."

I felt an odd pride that Sarah could instill in others that sense of pleasure at feeling singled out and noteworthy. And while it didn't diminish my appreciation for her ability, I'd forgotten I wasn't its sole beneficiary. The reminder stung because I'd wanted to believe what Sarah and I had forged together long ago was extraordinary enough to render me distinct from other people in her life. Apparently that wasn't the case. In any event, I needed to finish my fishing expedition.

"You don't farm out any of the work overseas or something?"

Carol laughed and stood. "You're the one paying the bills now, Cassidy. You should know." She tossed her tray into the trash and set her fork in the dishwasher.

I didn't see Sarah at all during the workweek. She hadn't called me for racquetball, returned a voice mail I'd left, or gone into the office the entire week as far as I could tell. At one point, because I had to leave a document on Sarah's desk that required her signature, I asked Carol whether I could enter Sarah's office since her door was shut. Carol assured me it was okay, that she herself came and went when she had to, and Sarah was fine with it. I softly knocked out of habit and entered Sarah's office for the first time.

After crossing to her desk and dropping the file folder into a silver tray that appeared to be an "in box," I surveyed the room. On a nearby file cabinet were two framed pictures: one of her parents, the other of Sarah and her father. On the wall behind the door was an array of letters and cards pinned to a large, framed corkboard. I peeked at a few. Some were addressed to Sarah, others to the Foundation, and the rest were various shades of To Whom It May Concern. All were personal "thank you" notes from numerous people the Foundation had helped over time. They were stories of tragedy overcome, hope restored, and deep gratitude for the Foundation's support. The Foundation was very clearly a labor of love for Sarah.

Her work was making a difference in people's lives. I felt renewed sympathy for the immense loss Sarah must feel without her father by her side. It helped dissipate but not extinguish my hurt at feeling ignored.

❖

Thursday afternoon, Morrison stopped by my office. "Cassidy?"

I looked up from my computer screen. "Hi, Greg."

"I've got a proposal for you."

I raised an eyebrow.

"If you're free, I'd like you to take tomorrow off and attend one of our fund-raising events tomorrow night instead. You'd only need to be there a couple hours, but you'd be one of the employees representing the Foundation, if anyone asks."

"Why me?"

Morrison, still standing in the doorway, seemed uncomfortable, as if unsure of how to respond. Then he called out over his shoulder. "Carol? Carol, would you come here for a minute?" Moments later, she was in the doorway. Morrison took a step inside my office. "I wanted Carol to be here so this doesn't sound…crude." He paused, and an idea seemed to hit him. "In fact, maybe the better way to do this is ask Carol." He turned to her. "Carol, why would we want Cassidy to attend tomorrow night's fund-raiser?"

She smiled at me. "Because she's a total hottie who'll help grease the wallets of our donors." She looked at Morrison. "Is that what you mean?"

He nodded and extended his hands palms up in a "there you have it" gesture. "I couldn't have said it better myself."

"It's one of the reasons Sarah's such an excellent fund-raiser. She's a hottie, too," Carol said with a wink.

I laughed. Carol was a fifty-something mother of three who was still very much in love with her husband of thirty-some years. To hear her say "hottie" was amusing. To hear her call Sarah one was hysterical. And so very, very accurate.

"I see. I suppose that means I'd have to wear something...
um...racy?"

"No, no, no," Morrison said quickly. "Flattering, sure, I
suppose, but elegant, classic, approachable, that sort of thing."

"I'm sure you'll get plenty of attention in whatever dress you
wear, honey," Carol said. "Don't worry about that." She walked
back to her desk.

I shrugged. "All right. I'm game."

Morrison gave me the details and left.

I was betting the elusive Ms. Perkins would be in attendance.
Time to test the temperature of her cold shoulder and how indistinct
I was to her.

Chapter Fifteen

I was speaking with a petite, curvaceous, thirtyish blonde when I finally saw Sarah about ten yards away. She had just turned from a handsome, gray-haired man in his late fifties or early sixties, and they were both laughing. The friendly blonde, who was easy on the eyes in her flattering scoop-neck cocktail dress, looked like a stagehand compared to the main event at a beauty pageant starring Sarah. She was devastatingly gorgeous in an eye-popping red, V-neck, sleeveless gown with draping ruffle details. Her hair was gathered in a stylishly messy bun, leaving loose strands to fall glamorously alongside her ears. My cheeks flushed and my body stirred as I watched her, nearly hypnotized by her exquisite fluidity and magnetism. When she glanced up and noticed me, her laughter ceased and the delight in her face dissolved into a scowl as she surveyed my companion and me.

The blonde asked me a question that called my attention back to her. I had to ask her to repeat what she'd said. "Is this your first time at a Foundation fund-raiser? I don't recall having seen you at other events. I would have remembered you." A predatory smile crossed her lips. She held a glass of sparkling wine while her other hand languidly toyed with her necklace. She was an attractive woman, but her evocative gesture and tone were lost on me. There was no competition.

"I went to one years ago, but I don't remember much about it except the incredible view from the rooftop perch." I tried to focus on my conversation instead of how scrumptious Sarah looked tonight.

"Enclosed in glass?"

"That's it."

"That's at the Grand Biltmore, downtown. It is an amazing thing to behold." The woman's tone was as flirtatious as her smile, and she examined me slowly from head to toe as she said this. Suddenly someone took my elbow and stepped between the blonde and me.

Sarah smiled disingenuously at the woman. "Excuse us a minute, Caitlin." Sarah pulled me across the room and out onto an empty, enclosed patio. She gave me a light, twisting shove that spun me around to face her.

"What the hell are you doing here?" Sarah snapped.

"Why the hell are you ignoring me?"

She continued to glare at me. Enunciating each word with impatience, she practically growled. "I. Asked. You. A question."

"Greg told me I could take the day off if I'd come here and mingle for a few hours tonight."

She crossed her arms and took stock of my ensemble. "In *that*?" she asked disbelievingly.

Suddenly self-conscious, I looked down at what I was wearing, then crossed my arms as she had done. I felt defensive. "I thought it looked okay." It was my best dress.

"What did he tell you to wear?"

"I asked him that and he said classy, approachable, and flattering."

She snorted. "Flattering? Jesus." She shook her head in what I took as disgust. "And so you made a beeline to the first lesbian you saw to test out how *flattering* you look?"

I put my hands on my hips, moving from defensive to angry. "What is your problem? I have no idea who that woman is or whether she's gay. I just met her, for God's sake."

"Oh, she's gay all right. I'm sure she's loving the new *accountant*," she said sarcastically.

"Well, isn't that the idea? To flutter around the party, acting interested in everyone and everything so they feel happy and satisfied and very generous with their wallets and purses?"

"We're not high-class hookers, Cazz. We're not trying to bed them."

My nostrils flared and I took a deep breath before stepping away from Sarah, afraid I'd say something hurtful in retaliation for feeling she'd sucker punched me. I turned and stalked toward the door we'd come through.

"Wait." Sarah rushed to my side and tried to stop me with a hand on my arm. "I'm sorry."

I shook her off and kept moving. I opened the door and felt another pull at my elbow.

"Cazz, please." She kept her voice low, obviously trying not to draw attention to us yet beckoning me with another light tug on my arm.

Now that we were back in the party, I didn't want to make a scene, so I relented and followed. She led me to the elevators and pressed the up arrow. One of the four elevators immediately opened and I entered behind her. She pressed the button to the 22nd floor and the elevator made quick work of the ascent. Her eyes were on me during the brief ride, but in my anger I refused to meet them.

She exited to her right and I followed as she walked down the hall. Though I tried to be unaffected, the toned arms, confident shoulders, graceful sway of hips, and splendid sweep of neck and back before me all began undermining my annoyance. I nearly snorted at how ridiculously easy she could manipulate me, and damn it, she wasn't even trying.

When she stopped in front of room 2214, she bent down slightly and gathered some of the elegant red ruffle of her dress. Feeling for something, she pulled out a key card from a tiny hidden pocket inside the ruffle below the knee and inserted it into the door lock. The light flashed green. She pushed open the door and stood aside to let me through.

As the door closed behind us, Sarah grabbed me around my waist with one arm and threaded her fingers in my hair as she pulled my mouth to hers. She pressed her body to mine and forced me against the door in a fierce kiss that sent wonderful shivers through me. If I hadn't had an object to lean against, I'm sure Sarah would have brought me to my knees as I wouldn't have been able to stand on my own. My irritation gave way to confusion, then to desire, and soon I returned her kiss with an intensity to match hers. Our lips and tongues moved together like the flowing of an ocean tide, alternating between moments of raging passion and gentle tenderness. It seemed as if we were both acknowledging the gamut of feelings we elicited in each other: there was no right or wrong way to kiss or touch, simply an overpowering need to do it.

I slid my hands from her back down to her waist and drew her harder against me, molding our bodies together. She began tracing a path with her lips and tongue along my neck and under my chin, covering me with delicious nips and kisses that made me yearn for more. My head tilted back against the door and I moaned from the pleasure her hot, moist mouth incited throughout me. She stepped a thigh between my legs and gently rocked against me, setting my body aflame. She licked the skin below my left ear and moved her mouth over my earlobe, teasing it with her tongue until I could no longer breathe. Goose bumps erupted over the left side of my body. I reached for her and claimed her mouth with mine, wondering how it was possible to want someone as much as I wanted her.

As we kissed, Sarah continued her gentle rocking motion and moved her hand to lightly cup my breast, brushing her thumb across the thin materials that covered my nipple. I moaned again and slowly broke the kiss, cradling her face with my hands.

"God, I want you," I said in a breathy whisper.

Sarah stilled in my arms and removed her hand, wrapping both arms around me. "I want you, too. So much." She sighed, released me, took my hands from her face, and held them as she stepped back. "But Cazz, look around you. This isn't what you want." She dropped her hands from mine and took another step back.

Reeling from the parting of our bodies and the yearning mine now screamed for, my brain seemed unable to process information at its normal speed, and I couldn't understand what she was saying. I shook my head in confusion and concentration.

"I didn't know you were going to be here, Cazz. I didn't ask you to come."

I scanned the hotel room and after several moments my brain kick-started into gear. "Who…who is this for?" I stammered, feeling a sharp pain in my abdomen at the prospect of Sarah sharing this room with someone else.

Sarah kept her eyes on me. "I don't know. Maybe no one. Maybe not." She let that sink in. "I don't…fraternize with Foundation donors, but sometimes after an event like tonight, I'll see if there's anything…interesting happening nearby."

"You mean you'll see if *someone* interesting is happening nearby."

She nodded.

"A distraction?"

She nodded again.

Part of me felt disgusted by the idea of Sarah's one-night stands, part of me desperately wanted tonight to be my first, and part of me felt a twinge of disappointment that my personality wasn't similarly calibrated to seek them and never would be.

"Then why did you bring me up here?" A rising tide of anger swelled within me, as if I'd been set up to fail.

Sarah responded with a guilty smile. "I'm only human." She put her hands on her hips, and her eyes deliberately roamed the length of my body, undressing me. She licked her lips. "Cazz, you're sexy as hell in that dress." She shook her head slightly and her eyes widened a bit. "Damn." She shrugged, and her smile turned slightly sheepish, managing to dissipate my anger somewhat.

Momentarily distracted by her admission, I glanced down at my dress. "I thought you didn't think it was flattering."

"Oh, it's flattering all right. But that's the understatement of the year. You're stunning."

I stared at her, wondering how this beautiful woman in this incredible dress that accentuated her curves and the glorious triumvirate of her arms, neck, and shoulders could say I was the one who was stunning.

Emboldened by the compliment and stirred by her honesty and concern for my feelings, I stepped toward her and took one of her hands in both of mine. I brought it to my mouth and slowly kissed each knuckle, lightly brushing them with my tongue, never taking my eyes off hers. I turned her hand over and gently kissed her palm before holding it in my hands.

I continued to look into her surprised eyes. "I can't interest you in something that might evolve into more than a momentary distraction? It might not, you know. It might end tonight. You don't have to promise anything more than a willingness to keep the door open to the possibility."

I searched for a hidden passage that would take me past her defenses, but Sarah pulled her hand away, drew her arms around her waist protectively, and moved away, no longer willing to meet my eyes. I could tell from her body language she was emotionally as well as physically withdrawing from me, and my stomach tightened at the thought of losing our closeness. I was grasping.

"Then what if I throw caution to the wind and decide I want to be your distraction for the night anyway? No promises. Nobody gets hurt."

She shook her head and took a deep breath. She turned to me with a serious expression that seemed laden with regret.

"You could never be that to me."

Her words threw me into an untenable position. She wouldn't give us a chance at something beyond one night or accept me as a plaything for an evening's romp.

"Damn it, Sarah! What? You wanted to see what was between us long enough to confirm it might be something special so you could run as fast and far away from it as possible?" I stepped into her personal space and glared at her, demanding an explanation.

She stayed in place and spoke in a flat tone. "You're right. This was a mistake. I'm sorry I dragged you up here."

Great. Now she was apologizing. I wasn't getting anywhere. Though stunned by the whiplash I'd just experienced going from the fierce heat of our connected bodies to the cool distance of the indifference she projected, I wasn't sorry she'd brought me here. The miles that suddenly seemed to separate us disappointed me, but she'd breathed life into every nerve ending in my body and instilled within me a longing I was loath to lose, a hope I wasn't ready to sever. I softened and sighed.

"I'm not sorry." I reached out, holding her shoulders since her arms remained crossed. I slowly kissed her right temple, right cheek, the tender skin below her right ear, and her chin, then mirrored the same kisses on her left side. As I used my tongue, lips, and teeth against the delicate skin below her ear, she released some tension. I delivered soft, caressing kisses on her delectable neck, moving under her chin to give each side equal consideration, while tracing my hands along her sides and stomach.

She let out a low moan as she tilted her head back to give me greater access and wrapped her arms around my shoulders. "This is not helping to shore up my resolve." Her voice was thick, irresistible.

Lifting my gaze to meet hers and bringing my arms around her waist, I said, "Perfectly harmless," before moving my mouth over hers.

We kissed tenderly, exploring each other with sweet abandon, and I marveled at the wealth of emotion and need that can be communicated by soft, moist lips touching. The underlying intimacy between us made me feel slightly scared yet inexplicably and entirely full—a kind of soaring and belonging. If she was feeling half the things I felt, I knew—well, hoped—she wouldn't close the door on us forever. So I was willing to lose round one of what I hoped would be a contest that would go the distance—at least a further distance.

I forced myself to pull back, still holding her waist. Light-blue eyes slowly greeted me from behind long eyelashes. "Okay," I said. "We'll compromise." Sarah raised her left eyebrow in that trademark curious, questioning expression of hers. "I leave, and you don't consider this a mistake."

She shook her head slightly and sighed, removing her arms from around my shoulders and holding me at my hips instead. She wasn't jumping at my offer.

"Maybe it's not a mistake. Yet." She said it as if it were inevitable.

"What makes you think it will be? Am I so horrible?" Did Sarah find something frightening about me? Maybe the fact that I was a woman? Various emotions played across her face: fear, arousal, determination.

She finally answered by plastering me against the door and kissing me so thoroughly my head swam. When she eventually broke the kiss, gently tugging my bottom lip with her teeth before releasing me, I was breathless and overwhelmed with sensation. She trailed her long fingers down my arms until she held my hands with hers, lightly rubbing my palms with her thumbs.

"That's the trouble. You're completely irresistible," she said. She smiled as she took her hand and brushed the hair from my forehead, then traced my cheek with the back of her fingers. She turned her palm and cupped my cheek, regarding me with utter tenderness. I wondered at the emotion in her eyes. "You scare me, the way you make me feel," she said softly.

She had rendered me so powerless with her kisses I could barely make out what she was saying, dazed as I was from desire. Then her smile faded and her expression turned sad. A hint of liquid appeared in her eyes, and I quickly roused myself from my lust-filled haze.

"I'm not going to hurt you," I said, trying to read her thoughts.

She immediately willed away her vulnerability and stiffened, her eyes suddenly dry. "First of all, you don't know that. And second, I might hurt you. I really have no desire for either of those things to occur."

"I'm willing to take the risk." Where was my courage coming from? I never believed I'd ever be this close to Sarah to disclose such a thought, let alone be so certain of my willingness to open myself up to potential devastation.

"I'm not." With that succinct declaration, she moved away from me and averted her eyes. She straightened out her dress. "I have to get back," she said, her voice catching. She reached for the door.

"Wait." I put my hand on hers and pulled it away from the handle. I didn't understand what she was so afraid of and needed to know. "Sarah, please."

She lifted her eyes to me briefly, and the anguish in them terrified me. Whatever I was doing to Sarah, I didn't like it. I didn't want to hurt her, yet the only thing reflected back at me was pain. She quickly opened the door.

"I need to see to my guests." She swept past me into the hallway.

Her abrupt departure and tormented countenance left me baffled. I couldn't shift my focus to the surrounding hotel room for several moments. When its purpose occurred to me, I was suddenly the one fighting back tears. I was distressing Sarah in a way I couldn't comprehend, and she was upsetting me with her preparations for a night of...*ugh*. I didn't want to think about it. There was little chance of that, but remaining in this rendezvous chamber sure wasn't helping, so I left.

❖

I got home after two o'clock in the morning, having stayed until the end of the event after feeling an unexpected obligation to the Foundation to be pleasant company to any attendees desiring small talk. And who was I kidding? I also stayed because I was desperate to lay claim to more time with a certain gorgeous woman promenading among the guests in a striking red dress. Unfortunately, I couldn't get any more time with Sarah without appearing as desperate as I felt. Instead, the pretty, petite blonde cornered me twice more during the evening, going so far as to hand me a business card and suggest we have dinner soon.

Once I was through my apartment door, I immediately kicked off my heels, then unzipped and stepped out of my dress, all the while walking toward my bedroom. I threw on a T-shirt, jumped onto my bed, and screamed into my pillow. The idea that someone else might be sharing hotel room 2214 with Sarah was maddening, disheartening, unthinkable. How could she be so callous as to let me know why she'd gotten a room? She hadn't intended to tell me, but it wasn't my fault she decided to kiss me.

And what kisses they were. Merely recalling her luscious mouth on mine made me tremble. God, the things she made me feel. How could she go from that—from what we shared together—to getting it on with some stranger? And if that wasn't bad enough, why did she appear so distraught when she said she wasn't willing to take a risk with me? Did she want to but felt conflicted? Was she saying in broad terms that she couldn't get hurt again, or was she saying specifically she couldn't get hurt again *by me*?

She couldn't possibly be talking about high school. *Could she?* It had broken my heart to leave Claiborne. To leave Sarah. It had taken years, Alex, and a couple of short-lived relationships with women for me to understand, in hindsight, that I'd fallen madly in love with Sarah in high school. But even at the time, before the lightbulb went off, there was only Sarah.

Only ever Sarah.

I'd been forced to abandon my feelings for her and my connection to her when my parents moved us to Texas. Of course, all those old feelings were now bubbling up inside me and threatening to turn my world upside down again because I was clearly never going to get over loving Sarah. But surely that was my issue, not hers. After all, she'd been going steady with Dirk the entire time we'd known each other in our youth.

Though tonight confirmed we were attracted to each other, did she ever think about me the way I thought about her back then and all the years in between?

No, that wasn't possible. I was certain my feelings for her were different than anything I'd ever known. But it never occurred to me she could feel similarly. That couldn't be it.

My cell phone rang. Who the hell was calling at this hour? I ran down the hall and pulled the phone from my purse but didn't recognize the number.

"Hello." My sharp tone belied the greeting.

"Why so grumpy?" Sarah asked. "You're not the one sitting all alone in a fancy hotel room."

"You're alone?"

"Yes."

I exhaled a sigh of relief. "Why are you telling me this?" Several moments of silence followed and I wasn't sure if our call had been dropped.

"I honestly don't know," Sarah said. "Some part of me wanted you to know."

"I'm glad."

"That I told you, or that I'm alone?"

"Both. Definitely glad you're alone." After a moment, I said, "No, I take that back. I'd rather you weren't alone." I wanted to be with her.

"Isn't that a mixed message?"

By phoning, she'd taken a risk. It was my turn. I decided to be direct. "Let me clarify. I don't want you to be alone tonight. I'd rather you were with me. But I don't care if that means we stay up all night drinking coffee and playing Monopoly, or drive to the beach and listen to the ocean while we talk about our hopes and dreams, or play truth or dare until I learn all your secrets and fantasies, or rip each other's clothes off and make love until we're blissfully exhausted. I want to spend time with you, Sarah. I want to know you in every way imaginable.

"And you were right. I shouldn't have said I'm not going to hurt you. What I should have said was: I'd never hurt you on purpose. It's up to you whether I could ever get close enough to hurt you, but maybe it's up to me to prove to you it's a chance worth taking."

I don't know why I felt the need to say all that—not at that moment, anyway—and the extended silence on the line made me feel extremely exposed and not a little terrified. The words were out now and couldn't be recalled. Fear crawled up my spine. I'd gone too far, too fast. Pushed too soon. Revealed too much.

When Sarah still said nothing, I laughed uneasily. "Isn't this where you're supposed to act like you didn't hear me and say, 'Cazz? Hello? Are you there? Cazz? Can you hear me?'"

Sarah chuckled softly. "Sorry. I heard you. I…I don't know what to say. I got stuck on the part about ripping each other's clothes off and had trouble concentrating on the rest."

I couldn't help but laugh. She could have left me to suffer with my anxiety, but instead she'd chosen to keep the lines of communication open by allowing a trace of flirtatiousness through.

"I'm kidding," Sarah said. "I did hear you. I don't want to hurt you either, but I don't think I can give you what you're asking."

"I haven't asked anything yet, but now that you mention it, I am going to ask for something."

A few quiet moments elapsed and Sarah's voice came across the line. "Hello? Cazz? Can you hear me?"

"Very funny, Perkins."

Sarah chuckled again. "Sorry. Couldn't resist." I heard her exhale. "Okay. Ask away."

"Please don't avoid me. That's all I ask."

She barked a laugh. "It's funny you'd say that."

"Why is that funny?"

In a low and sultry voice, Sarah replied, "I don't think I can stay away."

It was a dream, hearing those words, and suddenly I was floating from relief and happiness. I couldn't think of anything to say except to thank God, when her voice came back over the line.

"Good night, Cazz."

"Night, Sarah."

I hit the button to end the call and set the phone down. I had to smile. She was still torturing me by not being with me, but at least she wasn't tormenting me by letting me think she was with someone else.

CHAPTER SIXTEEN

Saturday morning—rather, later that morning—I awoke, consumed by thoughts of Sarah. I wanted to spend every waking hour with her (though I'd hardly mind the sleeping ones, too). On a whim, after my morning spin class, I called her around eleven.

She answered her mobile phone. "Hello?"

"I don't suppose you're free this fine afternoon?"

"My plans got cancelled an hour ago, unfortunately. Why?" She sounded a little down.

"And tonight?"

"Same."

"What's wrong? You sound bummed."

"I am. I was supposed to do eighteen holes with the CEO of Pipeline Technologies but he sprained his wrist, and the other two from our foursome opted for a shorter day playing tennis instead."

I pounced on the opportunity. "Perfect. I'll pick you up at one."

Silence on the line. Finally, Sarah spoke. "Cazz, I'm in a foul mood. I've been trying to get on this guy's calendar for months. Pipeline donates one percent of its profits to foundations like ours, and I want Kindle Hope to be one of its three charity beneficiaries. Let's do this another time."

"Trust me, I have the perfect thing for you. One o'clock. Grab some lunch, and be sure to wear comfortable clothes and shoes. And sunscreen." I hung up. If she truly wanted to be left alone to sulk, she'd call back and tell me. But the phone didn't ring, and after several minutes of waiting, my ears lifted in a telltale sign of the huge grin on my face.

Sarah was ready to go when she opened the door at one. She wore a white, sleeveless blouse over low-rise, sycamore-colored chinos. With a matching cardigan tucked under her arm and her hair in a loose ponytail, she was adorable yet sexy. She locked the front door and followed me to my Toyota.

We didn't speak much as we made our way down a blessedly traffic-free I-5. Sarah spent most of the drive with her eyes hidden behind sunglasses and her head against the headrest. It was a long drive, but rather than complain or require I reveal our destination, she seemed comfortable letting me lead. I exited on Disneyland Drive and continued until I found parking. Sarah took all this in and finally graced me with a smile, lifting herself out of her funk.

"It's better at night, but it's still fun during the day. You've been to the Downtown Disney District, right?" I asked.

"I have. I love it."

"I thought we could wander around, shop, snack, whatever. And if you're up for it, we could go on a few of the rides across the way." I tried to read the appeal of that suggestion by her expression.

"Kind of expensive for an afternoon, isn't it?"

I smiled sheepishly. "I splurged a few months back and bought an annual passport. And they were having a special when I bought it, so I have a free ticket." I pulled the ticket out of my back pocket and handed it to her.

She didn't take it, instead removing her purse from her shoulder and rifling through it. She extracted a card from her wallet. "I have one, too," she said, and smiled as sheepishly as I had. "Guilty pleasure."

"Favorites?" I returned the ticket to my pocket.

"Of course. You say one and I'll say one." She lifted her left eyebrow as the right side of her mouth curled up mischievously.

I felt like I was back in high school, but in a good way. "Space Mountain, obviously," I said.

"Matterhorn," she replied.

"Haunted Mansion."

"Pirates!"

"Old school of me, I know, but those are my top four." I shrugged.

"Mine, too."

"Shop first, or ride first?"

"Shop, of course!" She laced her arm through mine at the elbow and started us down the lane.

The afternoon was perfect. We were like two kids, pointing and giggling, each occasionally eagerly pulling the other by the hand toward a destination of particular interest. We got lucky with the lines for our favorite rides and even went through Space Mountain twice using the FASTPASS system. We goofed around with Winnie the Pooh characters in Critter Country, enjoyed espresso and beignets in New Orleans Square, and shopped along Main Street USA. We even helped a lost child find her extremely worried parents.

Sarah had spotted the little girl crying outside Café Orleans after we left Pirates of the Caribbean. Sarah squatted next to her and asked if she was lost. The little girl nodded and rubbed her wet, red eyes with her knuckles.

"Would you like me to help you find your parents?" Sarah asked gently.

The girl, who was no more than six years old, shook her head and became more upset.

"No?" Sarah asked.

"I'm not…I'm not supposed to talk to strangers," the girl managed to say through her sobs.

I was standing next to Sarah, who glanced up at me briefly and smiled. "Your parents are very smart to tell you that," she said. "We'll stay right here out in the open and won't go anywhere scary, okay?" The child nodded. "Let's be friends so we're no longer strangers. I'm Sarah. What's your name?"

The girl's staggered breathing made it hard for her to speak. "Em…Em…Emily."

"Hi, Emily," Sarah said. She waved me down and I crouched next to both of them. "Emily, this is my friend Cazz. Cazz, this is my friend Emily."

I didn't think Emily was up for a handshake, so I lightly and briefly touched her shoulder as I smiled. "Nice to meet you, Emily."

Sarah attempted to make the child feel more at ease. "Cazz and I were talking about our favorite Disney characters, cuz that's what friends do. Mine's Cinderella. Who's yours?" Sarah asked. I'd always admired Sarah's ability to make people feel comfortable, and apparently she could do it for anyone of any age. How she managed to seamlessly insert the little white lie about us discussing our favorite characters, I'll never know, but it worked wonders on Emily.

Emily looked at Sarah for reassurance, then to me, then back to Sarah. Then Emily pointed to me. "She is."

Astonished, I glanced over my shoulder but no one was standing there. "Me?" I asked Emily, thinking she must be so distraught over being lost, she didn't comprehend Sarah's question.

She nodded. "Belle. From Beauty and the Beast," she said in a more confident tone, proud of knowing her Disney characters. "'Cept your hair's darker and your eyes are greener."

I opened my mouth to speak but closed it and turned to Sarah for input, giving her a shrug and a look that told her I had no idea what to say or whom the girl was talking about.

Sarah smiled. "You're right. Cazz is very pretty like Belle, and I promise she's just as nice. Would it be okay if Cazz stayed here with you while I go find someone who can help us locate your parents? I promise I'll be right back, and you can tell her all about Belle, okay?"

"Okay," Emily said, appearing more relieved. She reached a hand out toward me. I took it and tried to relax by smiling at the child. I knew as much about kids as I did about this Belle character, whom I could only hope had more to her than dreams of fancy balls and handsome princes.

Sarah stood and I glanced up at her with a *thanks a lot* smirk before returning my focus to my small charge and getting the skinny on my animated double. A few minutes later, Sarah arrived with two harried-looking parents in tow. The mother scooped up Emily and lavished kisses on her cheeks, then extended a hand to me in gratitude. We said our good-byes and continued toward the Haunted Mansion.

"Thanks for leaving me with the kid," I said dryly.

"She was smitten with you. It made sense for you to be the one to stay, Princess." Sarah chuckled and gave me a light, teasing shove on my shoulder.

"I guess I do have at least one thing in common with Belle, from what Emily said."

Sarah turned to me curiously as we walked side by side. She contemplated my comment for several moments before replying. "Oh, that's right. She's a voracious reader. You still a bibliophile?"

I shook my head. "That's not what I meant."

She stopped and was nearly run into by a petite brunette who was laser-focused on the Mark Twain Riverboat. Sarah called out an apology to the woman, who was so intent on her destination she didn't acknowledge her. Sarah turned back to me with a raised eyebrow, waiting for my explanation.

I offered a playful smile. "Apparently, Belle fell for a beast, too."

Sarah bit her bottom lip, trying unsuccessfully to hide a smile. We stared at each other for several moments, simultaneously reveling in the flirtation while trying not to crack up. We both broke at the same time, bursting into laughter. Sarah lightly smacked my upper arm and shook her head. With a grin, I threaded my elbow with hers and gently tugged her into the switchback queue at the ride's entrance.

We even lucked out with the return freeway traffic on both I-5 and 101. As we neared Sarah's exit, I glanced at her briefly and made a suggestion.

"I don't suppose you're hungry?"

"Starving. I was thinking of asking whether you wanted to grab a bite, but I thought you might be sick of me by now." Her voice was teasing and animated.

I laughed. "Aside from your subjecting me to "It's a Small World," which hasn't stopped playing in my head since we left that damned ride, I had a lot of fun today. You've been great company. Do you like Italian?"

"Love it."

"Excellent. I know just the place."

We only had to wait ten minutes for a table at Little Liguria, my favorite Italian restaurant in L.A. It was a small yet intimate establishment with red-and-white-checkered tablecloths, votive candles, paper napkins, and reddish-hued overhead lights that illuminated the tables in a sufficiently Goldilocks way: not too bright, not too dark. We got a table in the back and promptly ordered a half carafe of the house Chianti while we perused the menu.

Once we ordered, Sarah eyed me with curiosity. "I forgot to ask. How'd it go with Caitlin?"

I furrowed my eyebrows, wondering whom she was talking about. "Caitlin?"

"Blonde bombshell from last night. I assume she hit on you?"

I took a sip of wine and set my glass on the table. "Wow, that was last night? Feels like a long time ago already." It didn't seem possible that merely twenty-four hours ago I was in a hotel room kissing Sarah.

"You're stalling." She arched her eyebrow. "Not that it's any of my business."

I smiled. "Not that it *is* any of your business, but I'd say she was…tenacious."

Sarah shifted uncomfortably in her chair and narrowed her eyes briefly before catching herself and relaxing her expression. She lifted her glass and replied before she took a sip. "She is beautiful."

I nodded.

"And rich," Sarah added.

"Even better. And I'm already in her debt, so maybe I'll have to consider my…repayment options." I enjoyed harmlessly toying with Sarah, pleased by the trace of jealousy in her body language.

"In her debt?" There was a slight edge in her tone as she set down her glass, waiting for an explanation.

"If it hadn't been for her, I don't think I'd have been accosted in a hotel room and subjected to the most amazing kisses of my life. I owe her big-time." I pleasurably recalled my all-too-brief embraces with Sarah.

Sarah tilted her head, leaned slightly forward across the table with a quizzical expression, and searched my face as if assessing my sincerity. Then she sat back and momentarily bit her lower lip.

"You're serious," she said, seeming confounded. "How do you do that?"

"Do what?"

Our waiter chose that moment to bring us a small basket of freshly baked focaccia and a metal caddy holding olive oil and balsamic vinegar. "Ladies." He interrupted us to set the items down.

Once he left, Sarah continued. "Make me not doubt you."

I sat back and studied her with concern. "You say that like you're surprised."

She seemed to choose her response carefully. "I am."

"Surprised? Surprised you can trust me?" A knot formed in my stomach, and I needed to make sure we were talking about the same thing.

Sarah shifted in her seat, reached for her glass, and stared at the red liquid as she swirled it several times before looking across to me. "I know it isn't fair of me, Cazz, because you couldn't help it. Your parents moved and you had to go with them. But part of me never forgave you for leaving without saying good-bye. I felt betrayed. You didn't have a choice in leaving, but you had a choice in keeping in touch. And you didn't. You just…left." She took a sip of wine and set her glass down before meeting my eyes. "I think to a certain extent, it still colors my interaction with you, whether or not it's fair of me."

The hurt took over and made me choke down the apology I wanted to offer. We were in a public place, and I couldn't begin to explain to Sarah why I didn't call or write after my family left L.A. I picked up a piece of focaccia, dropped it onto the plate in front of me, and tore off a little section. I was suddenly not hungry, but wanted a socially acceptable reason to avert my eyes in an effort not to call attention to how it felt to hear her say she didn't trust me. I tossed the bread into my mouth and chewed thoroughly, staring at the plate all the while, willing myself not to shake my head in frustration. My throat felt constricted and swallowing was difficult.

I tore off another piece, preparing to repeat the process, when I felt a hand on my forearm.

"Cazz." Sarah kept hold of me until I met her eyes. "Don't." She released my arm.

I dropped the bread back onto the plate and forced myself not to cross my arms. "Don't what?"

"My having an issue trusting you isn't the same as you not being trustworthy. It's also not exclusive to you. Don't assume I don't trust you. It's just not easy for me, for a variety of reasons."

I shifted uncomfortably in my chair and stared into my lap, wondering how to respond. I felt her hand on my forearm again and looked up.

"Can you accept that? And know that I'm trying?"

Those last two words were a salve to my distressed ego. They helped dissolve the tightness in my abdomen and made me feel I'd received some sort of special pardon. Sarah wasn't asking for anything unreasonable. Plus, my silence after leaving L.A. wasn't exactly easy to understand, even if I'd bothered to explain, which I never had. And she was telling me how she was feeling, which in and of itself was a good thing, versus closing herself off from me.

I gave her a tiny smile and nodded.

At one point during dinner, Sarah asked how I liked my work at the Foundation. I hadn't wanted to discuss it with her because I didn't want to have to lie. I already felt guilty for withholding information from her, and it grew exponentially when she said she wanted to trust me, especially knowing now how difficult it was for her. I was loath to do anything to break that trust, however tenuous, but felt obligated not to come clean about my assignment since success in my field demanded total confidentiality.

Part of me felt I could trust her with the truth, but another part of me was all too aware that I knew virtually nothing about Sarah's relationship to her colleagues. Especially Gregory Morrison. I didn't want to plant any seeds of doubt that might cause her to become skeptical of anyone she worked with. I recalled Carol telling me that most of the Foundation's employees had worked there over ten years, and I was sure they were a tight-knit group. I didn't want

Sarah's knowledge of my assignment to come between her and anyone she cared about, especially before I was one hundred percent sure about what was going on and who was responsible. After everything Sarah was going through with her father's recent death, I'd even begun to regret the investigation since I didn't want her to experience any more loss in her life, should the case conclude with one of her associates being taken into custody. However justified from a criminal-wrongdoing standpoint, such an outcome would wound her deeply.

I tried for nonchalance. "It's fine. The people are nice. The work's steady."

"And how's the job hunt going?" Sarah asked as she took a bite of caprese salad.

My eyebrows lifted as I repeated her words. "Job hunt?"

"I thought this was an in-between thing for you."

I glanced down to my plate and pushed some butternut-squash ravioli around with my fork, racking my brain for the background details of my assignment. I couldn't recall Commander Ashby or anyone telling me I was at the Foundation under the guise of temp work. Customarily when my pilot-program colleagues and I were hired into a finance organization, the premise was that ours was a new, permanent position, even if we were on the temp-to-perm track. Although we would ultimately end up leaving the organization within a matter of weeks, we never let it be known that we expected anything other than full-time, long-term employment.

"Um, well, I guess it's true that nonprofit accounting isn't my expertise," I said, cutting a piece of ravioli with my fork.

"Hmm," Sarah murmured. I assumed she expected me to expand on my comment as several moments passed before she spoke again. "And how do you know Jim?"

"Jim?"

"Ashby."

Sarah swirled the wine in her glass, her eyes focused on the deep-red liquid. It was the color certain to be rising to my cheeks right about now. *Damn.* Sarah had confirmed what I suspected: Luke Perkins was the personal friend to whom Commander Ashby had alluded. I focused on my plate and again fumbled around in my head trying to come up with the tidbits of how I was supposed to be connected to Jim Ashby. Nothing registered. Commander Ashby had failed to disclose several important pieces of information that would have prepared me for such questions. At a loss as to how to respond, I opted for a minimal, honest reply.

"I don't, really. Know him, that is. We've met."

"Interesting. Greg mentioned you're the niece of a friend of my dad's, but Dad told me you were referred by Jim, who has no siblings."

I kept my eyes on Sarah, trying not to give away my discomfort with the cracks in my story. She arched an eyebrow and studied me. It seemed to dawn on both of us that Sarah's father must have told Morrison and Sarah two different things when he opted to bring me on board. That was intriguing for a couple reasons. First, it meant Luke had reservations about Morrison. Second, it meant Luke had given both of them a heads-up of my hiring, which accounted for Sarah's override of Morrison when I initially arrived. Unfortunately, it was also painfully obvious I hadn't been forthcoming with Sarah as to the true nature of my employment.

"Huh," I said, refocusing on my food. Thankfully, she let it go. It was good I hadn't been forced to lie to her, but unsettling because her line of questioning indicated she knew I was withholding information.

"Tell me more about the grant-making side of the operation," I said, as we browsed the dessert menu.

Sarah's eyes darted up and she cocked her head to the side. "Why?" There was no sarcasm or irony in her question, only genuine curiosity. "It's hardly glamorous. Not like the fund-raising events."

I set my menu down to focus my attention exclusively on Sarah. "Because it's important to you. If I had to guess, I'd say if you never had to attend another fund-raiser, it couldn't be too soon. And if I had to make another guess, I'd say finding ways to help the people the Foundation supports is the reason you wake up in the morning, the last thing on your mind before sleep, and the only thing that explains the gleam in your eyes when you press the flesh at those events. It certainly isn't the scintillating conversation." I rolled my eyes, then finished my train of thought. "Thank God you're able to keep it all in perspective when you attend those blasted soirees and feign delight all evening. You amaze me. Truly. I don't know how you do it."

I scanned the dessert options for a few seconds before peering back up at Sarah, growing concerned as her lips slightly trembled and she bit the lower one as if trying to still it. Telltale moisture crept into those wondrous light-blue eyes, eyes that hadn't left me during my little monologue. Shit. I'd probably offended her.

"What is it?" I asked.

She slightly shook her head as she lowered it to refocus on the menu.

"Did I say something wrong?"

She shook her head again but didn't speak.

"I'm sorry. I shouldn't have assumed." Time to backtrack. "Those events are probably super fun, and it's only me that finds them a little trying. I know how important they are to the Foundation and I shouldn't be so quick to—"

Sarah put her hand on mine. "Stop."

"I didn't mean—" I started anew and tried to pull my hand away, but she tightened her grip.

"Just…stop," she said, her attention shifting to where her hand rested on mine. Turning my hand palm up, she cupped my fingers in hers. She focused on our hands a moment longer before meeting my eyes and gently squeezing my fingers. "Thank you," she said with a small, sad smile. She squeezed my hand again before removing it. "You nailed it," she said softly. "All of it."

But if I was right, why did she look so sad?

The waiter swung by to inquire whether we were interested in dessert.

"Share?" Sarah asked me.

I nodded. "Absolutely."

"Tiramisu or profiteroles?"

Either sounded heavenly. I looked up at the waiter. "What do you recommend?"

"If you're only ordering one, go with the tiramisu. If you don't like it, I'll comp it," he said.

I took the bait. "How many have you comped this week?"

He waggled his eyebrows and grinned.

That sealed the deal. "Tiramisu, please. Two forks." I grinned back.

"Excellent choice," he said as he plucked the menus from our hands and left us again.

My smile waned as I settled my gaze on Sarah's face. "As much as I like to be right, I've obviously said something to upset you, and I'm sorry."

"You haven't upset me." Smiling that doleful smile again, she set her wineglass in front of her and started to spin it clockwise in small increments, giving it her full attention. She spoke to her glass. "I'm just…it's a little disconcerting how well you seem to…In any case, I'm not upset. Maybe a little sad, but not because of anything you said." She tried to lighten the mood by offering a tepid smile. "Probably premenstrual."

Sarah was clearly bothered by something but seemed to want to spare me the gory details.

I took a few moments before responding. "Fair enough. But, please. Enlighten me. Tell me about your work. Educate me about the grant-making side of things. Please."

She gave me a long stare before returning to the important task of spinning her wineglass via snaps of her fingers along the stem at the base.

"As you know, the Kindle Hope Foundation focuses on issues like human rights, education, civic engagement, reproductive health, community sustainability, and freedom of expression. We focus our giving on niche areas and organizations that have difficulty getting funding from other sources. Our preference is to make small grants that can have a large impact on individual lives." Sarah stopped turning her wineglass and shifted her gaze to me. "Bored yet?"

Sarah was nothing short of captivating when she talked about her work, so I was anything but bored. I gave her a smile but held my verbal reply as the waiter approached. He set down two forks and a small white plate housing a generous piece of tiramisu dribbled with chocolate sauce. "Enjoy," he said as he departed.

I lifted a fork and sliced a piece of the decadent-looking dessert. "Please, continue."

She narrowed her eyes warily at me for a moment before proceeding. As she progressed with her narration, she became more animated, using her hands for emphasis as she explained how impactful the Foundation had been and could continue to be a driving force for hope and change for hundreds of thousands of people worldwide. With almost childlike reverie, she lost herself in stories that told of myriad ways the Foundation was making a positive difference in people's lives. Watching Sarah tell me about this aspect of her life was like imagining myself sitting in the eye of a hurricane from where I could safely watch the flurry of movement surrounding me, be amazed at its power to transform everything it touched, yet feel completely secure in the knowledge that nothing could impact its progression. Sarah was indeed a force of nature. A force for good.

I'd eaten my half of the tiramisu long before she took her first bite, so engaged was she in telling me about certain organizations she'd located that helped further the Foundation's mission. She finally lifted her fork. "Now aren't you sorry you asked?" She ate a bite, closed her eyes, and moaned with pleasure. In and of itself, the sight and sound was incredibly tantalizing. But coming on the heels of hearing what moved her so deeply, what she'd dedicated her life to, the compassion in her voice as she talked about the hardship so many of the Foundation's beneficiaries endured, and the humility she conveyed as she downplayed her role in helping them, Sarah was the epitome of sexy. Hearing that moan made me have to stifle one of my own.

For the last umpteen minutes, all traces of sadness, stress, and hard work faded, giving her face a youthful glow. Her eyes had transformed into wondrous pools I wanted to dive into. She spoke with insight and confidence, and exuded an energy and excitement that was truly joyful. She was absolutely riveting. When her eyes landed on mine and focused on me, she swallowed hard and raised an inquiring eyebrow.

I must have been looking at her like she was the next course. At this realization, I fumbled for something to say and dumbly ignored her question. "Tasty." Sarah gave me a mischievous smile as her other eyebrow joined its counterpart. Warmth rushed to my cheeks as I realized how that might have sounded. "The tiramisu," I quickly added. "It's tasty, isn't it?"

Sarah dabbed her mouth with her napkin. "I have to say, that's not the reaction I typically get when I talk about grant-making. Usually I watch as eyes roll back into heads, not burn into me like lances."

My hand shot out for my water glass in a desperate attempt to get my hormones to chill. After taking a large swig, I briefly offered my best apologetic smile, then focused on the napkin in my lap that was suddenly incredibly interesting.

"I much prefer your reaction," Sarah said.

I glanced at her dubiously, but her heartfelt smile, which made her eyes twinkle, put me at ease. I exhaled in relief, pleased she'd forgiven my lecherousness. "You can't moan like that," I said, lightly chastising her. "You do that, after engaging me with stories of the great things you're doing at the Foundation, and, well…damn."

Sarah's face fell. I should have kept my mouth shut. "You misunderstand me," she said. "I wasn't trying to toot my own horn. It's a team effort. We couldn't achieve half the—"

"Sarah." I raised a hand to cut her off. I was thankful she wasn't upset by my half-assed flirtation but annoyed by her tendency to slight her magnanimity. I spoke with more bite than I intended. "You're so far from tooting your own horn, you border on pathological. Suffice it to say I'm sure your father was—and is, from wherever he's watching—extremely proud of you and everything you continue to do for the Foundation."

My irritation quickly faded as I focused on her face and saw the emotion there, emotion I was sure stemmed from my mention of her father. I leaned forward, reached out my hand, and though neither of hers was on the table, she lifted one and placed it in mine. I squeezed it gently and spoke in a softer voice.

"You know it's true."

Although I hadn't really known Luke Perkins, I'd never been more certain of anything. Their complementary roles at the Foundation, the esteem for the father-daughter duo held by all their colleagues, their years of working together, the continued financial support they received from old and new donors alike that told of unyielding respect for and trust in them—all these combined into indestructible proof of the mutual love and admiration Luke and Sarah held for each other.

Sarah lifted her other hand and dabbed a knuckle at the corner of her eye where a tear threatened to crest. She nodded and squeezed my hand in return. "Thank you." She pulled her hand away and swapped her napkin for her knuckle.

"Shall we?" I indicated the door. Sarah nodded again. Though reluctant to end the evening, I signaled the waiter for the check.

CHAPTER SEVENTEEN

Once we got back to her place, I stayed seated in the Toyota as she opened the passenger door. It was well after ten o'clock. After placing a foot on the driveway, Sarah turned to me.

"I know it's late, but would you care for a glass of wine?"

"You sure?" I didn't want our day together to conclude, but didn't want Sarah to feel pressured to extend it, especially given our proclivity for moving into emotionally charged territory.

"Please. Besides, I never gave you the tour." She exited the car and stepped to the front door, letting us in with her key. She tapped her shoes off toe against heel, and I removed my sneakers.

"You've already seen downstairs, so let's go upstairs." She took the stairs at a quick clip and I followed. At the top of the stairs to the left was a bathroom and straight ahead was a guest bedroom. We turned right down the hall and she opened a door on her left. "Office," she said, standing aside to let me peek in. Along with the usual accoutrements of a desk, bookshelf, and chair, the room was similar to her office at the Foundation in an important respect: it was covered with corkboard full of letters and cards that presumably were written with gratitude and appreciation from Foundation beneficiaries. I was too far away to read them but knew exactly what they were. Though I had no hand in her accomplishments, I was strangely proud of Sarah and what she did for the Foundation. And I was happy to see her take private pride in her work as well.

We walked to the end of the hallway, where she stepped inside of what was obviously the master bedroom. I peered in. She gestured to a couple of doors with her chin. "Bathroom. Walk-in closet. The usual," she said, glancing around.

My eyes landed on the king-size bed beneath a delicately carved cherrywood headboard. Although we'd shared many playful moments together in the theme park, I doubted she'd be much amused if I indulged my sudden shameless fancy of diving onto the bed, burying my face in a pillow, and inhaling the Sarah scents to which I'd be treated. Following quickly on its heels were far less chaste imaginings involving my hostess, and while hardly troubling, they weren't exactly in the spirit of the house tour. Before I said or did something foolish, I hastily backpedaled and let her lead the way downstairs to the kitchen.

"Home sweet home," she said, pulling a couple glasses down from the cabinet and grabbing an opened bottle of Cabernet Sauvignon from the counter.

"It is sweet." I took the wineglass she offered and followed her to a couch that overlooked the city below. We didn't sit on opposite ends of it, but didn't cozy up to each other in the middle either. We maintained a casual, comfortable distance and spent a few quiet minutes enjoying the view, the wine, and the company.

"Today was fun. Thanks for taking me," Sarah said, breaking the silence.

"Thanks for coming out to play."

"It made me feel like a kid again."

"Speaking of which, you were really good with that little girl. Emily."

"So were you."

"Hardly, but thanks." I turned to her. "Ever want one of your own?"

She gave me a look that told me I'd crossed a line, but tried to hide it by glancing away. She picked up her wineglass and swirled the contents, seeming to mull over a response. I stopped myself from apologizing for my directness, given everything that had transpired between us since our reconnection at the bar two weeks prior. Sarah had asked me all sorts of personal questions.

"Not any more," she said stiffly.

Ouch. That couldn't be good. And it did nothing to curb my curiosity. My question was out before I could stop myself. "Will you tell me what happened between you and whoever hurt you so badly?"

Seeming annoyed and disappointed, she set her glass down. "It's water under the bridge, Cazz. It doesn't matter." She waved her hand as if to settle the question.

I stared at her. "Doesn't matter? It hugely matters. Whatever happened deeply affected you, and I want to know what it is."

She narrowed her eyes. "Talking about it makes it seem more important than it is. I don't like to give it that weight."

Trying to rein in my rapidly rising irritation at her stubbornness, I adopted an even tone I wasn't feeling and kept my voice low. "Whether or not you talk about it doesn't change how you feel about it. It's a weight you live with regardless."

"Not if I can help it."

"Damn it, Sarah!" I jumped to my feet, gesticulating and losing all pretense of calm. "You need to get over whatever the hell it is, and ignoring it isn't going to make it go away!" I spoke louder than I'd intended, wondering at the depths of my frustration.

"No," she said coolly, slowly getting off the couch and crossing her arms. "*You* need me to get over it. I need to do no such thing. I told you before that I wasn't looking for anything complicated, and I meant it. But you ignored me because it's not something you wanted to hear."

I shook my head in exasperation at hitting the cement wall that was Sarah. "Shit." I pinched my tear ducts with a thumb and forefinger, trying desperately to maintain some composure. "Okay." I was reeling from the rapid turn of events, displeased with myself for being the instigator of an argument I hadn't intended to start. I crossed my arms and studied her, mirroring her stance. Then I shook my head again and dropped my arms, knowing my welcome was worn out.

"You're partially right." I moved to the entryway. "I do need you to get over it." Dropping to the floor, I tied my laces. "I think you're remarkable and phenomenal, and I can't get you out of my head," I said with annoyance instead of appreciation. "But you do need to get over it." I popped up to my feet and stood inside the door. "For you, not for me." I was on a roll now. "If I'm not in the running, so be it. Let's take me out of the picture altogether." I swallowed hard, not wanting to say the words but believing the truth in them. This wasn't about me. It was about a one-of-a-kind, generous, and loving woman who deserved to be loved.

"You have so much to offer, Sarah." My tone was softer, more resigned. "You're selling yourself short. People get hurt, absolutely they do, but love is worth the risk. I can't imagine cutting myself off from it like you're doing." I pressed the heels of my palms to my forehead in a display of frustration. "Fuck, listen to me." I sounded like an idiot. I pivoted away from Sarah, turned the knob, and tugged the door open, only for it to be ripped out of my hand and slammed shut in front of me. The loud noise punctuated the gulf between us. Sarah had thrown herself between the door and me and was standing before me, seething.

"You hypocrite! How dare you tell me you can't imagine cutting yourself off from loving someone! You're going to stand there and honestly tell me you've never done it? That you've never been afraid to risk your heart when you loved someone?" Her light-blue eyes were wide and threatening with fury.

"No!" I replied sharply. "God damn it, no. What are you even talking about?" Her intensity and insinuation completely took me aback.

"Okay, then tell me this. Why didn't you ever call or write?"

I took a step back as if she'd slapped me. The question lay before me like a minefield. "Jesus. What does that have to do with anything?"

"Answer me." Sarah's expression was punishing.

I shook my head, wondering how to respond and dreading the possibility of irrevocably alienating her. It was one thing for her to be angry with me. It was one thing to tell her some of what I'd been feeling since seeing her again. Those were adult feelings, and given our scene in the hotel room, she'd been feeling at least a little of the same toward me. It was a wholly different thing if she were to freak out because of how I felt about her—how I'd always felt about her. It would make me seem pathetic if she knew I'd never gotten over her. I felt ashamed. A stronger person wouldn't have clung to her teenage memories as sacred treasures the way I had.

I leaned against the door and bowed my head. No. I couldn't answer.

"Hell, Sarah, I don't think you need to hear that. I need to go."

She pushed off from the door and stood in front of me. "I thought I meant something to you back then." Her expression was laced with hurt and there was an edge to her voice.

"Jesus Christ." I tugged off my shoes and threw them down. "Meant something to me." I muttered as I marched to the living-room window and, pacing, pulled my hand through my hair.

"Jesus, Sarah. Are you kidding? You didn't mean *something* to me. You meant *everything* to me." I gulped and spoke softly. "You really want me to say this?" I stopped pacing and looked at her, desperately hoping for a reprieve.

She didn't give me one but simply nodded. She'd moved away from the doorway and was standing next to the couch in the living room, her eyes following my every move.

"Sarah, I…fuck." I started pacing again, shaking my head and crossing my arms protectively. "I didn't call or write because I boxed it up. I had to box it up. I…I don't know how to explain it. I was…devastated. Devastated when we left L.A. You had Dirk. I had…feelings for you that I shouldn't have. I had no money, no transportation, nothing to offer you after that except grief. And I couldn't grieve because that felt wrong. So, I boxed up that time in my life for what it was: a gift. I finally found happiness when I thought about it that way. Finally found…" I stopped moving and faced her.

She was watching me, listening intently.

I put my hand out, palm up, and gestured in her direction. "You. I found you." Tears stirred in my eyes and I resumed my pacing. "I couldn't ruin that gift—your gift—by turning it into a sad thing. A desperate, pining thing. College was around the corner and we'd both be going our separate ways anyway. I didn't…I didn't keep in touch because I didn't want to taint my memories of you with sadness or sorrow. If I kept in touch, I'd feel emptiness because I'd want you with me. And empty was the furthest thing from how I felt when I was with you. I'd never felt so full. I didn't call or write because I just wanted…"

Now the tears were rolling, and I could only whisper. I stopped and gazed out the window, holding myself tightly. I involuntarily shook my head again and wiped my eyes with the back of my hand. "I know this doesn't make sense, but I just wanted to hold onto my beautiful, amazing Sarah."

Excruciating silence met my confession.

"Damn," Sarah finally said softly behind me.

I was frozen in place, wondering how I'd managed to tell her how I felt about her back then and frightened at the repercussions. Scared she would freak out and leave me with only my memories. Then I suddenly had so strong an urge to escape, it eclipsed everything else. I wiped my eyes again and rushed to the door, wedging my foot into the first of my sneakers.

Sarah was suddenly blocking the door again. "I'm not letting you leave like this." She pressed her back against the door handle.

I felt like a trapped animal. My foot wouldn't slide into my other shoe, so I crushed the heel down with my body weight. I struggled futilely to suppress my crying, embarrassed I couldn't speak and mortified by my admission.

Sarah entreated me to stay. "Cazz. Please."

I shook my head again and gave her a look that must have conveyed my desperation to depart, because she reluctantly stepped aside. I immediately reached for the doorknob and heaved the door open, then bolted for my car without glancing back. Shoving the key into the ignition, I threw the car into reverse, then forward as a trail of tears coated my cheeks. Though it was difficult to see along the dark and narrow streets with water pooling in my eyes, I couldn't extricate myself fast enough.

I was in agony, fearing Sarah would put two and two together and realize I was in love with her. It was a bitter irony, wanting so much to let her know, yet not wishing to admit I'd never wavered from the feelings I'd developed all those years ago. Doing so would make it sound like an unrequited, forbidden, tormented thing that spoke of endless longing and regret. I never felt that way myself: my love for Sarah was a special, joyful, bursting thing. Having told Sarah how I had to isolate my teenage feelings for her in order to hold onto the tenderness and hope they instilled in me, I feared she'd make the logical leap and conclude that I'd never stopped loving her, and, as a result, that I was pitiable and unworthy. After all, it had been *ten years*! Who wouldn't have let go long ago?

I couldn't believe I'd allowed myself to tell her I'd boxed up her memory as the gift it had always been to me. Why had I been stupid enough to tell her something that would make her want to run as far away from me as possible?

CHAPTER EIGHTEEN

Sunday afternoon, my cell phone rang. I'd just come from a noon spin class and grabbed the phone out of my gym bag without checking the display.

"Hello?"

"Detective." The deep, booming voice surprised me and grabbed my attention.

"Commander." We hadn't spoken since the day he gave me the case. Our only contact had been a brief midweek voice mail in which I'd informed him that although I was still actively investigating, I'd seen enough to know some sort of financial irregularity had been and likely continued to be perpetrated at the Foundation.

"There's been a change in plan. Do you have what you need from the Foundation? I'm pulling you from the field," Ashby said.

"Uh, yes sir, actually. I have several strong leads and can do follow-up work away from the office. I wasn't intending to stay much longer."

"Good. You're not to return there. Section ninety-two. You need to drop it or close it, in short order."

This was bad news. Section ninety-two was the paragraph in the pilot program's charter that precluded civilian investigators from handling violent crime, even indirectly. Since we weren't sworn police officers—we weren't armed and didn't make arrests— the section was created for the safety of the program's participants. Forbidding an investigator from returning to the premises made sense: suspicious perpetrators of ongoing crimes would be far more interested in following the activities of existing employees than of former ones. Section ninety-two had never before been invoked.

"I need a week, sir. Two at the most. I'm close."

"Make it one, Detective."

"What's happened?"

"Perkins," he said, giving me a jolt of concern over Sarah. "Luke Perkins, managing director of the Foundation. I'm sure you've heard by now he was killed in a car crash several weeks ago. We got a call from a man who said his van had been stolen while he was out of town. Turns out he rarely uses it, so he hadn't noticed the damage that couldn't have occurred while it was parked on his street. His story checked out."

"Sorry, sir, I'm not following."

"The guy's van was stolen and used to take out Luke Perkins. We confirmed the paint match with the Perkins car. The Perkins car crash was no accident, Detective. This is now a homicide investigation. I can't put you at risk." Ashby clicked off.

Homicide? Whoever was embezzling from the Foundation had taken out Luke Perkins. It had to be. I didn't believe in coincidences like that. Apparently Ashby didn't either. If Luke Perkins was purposely killed, his suspicion about what was going on at the Foundation was surely linked to it. Although I could safely continue my legwork away from its headquarters, Sarah was potentially in danger from the same person who'd targeted her father. I shuddered at the prospect. I had to wrap up this investigation ASAP—an investigation I was sure would lead me to the killer.

Early Monday morning I arrived at LAX and waited standby for the first flight to Phoenix, the only location where I'd finally tracked down a Broderick LLC CPA firm. The licensure of the CPA, a man named Jack Broderick, was in Arizona, not California. Time to pay him a visit. I rented a car and headed straight to the Broderick LLC office, located in a dated strip mall housing a ninety-nine cent store, a convenience store, a greasy-spoon diner, and a handful of other no-name-brand businesses. A bell sounded as I entered a few minutes after ten o'clock local time. A fortyish brunette coming from around the corner appeared startled by my entrance, as if surprised to have a visitor. Business must be booming.

"Hi," she said. "Can I help you?"

"I hope so. I'm looking for Jack Broderick."

"Do you have an appointment?"

I shook my head. "Do I need one? The sign says 'walk-ins welcome.'"

She smiled. "Of course. Jack will be here any minute. He's dropping something off at the post office. Please, have a seat. Can I get you some coffee or water?"

"No, thanks. I'm fine."

The bell jingled and I turned around to see a heavy-set Caucasian man in his mid-fifties, wearing belted khaki pants partially hidden below a massive gut covered by a drab white oxford shirt. He sported a thick mustache to compensate for his thinning hair.

"Jack." The brunette spoke over my shoulder. "This woman is here to see you. I'm sorry, I didn't catch your name."

I stuck out my hand to Jack. "Cassidy Warner."

He shook it. "Jack Broderick. Come on back." I followed him to his office, and he motioned for me to take a chair opposite his desk. As he sat, the chair groaned under his weight, and I wondered how long it would hold before breaking.

"What can I do for you, Miss Warner?"

"Do you perform the annual audit for the Kindle Hope Foundation in California?"

He didn't hide his surprise. "Yes, I do. Is that how you got my name?"

"Yes. I was hoping you could tell me about your audit techniques specific to the last audit you conducted for the Foundation and whether you noticed anything out of the ordinary during your fieldwork."

He furrowed his brow. "I'm afraid that's confidential information, Miss Warner."

I withdrew my badge and ID from my purse and handed them to him. "I'm investigating the possibility of embezzlement there and could use your cooperation. I have no desire to bring your firm any trouble, but I can make this as easy or hard as you wish."

He studied my credentials and returned them. "We follow standard AICPA audit techniques, Detective. I sincerely doubt anything out of the ordinary's happening at the Kindle Hope Foundation."

"Did you physically inspect the deeds for the land?"

"Yes, indirectly. Due to the materiality of the holdings this past year, we inspected them through a sister firm located in the area."

"Where is the bulk of the land owned by the Foundation?"

"Colorado. Grand Junction vicinity."

"Did you confirm the securities and mutual fund holdings?"

Broderick nodded. "Of course."

"What does Mastick Consulting do for the Foundation?"

"You'd have to ask management that question. We don't ask why a particular firm is used. As long as the money ties out, we're satisfied."

"Satisfied? Those consulting costs made up eighteen percent of last year's G&A expenses and nearly five percent of all expenses. Tell me, Mr. Broderick, what was the materiality threshold you used for the audit and how was it determined? With those numbers, I'm curious as to how you could not know the nature of the services Mastick performs or determine it wouldn't be useful information to someone reviewing their annual report."

Broderick tapped his fingers against the desk, then, after several moments, said, "Materiality thresholds are a matter of professional judgment, Detective. There's no bright line to their determination."

"Indeed." This man knew enough auditing lingo to understand that the percentages I'd laid out would be troublesome for his firm should the audit work be peer reviewed. If I hadn't already had his attention, I was certain I had it now. "How did your firm get involved with the Foundation?"

Broderick leaned back in his chair, making it groan loudly. "I went to college with Greg Morrison."

It was starting to make sense. "Do you audit any other non-profits?"

"No."

"So you have no expertise in auditing that type of organization, yet you render such services to Kindle Hope. Were you paid to overlook certain irregularities?"

"You're overstepping, Detective. Every service business out there gets clients through referrals. The fact that I know Greg Morrison has no bearing on my firm's professional conduct."

"I see. By professional, you mean how your firm is operating illegally by not being registered with the California Secretary of State, for example."

Broderick steepled his fingers. "An accidental oversight, I can assure you."

"Your firm is required to be registered with the California Board of Accountancy if it's practicing public accounting in the state, which it is. Furthermore, while your firm is no longer required to be licensed there due to the recent change in law, such was not the case when you performed your prior audits of the Kindle Hope Foundation. Accidental oversight?"

Broderick's lips tightened. "What can I do for you, Detective?"

"I'd like to borrow your electronic audit work-papers for a few days. I won't make any copies and I'll return them by the end of the week."

"Absolutely not."

"No?"

"That's a complete breach of confidentiality."

"I'll leave it to you to get comfortable with the idea. And I require you to keep it between us. I wouldn't want anyone to give Greg Morrison or anyone else a heads-up about this inquest. Is that clear?"

Broderick glared at me in silence.

I tilted my head to the side and raised my eyebrows, waiting for his assent. I repeated, louder this time. "Is that clear? Or do I need to *broaden* my investigation?" I had enough on his firm to shut him down for years, if not permanently, and he knew it. I waited for my not-too-subtle threat to sink in.

Broderick nodded and stood, releasing the chair from its burden. "I'll save them for you on a USB drive. Give me twenty minutes." He left.

Any time I made headway in an investigation, I'd get a little thrill. This time, Ashby's news about Luke Perkins dampened the charge. I'd met my share of white-collar criminals in my line of work, but this violent-crime aspect was new. I'd also never had a personal connection to a case before. Although I didn't like that these firsts were occurring on the same assignment, I was glad Ashby had selected me for it. I wouldn't stop digging until I was certain Sarah was out of danger.

Around eleven AM I was back on the road heading to the airport. My next destination: Grand Junction, Colorado. Although nonstops from Phoenix were available, there were only three a day. With the one-hour time difference, the next one wouldn't get me in until after the county courthouse closed. I had to wait more than three hours for the next flight. During the interim, I ate lunch and used my laptop to reserve a rental car and hotel room for the night. Next, I sifted through the audit work-papers until I found the audit files relating to the land. As expected, there were no copies of the deeds, but addresses of the properties purportedly owned by the Foundation were listed. That was exactly what I needed to start my search in the morning.

Settled in my hotel room, I finally drifted off to sleep wondering whether Sarah was safe. I longed to hear her voice yet fought the urge to call, because I didn't want to relive any moment of my confession or answer questions about my absence from the office. But I still worried about her.

After grabbing a bagel and coffee from the hotel restaurant, I arrived at the Grand Junction county courthouse at eight o'clock local time. The first property I searched for ended up mirroring the others. It was in the Foundation's name, the prior owner a single man named Paul Gunderson. In and of itself, that wasn't strange. But this

Paul Gunderson happened to be the prior owner of each of the three properties held by the Foundation in the Grand Junction area. Also, the same person—someone named Joseph Stein—had notarized the deeds in the Foundation's name as well as those in Gunderson's name. I didn't believe Gunderson existed any more than I believed the Foundation was the rightful owner of these properties. I was getting closer to the truth.

I hopped back in my rental car and returned to the airport. There were no direct flights to L.A., so I had to connect through Phoenix again. By the time I got home, it was nearly three o'clock and I was hungry. The two tiny bags of peanuts I received in-flight hadn't been much of a lunch. Since my freezer was bereft of frozen entrees and I had no time to cobble together a respectable meal, I boiled some edamame and booted up my laptop again. Hating the post-airplane/airport aura that cast at least a psychological, if not physical, film over my body, I desperately wanted to shower, but had to make some calls while it was still business hours in Colorado.

In some online real-estate listings, I found old pages of information on two of the properties purchased by the Foundation, which had completed the transactions using local real-estate agents. I called both agents but was sent to voice mail, whereupon I left my contact information without explicitly saying why I called. I'd be more likely to get a quick response if I sounded like a potential client. At this point, I wanted to confirm the identity of the seller.

My theory: Greg Morrison had searched Grand Junction county records for land owned by out-of-towners who'd held the properties for a number of years, likely decades. He then falsified deeds in the name of Paul Gunderson. He used a fake ID to play a man with that name and used the same notary on documents claiming him on the title. He then listed, FOR SALE BY OWNER, the properties he wanted the Foundation to purchase. As a Foundation representative, he would inform the real-estate agents what the Foundation was aiming for in terms of investments in land, which would conveniently mirror the features of the properties purportedly owned by Paul Gunderson. As the seller of those properties, Paul Gunderson, a.k.a. Greg Morrison, would receive a wire in his bank account upon the closing of the deals.

The true owners of the land hadn't yet discovered the ploy. It might be years before they did. And since the Foundation would be one of the victims of the fraud (in the event the real owners discovered the falsified documents), no one at the Foundation would likely be implicated since it wouldn't make sense that the Foundation would harm itself.

Moreover, although I hadn't yet connected all the dots relating to Mastick Consulting, my intuition told me Morrison had found a clever way to steal even more money from the Foundation. It was possible he kept things simple on the front end by sending payments from Mastick to the bank account he held as Paul Gunderson. On the back end, however, I suspected he'd set up entities and aliases to make his collection of payments from the Foundation to Mastick Consulting difficult to trace, based on the very fact that Mastick was set up as a Nevada Corporation. Once I could confirm Morrison's involvement in the land transactions, I could obtain a warrant to access the Nevada records.

I showered, having made my calls and marginally satisfying my hunger. Wearing jeans and a T-shirt, I was searching for pictures of Greg Morrison online when I heard the apartment buzzer notifying me someone was at the main door. I glanced at the wall clock and noted it was nearly five o'clock. I pushed the intercom.

"Yes?"

"Cazz, it's Sarah. Can I come up?"

Jesus, what was she doing here? I hesitated briefly, contemplating my options. There weren't many. I'd just confirmed my whereabouts, and if I claimed to be feeling under the weather, she'd want to check on me.

"Turn right through the main gate and then left at the top of the stairs. I'm in two twelve," I said, before pushing the pound sign into the intercom keypad that electronically unlocked the main door downstairs. I opened the apartment door and waited, surprised at how dark it was already.

When she reached the top of the staircase and walked down the hallway toward my door, my heart jumped. Her stride was its usual: fluid and confident. She was wearing a dark-gray woven blazer with black-accented lapel and pockets, black slacks, and a colorful scarf. She looked incredible, as always. I was still annoyed with myself for having opened up to her about the feelings I'd been harboring for so long, but hadn't come across a time when it wasn't damn nice to see her.

"Where have you been?" she asked as she approached.

I motioned her in and closed the door behind us.

"Greg said you quit and gave no notice. Are you okay?" Her look of genuine concern made me blush.

"I'm fine," I said, feeling guilty for not coming clean about my true role at the Foundation. But our last conversation was on my mind: her telling me she didn't want anything complicated, me telling her to get over her relationship hang-ups, and then of course my blubbering about how I'd treated her presence in my life as a gift all these years. I hardly felt things were comfortable between us and wondered why she hadn't simply called.

We both remained inside the doorway. Feeling her eyes on me, I stepped back until I was leaning against the door and motioned toward the living room with a hand. "Welcome to my castle." I looked absently toward the opposite wall. Anywhere but at Sarah. I could tell out of my peripheral vision that she kept her eyes on me.

"Are you sure you're okay?" she asked.

I glanced at her and nodded. "Yep. I'm good." I pushed away from the door and walked into the living room, needing separation. All I wanted to do was grab her and kiss her senseless, and that seemed a beyond-inappropriate way to thank her for her concern over my welfare.

"I'm sorry I couldn't provide more notice to the Foundation. Something came up requiring my immediate attention. I apologize for behaving so unprofessionally," I said in a stilted manner. I needed to focus all my attention on my case instead of how agonizingly beautiful Sarah was with her eyes ablaze with anger and worry.

"I'm not here as your God damn employer, Cazz. I'm here because the unprofessional behavior you've suddenly displayed is completely unlike you, the way you left my house the other night was—well, let's just say it was disconcerting—and you haven't returned my calls. I've been worried sick."

"You called? When?"

Sarah put her hands on her hips and glared at me. "I've left three messages over the past two days. Haven't you checked your voice mail?"

I walked over to the kitchen table where I'd tossed my cell phone and checked the display. The message icon was lit, which I hadn't even noticed when I'd made my calls. After pressing the voice-mail button, I heard the robotic voice inform me I had three new messages. Sure enough, Sarah's voice came through the speaker. *Crap.* I'd been too preoccupied with my travels and too reliant on my laptop to check. Until I'd contacted the realtors, I hadn't expected any calls. Thankfully, from the standpoint of not having dropped the ball on my investigation, the only new ones were those Sarah had mentioned. Yet all of them sounded similar to what she'd just told me in person, and I felt like a heel. She really had been worried.

I set the phone down and faced Sarah, who stood in the adjacent living room with her arms crossed, exuding irritation. I didn't have a good excuse and was upset with myself for potentially having delayed progress on the case due to my cell-phone snafu.

"I'm sorry. I didn't get your messages until now. It was very thoughtful of you to stop by to check on me." I continued my robotic responses and walked past her before stopping in the foyer. "As soon as things get settled for me, I'll call you," I said, not making eye contact. The only way I could have been more rude was if I'd tugged open the door and held it. She didn't deserve any of it, but I was in a jam. I couldn't tell her why I'd made my hasty exit from the Foundation because I couldn't expose my investigation. And I couldn't make many excuses because I didn't want to lie to her. Being rude was somehow more forgivable than being dishonest, especially knowing how much it upset me when she told me she didn't trust me. Not that I'd get a chance to ask for forgiveness after tossing her out on her ass.

"I'm going to ignore that big brush-off, thank you very much," Sarah said. Through the corner of my eye, I saw her edge closer. Then her fingers lightly cupped my chin and tugged, gently forcing me to look at her. When I brought my eyes to hers, the full force of her light-blue eyes bore into me. "Tell me what's going on," she said in a soft tone that belied the command.

Though I had to face her because she was physically forcing me to, my eyes drifted down, away from her. I couldn't speak. I shook my head as much as her grasp allowed.

"Look at me," Sarah said.

I did.

"Tell me."

"It…I…" I blinked. Sarah's gaze penetrated me. I felt certain she could read my thoughts. It was ridiculous yet unsettling at the same time. I cleared my throat and flicked my eyes away again. "It doesn't…" I couldn't say it didn't concern her. "I can't…It's something I have to handle on my own." Time ticked by in silence. Finally, she released me and I slid my eyes back to hers. Her level gaze said she was expecting more. "Can you please leave it alone?" I said hoarsely.

The ringing of my cell phone interrupted my discomfort.

"Excuse me." I headed to the kitchen counter and grabbed my phone. "Hello?" I listened to a woman's voice wishing to confirm she'd reached Cassidy Warner. "Yes, this is Cassidy," I said as Sarah walked to my laptop and glanced at the open browser page. After the caller identified herself as one of the realtors who'd acted on behalf of the Foundation, I asked whether she could describe the seller. She described Greg Morrison perfectly. Sarah could hear my end of the conversation, but I couldn't do much about it. "Do you think you'd be able to recognize him if you saw a picture of him?"

The realtor thought it likely she could but, before doing so, requested further information from me as to the reasons for my inquiry and my role in it.

"I'm afraid I can't go into it at the moment, but you'll have all the information you'll need by the time you see the photograph," I said. I confirmed the realtor's e-mail address and told her I'd be in touch shortly. I clicked off the phone and looked at Sarah, whose mood had further soured.

She crossed her arms and briefly pointed to my screen. "Mind telling me why you're searching for information on Greg?"

"Do you have any good photos of him? The few I've found online are blurry at best."

"I have some at home." Sarah's tone was cool, her stance unchanged.

"Do you have a scanner there? And high-speed Internet?"

"Yes and yes. Are you going to tell me what's going on?"

I ignored her question. "I'll follow you in my car." I grabbed my laptop and slid it into my messenger bag along with my cell phone. "Let's go."

Sarah gave me the evil eye before acceding to my wishes and walking out my door in front of me. I could handle her ire. But I could never forgive myself if something happened to her. The homicide investigation and the pace at which it proceeded were outside of my control. My investigation, however, was very much within it, and I was rapidly closing in on my target. With a little more evidence, I could give Ashby enough to take Morrison into custody without us having to await the outcome of the Perkins case. Above all else, even if it meant Sarah might never forgive my deception in the form of my cover, I needed to nail Morrison and keep him away from her.

CHAPTER NINETEEN

As soon as we arrived at Sarah's house, we doffed our footwear and took the steps two at a time up to her office. While Sarah searched boxes of photographs for a quality picture of Morrison, I drafted an e-mail to the real-estate agent that included a copy of my credentials. I informed her I was working on an investigation whose details I wasn't at liberty to disclose and asked her to confirm whether the man in the attachment was Paul Gunderson. When Sarah returned with a large photo, I scanned it to my laptop and attached it to the e-mail. I sent the information off to the realtor and turned to Sarah.

"What can you tell me about Mastick Consulting?"

"No, no, no. You're going to tell me what the hell's going on first."

I ignored her. "What does Mastick do for the Foundation?"

She huffed in disgust and stalked away. I followed.

I caught her upper arm and stopped her from heading downstairs. "It's important."

She whirled around to face me, her eyes wide and angry. She pointed at my chest. "Listen to me very carefully." Her voice was dangerously low and modulated, as if she were wrestling back a very powerful beast poised to rip me to shreds. "Asking me questions about some company I've never heard of does not qualify as important. What is important is that if you don't start telling me the truth, we have nothing to say to each other."

"I haven't lied to you." I felt guilty, knowing I hadn't been forthcoming either. I was glad she'd confirmed my suspicion that Mastick was one hundred percent Morrison's baby, since Sarah would have surely known about any viable services for which the Foundation paid hundreds of thousands of dollars annually. But I wasn't happy with her insinuation that I'd been lying.

She glared at me, spun back around, and rapidly descended the stairs. Again I followed. She reached for two pint glasses from a kitchen cabinet and began dispensing ice and water from the refrigerator into one. She seemed to need something to do with her hands besides throttle me, and getting us water was a far preferable choice.

"You said you're an accountant." She filled the second glass.

"I am," *among other things*.

"Fine." She shoved a glass in my hand, managing somehow not to spill its contents. "I see how it's going to be. I have to be very specific, don't I?"

I met her eyes but didn't answer.

"What else do you get paid for, professionally, besides being an accountant?"

"I can't talk about it." I focused on my glass.

"So you admit you're not what you seem?"

The subject moved away from the professional arena and I met her gaze. "This isn't personal."

"It's completely personal!" Her glass came down hard on the counter, splashing water but miraculously not shattering. "You're asking for information about a man I've worked with for more years than I've known you. You're taking advantage of your position at the Foundation to look into something you're not telling me about, and I don't have to remind you that anything concerning the Foundation is personal to me. And you're making me feel like a fool for wanting to trust you. Not just wanting to, damn it."

She surveyed the corner beyond me where the wall and ceiling met, focusing on nothing, appearing to gather her thoughts.

"What else has been a lie, Cazz? Was getting close to me all part of this plan? You thought you'd take advantage of having known me in the past in order to help you find whatever it is you're searching for?"

Astonished, I glared at her with incredible indignation and took some steadying breaths, trying to contain my rising anger at her suggestion that I'd lied about my feelings for her. I walked to the sink, took a few gulps of water, and set my glass on the counter, wondering how to respond.

An unbelievable tightness was weaving throughout my abdomen. Was it even possible to break down Sarah's walls—walls that reminded me of myself at an earlier age, walls that never seemed to be part of Sarah's repertoire in our younger days? The irony of our having switched roles, or rather, that she found it so difficult to trust, saddened me. I wanted to show her how I felt, though she was far from giving out "kiss me" vibes and my anger wasn't leaving me feeling particularly tender. I also wanted to opt for the simplicity of honesty since I didn't feel I'd ever lied to her about my feelings.

Deciding on honesty, I slowly turned and pressed the heels of my hands onto the counter, physically bracing myself for her reaction to what I was readying myself to say. I took a deep breath to settle my nerves and calm the tide of frustration that had washed over me. I looked at Sarah, who was facing me with her arms crossed, and kept my voice controlled.

"Since you're not going to believe me anyway, I have nothing to fear by telling the truth. Since the day you first hugged me on the tennis court, then listened to me tell you why I wasn't good with compliments, to the day we kissed at your parents' house ten years ago, there's never been anyone else for me. Then to reconnect with you after all these years, and feel you against me, and know how right it feels to be with you, it's all come back, stronger than ever. You're the only person I've ever been in love with, Sarah. The only one. Don't ever—*ever*—insinuate that any of it was a lie."

In classic Murphy's Law fashion, my cell phone rang. I groaned, annoyed by the interruption yet relieved for the reprieve. The surprise on her face told me she'd at least heard me, but I didn't have time to study her for further reaction. I jogged past her and ran upstairs to my phone, hoping it was already the realtor.

"Hello?"

"I hate to interrupt a good argument, but it's time for you to leave." The male voice was unfamiliar.

"Who is this?"

"Your friendly neighborhood voyeur. Get your stuff and go back to your apartment. I've seen enough and I'm sick of waiting."

"You must have the wrong number," I said, concerned he didn't.

"Don't. Test. Me." Something in his tone made it clear he had the right number.

"What do you want?"

"The great thing about some of these houses is I can see in as well as you can see out. Now get back downstairs, say good-bye to the lady in the scarf, and go back to your apartment. I don't like to repeat myself."

I was briefly immobilized with shock. I didn't know whether he was using a telescope or binoculars or what, since I'd never seen the back of Sarah's house during daylight, but the man on the phone was clearly watching us from somewhere outside. The idea frightened me. Who the hell was doing this? And why? Was this guy connected in any way to Luke Perkins's demise? At the terrible prospect, getting him away from Sarah vaulted to the top of my priorities, which was enough to prompt me into action.

I threw my laptop in my messenger bag, tossed it over one shoulder across my back, and ran downstairs with the phone still pressed against my ear. Rushing to the massive windows, I moved the curtains away from the first set of blinds I could find, needing to end the show we were unwittingly giving this crazy bastard.

"What are you doing?" Sarah asked from behind me.

The moment I found and reached up for the cord to send the blinds zipping down to cover the window, I heard his voice. "Don't even think about it, or I'll shoot." I pulled my hand away as quickly as if I'd burned it. *Shoot?* I stared out into the darkness but couldn't see anything except the glare from the window. My thoughts turned to the indoor lights. I wondered whether one panel controlled all the lights in Sarah's living and dining rooms, and where I might find it.

If I could throw us into darkness, maybe we could call the police and find a place to hide until they arrived.

"Cazz, what's going on?" Sarah asked with an anxious tone I hadn't heard before, probably concerned by whatever strange or terrified expression I had on my face.

Before I could act on my idea to locate and kill the lights, the man laughed. "Stop looking for me and turn around, Cassidy." His use of my name sent chills up my spine. This man knew my name, my phone number, my exact location. I turned slowly and focused on Sarah. "That's better," he said. My anxiety level was at a lifetime high, and I struggled to stay focused on what he was telling me.

"Who is that?" Sarah motioned to the phone, searching my eyes for an explanation.

"Tell the pretty woman you're leaving and get out. You have three minutes if you want her to live." He clicked off.

I stared at my phone, trying to concentrate. I had to get this guy as far away from Sarah as I could, and needed to tell her something to convince her to let me leave and not to follow. If she suspected I was in trouble, even if she was upset or angry with me, she wouldn't let me leave and would want to call the police. Unfortunately, the police wouldn't get to us until it was far too late, if the guy could be believed. And given that he knew my name and had been watching us, it didn't seem much of a stretch that if someone was going through all this trouble, it was highly likely he was armed.

I didn't have much time to mull over whatever speech I intended to give to Sarah. I continued staring at the phone in my hand, wasting precious seconds sifting through various scenarios. I could try to be the biggest ass possible. It meant lying, which I dreaded doing, but if I said something hurtful, Sarah would berate herself for believing in me and then take time to lick her wounds. That would keep her from following me, at least for a while. But as I tried to muster some serious attitude, I looked at Sarah and all my fright dissipated. I was suddenly awash in something else entirely.

Instead of feeling forced into a game of Russian roulette, I felt like my number came up on a roulette wheel and the jackpot was mine. Right in front of me. Those beautiful light-blue eyes—

eyes filled with concern—made warmth radiate through me. They delivered me. Grounded me. I felt gratitude, or maybe wholeness. A sudden calm, a sudden peace enveloped me.

It was simple.

Sarah was the love of my life. She might not know it, but I did. If I was in danger—if something happened to me today—no one could take away this wondrous feeling of loving this extraordinary woman.

I had this chance—this final chance, possibly—to tell Sarah how I felt about her. And I could do it without compromising her safety. I looked into her worried face and smiled appreciatively. Brushing her cheek lightly with my knuckles before gently palming it, I leaned forward so our lips were mere millimeters apart. I closed my eyes, breathing her in, memorizing her scent and the feel of her warm breath near my mouth. I opened my eyes and saw confusion in hers. Without taking my eyes off hers, I closed the remaining distance and delivered the softest, most incredibly tender kiss to her lips I could manage, trying to convey without words what she meant to me. Trailing my hand down under her chin, I lightly held it as I leaned back, smiling again at the sight of her and the sweet ache in my chest only she could stir in me. My heart was so full, I couldn't speak.

Which was a good thing. I wanted to say so much but didn't have time. Mindful the clock was ticking, I turned abruptly. I couldn't let anything happen to her.

As I slipped into my all-terrain sandals and yanked open the door, Sarah rushed to me and called, "Ca-aazz!" Its two syllables pleaded for answers. "What the—" She tugged my messenger bag and spun me around to face her. "What's happening? Where are you going?" Her tone bordered on frantic.

I needed to say something to try to calm her. Pulling away and continuing toward my car, I walked backward so I could face her. "I'll be back as soon as I can." I tried to keep my voice light, telling myself the vagueness of my reply was appropriate under the circumstances. I tried not to think of my unlikely chances.

"Tonight?" Sarah asked with what seemed to be desperation.

I kept my eyes on hers for another moment before opening my car door. As I tossed the messenger bag into the passenger seat, I felt a tug on the back of my shirt and turned.

Sarah grabbed my shirt in both her hands, sternum level. "Look at me and tell me you'll be back tonight."

I didn't have time to argue. Three minutes was three minutes. I needed to say something to end the conversation and keep her there. I did the only thing I could: I lied. I kept my eyes on her and nodded.

She released me immediately, her expression one of fright. I didn't understand it and didn't have time to try. I started the engine, backed out in a U-shape, and put the car in drive. I might never see her again and had to force myself not to dwell on that dreadful possibility.

CHAPTER TWENTY

As I started home, I contemplated calling Ashby. Mobile-phone conversations were relatively secure but the call logs weren't, which was why we got new phones with each assignment. Plus I didn't know how much my stalker friend had on me. It was a risk I should take since I'd only recently been issued this one. My phone rang. I hit speaker and set it on my lap.

"Hello?" I spoke loudly, trying to be heard through the car noise.

"No phone calls, Cassidy. I'm monitoring you." The man hung up, and my hope of rescue ended along with the call. My thoughts flew back and forth between my impending demise and Sarah. I had no way to be sure nothing would happen to her. The thought was maddening.

After parking in the lot of my apartment complex, I got out of my car and waited. Moments later, a brown van entered. The driver slid from the van and stopped ten feet from me. He wore a ski mask that covered his head and neck, with holes for his eyes and mouth. I could tell he was Caucasian and, from his voice, guessed he was in his thirties or forties. He was about an inch taller than me, lean and muscular, coiled tight as a spring. In black jeans and a black T-shirt, he sported a small backpack and held a gun to his side.

My cell phone rang from inside my messenger bag. "Ignore it and open the door, Cassidy." He gestured to the main door of the building with a flick of his gun.

I unlocked it with my key, then entered and pushed it open for him to follow, allowing a few feet of space to build between us. As I reached the door of my apartment, he trained his gun on me.

"I'm right behind you," he said. He followed me into the apartment, closed the door behind us, and directed me to a kitchen stool. "Hands on the counter, palms down." He flung his backpack onto my coffee table and rummaged around for something in it. "Put these on. One on each wrist." Still holding his gun on me, he tossed me a pair of plastic zip ties and I put them on. "Too bad you investigative-types are all the same. I kinda hoped you'd tell your girlfriend what you've been up to, Cassidy. Bigger payday for me. But the boss would be very upset if I had to get rid of both of you, since he thinks she's a big breadwinner. Nothing from your phone or e-mail suggests anyone else knows what you do, and you weren't at her place long enough to get into it. So you get me all to yourself."

A few short ring tones from my cell phone told me I'd received a voice mail, but I was more distracted by what he meant about my communications. His voice interrupted my thoughts.

"Cross your wrists behind you. Face that way." He pointed me toward a wall. He used another plastic tie and cuffed my wrists together, first through the other ties and then over my wrists again, pulling all of them so tight they dug into my flesh. "Expecting a call?" he asked.

"No," I said truthfully, wincing from pain.

"Let's listen." With his empty hand, he searched my bag and removed the phone, holding the key for voice mail. He put it on speaker mode.

"Cazz, it's Sarah. Thanks to you, we've got enough to put Greg away for a long time. I'm really glad you told me about the investigation. We should call the police first thing tomorrow. I'm not sure why you suddenly had to leave, but I'm heading over now so we can coordinate. See you soon."

What on earth was she talking about? What the hell was she doing besides trying to get herself killed?

"Well, well, well. Guess I was wrong about you. You did spill the beans," he said with a glimmer in his eyes.

"I didn't tell her anything." I was mystified. Sarah's message made no sense.

It happened so fast I didn't see it coming. He backhanded me with such force I toppled over onto the floor along with the stool. I landed hard on my shoulder, hip and, to a lesser extent, my head. The dull ringing in my ears sounded as if someone in a nearby apartment had forgotten to turn off their alarm clock.

"Get up." The gunman barked at me from within what seemed like a tunnel.

I was dazed and my head was throbbing. Had he held his gun as he struck me? It sure felt like it. His words registered, but I couldn't move. Then strong hands lifted me and I was suddenly sitting on the righted stool again. He stood in front of me and patted my cheek patronizingly.

"Uh-huh." He smiled ruefully. "I'm sure." He pulled a mobile phone from his pocket and held one number, which speed-dialed a phone number. "It's me. The daughter knows. Listen." He pressed the voice-mail key on my phone again, hit speaker mode, and put his phone next to the speaker. After Sarah's message played again, he clicked off my phone and lifted his back to his ear. "Your choice." He then listened to whoever was speaking at the other end of the phone, presumably Greg Morrison. "No. No twofers. You know the price." He paused to listen some more. "Will do."

He hung up and grinned. "Good thing you told her after all. Your girlfriend's worth another hundred grand to me." He pulled a small rag from his pocket, balled it up, and shoved it into my mouth. Then he took a second rag from his backpack, rolled it snake shaped, wrapped it across my mouth, and pulled it tightly behind my head as he knotted it in back. It was difficult to swallow and I was drooling into the rag in no time.

I realized he had zero incentive not to check my messages. If they were irrelevant, it would take seconds for him to come to that conclusion. If they were relevant, he could have the opportunity to earn a lottery-size amount of cash without the tax bite.

"I have to hand it to you, Cassidy, you've been a busy gal." The gunman held up my phone. "You won't mind if I uninstall the software that's been tracking your every text, e-mail, and telephone call?" I watched in sick fascination as he expertly uninstalled some sort of software from my smartphone while he kept talking. "Don't act so surprised. It's simple to get access to a cell phone for a few minutes. Offices are the easiest, especially when it's a colleague who's interested in what you're up to. People don't have their phones with them twenty-four seven. All it takes is two minutes and a willing participant. You walk out of your office, they go in, grab your phone, open the browser, download and install the software, return the phone, and boom. I've got access to everything."

He held up my phone again, proudly. "Voila, no more spying. No one will know you were being tracked, assuming we leave your phone behind. Of course, I don't know who you met at that pissant little strip mall in Phoenix or why you were at the Grand Junction courthouse, but my boss found that GPS info all very interesting." The man removed another rag, latex gloves, and a spray bottle. He pulled on the gloves, sprayed some liquid into the rag, and started wiping down my phone and the side of the stool he'd picked up after he'd knocked me over. "Once you told that realtor you couldn't talk about it, I was convinced you hadn't told your friend what you were up to, and the body language between you at her house confirmed it. But after that voice mail, I'm very happy to be wrong."

He shoved the spray bottle and rag back into the bag. "Now the question is what to do with the two of you. I don't typically mix business with pleasure, but I'm not usually dealing with the likes of you and your hot little friend. The possibilities are endless, don't you think?"

Against the backdrop of his black mask, the mouth full of straight white teeth grinning at me was alarming and only served to remind me of how law-enforcement investigators occasionally used dental records to identify remains—in this case, mine. Such morbid thoughts were not calming me.

"Especially when we add a couple more of these into the mix." He grabbed two more plastic zip ties from his pack and bound my ankles to the kitchen stool. My knees were splayed and I was completely defenseless as he moved to stand between my legs.

He dug into my thighs with his latex-covered fingers and pressed his crotch into mine. I turned my face away so he couldn't see the fear in my eyes. Then my head suddenly snapped back as he grabbed a handful of my hair and pulled down hard, forcing me to look up at him. I stared at him, trying to douse the fear with as much fury as I could muster in an attempt to lessen his satisfaction. He unleashed an eerie grin and loosened his grip on my hair. He made a show of smelling me, inhaling deeply as he trailed his nose over my face. "Like I said. Endless." He patted my cheek and grabbed his gun. Then he leaned against the counter and propped a foot on the lowest rung of my stool. He watched the door while I tried and failed to keep the tears from spilling down my cheeks.

A few minutes later, the buzzer sounded. The gunman jumped up and over to the intercom and pressed the button without saying anything.

"Cazz, it's me." Sarah's voice came over the speaker. I tried to scream, but it came out as a weak muffled sound she had no chance of hearing. The man apparently read the brief directions posted below the intercom because he hit the pound sign to buzz Sarah up before returning to my side.

I was desperate with fear. I was bound and gagged, my temple and shoulder were throbbing, and the woman I loved was coming to help me finish an investigation I never should have taken on as soon as I knew she was involved. Every movement I made to try to get out of the makeshift cuffs dug them further into my wrists; they must have cut into me when I'd struck the floor. I was nearly gagging on the rag he'd shoved into my mouth, as it tickled the back of my throat and I couldn't move it with my tongue. A trickle of something, probably blood, trailed down my face from where he'd smacked me at the temple or from when I'd landed on the floor; I wasn't sure. I was full of snot from silently crying and wet with drool from the rag, both of which made breathing extremely difficult.

This was it. There was no backup plan. Sarah was out of time. We were both out of time. I was a civilian in a police officer's world. I wasn't trained for any type of physical confrontation or violence. This kind of thing simply didn't happen, wasn't supposed to happen.

Time moved in slow motion, leaving me wretchedly anxious and despairing, further exacerbated when I heard a knock on my apartment door. The gunman whispered in my ear, "Not a sound, Cassidy. Not one sound." He then quietly walked to the door and stood behind it so Sarah wouldn't immediately detect a problem until she was inside. His gun in one hand, he turned the knob with the other. He aimed the gun at chest level, ready to pounce on Sarah as she came through the door. More tears escaped, making it difficult to clearly view what was happening.

As the knob twisted, a thunderous cracking sound erupted as the door crashed inward in shards. Sections of wood flew everywhere. Following the imploding door was a massive human body in the unmistakable form of Commander Ashby. Behind him was another cop. Both had guns drawn. The sheer force of the door launched my captor onto his back and he fired aimlessly as he fell. Ashby fired a half-second later and the man stopped moving.

With his eyes and gun trained on the man, Ashby spoke to me while his partner surveyed the apartment. "Just him?"

I nodded, tears of pain and relief springing from my eyes. Realizing the officers were focused elsewhere, I tried to make an affirmative "Mm-hmm" sound in answer. Their stances perceptibly relaxed upon hearing my reply and glancing over for confirmation. As the other cop knelt next to the man to check for a pulse, Ashby holstered his weapon and spoke to me.

"Yeah. My team only saw this one. I've got guys there and there." He gestured with his chin to the two buildings across the street. "But they didn't have a clear shot, so…" The cop turned to Ashby and shook his head. The commander told him to call it in.

Ashby crossed to me in a few muscular strides and removed the gag and the second rag from my mouth. He pulled a Leatherman tool from his pocket and cut the plastic cuffs from my wrists and ankles as his cell phone rang.

"Ashby," he barked. "Yeah, send her up," he said into the phone while he fished something out of his jacket pocket with his other hand. I surveyed my bleeding wrists and rubbed around the cuts to get some blood flowing into my hands. "Here." He shoved a folded handkerchief into my hands to let me clean the blood, sweat, drool, and snot from my face. "You okay?" Though still a growl, at least it was a softer one. I nodded. "Need an ambulance?" I shook my head, which made the throbbing worse. My wrists hurt, but they would heal. Ashby looked at the side of my head. "He hit you?" I nodded again. "You're going to the ER."

"I'll be okay," I said faintly, coughing at the first use of my voice after the rags were gone.

Ashby strode to my freezer and grabbed a package of corn. "I'm sure that's true, but we're not taking any chances. Here." With far more gentleness than I could imagine coming from him, he placed the frozen corn in my hand and lifted, resting it lightly against my wound. "Hold that there." By this time, multiple uniforms were already swimming through my apartment taking videos and measurements, while I sat stunned.

"Commander," I said, finally finding my voice. "How did you…" I still couldn't comprehend what had just transpired.

"Don't look at me," Ashby said gruffly. "It was her idea." He tilted his head toward the doorway.

Sarah stood there, staring at me. I didn't bother to wipe my fresh tears away as she crossed the room in seconds and engulfed me in her arms.

Relief, gratitude, love all washed over me as I found solace in Sarah's embrace.

"It's okay, Cazz. It's all okay now," she said, rocking me gently.

CHAPTER TWENTY-ONE

An officer-involved shooting (OIS) required a lot of interviews and paperwork. Although Ashby told me I didn't have to go to the station immediately following my stop at the ER, I wanted to be done with it. I also wanted Morrison behind bars as soon as possible. Because OIS protocol required that Ashby, the other officer involved, and I be separated in order to be interviewed, I would need to wait until I was released from questioning to tell Ashby what I had on Morrison.

Sarah insisted that I not stay at home tonight, not after what I'd been through. Ashby concurred, saying the OIS investigation team needed at least a day—probably more—to clear the scene. Sarah offered to let me stay at her place, but I was feeling pretty raw and didn't think I could handle any additional emotional tangles with her tonight. Instead, I agreed to let her book me a room, given her familiarity with the local hotels. We weren't allowed to touch anything in my living room or kitchen, but thankfully the area cordoned off didn't extend to my bedroom or bathroom. We separated, each under strict supervision, Sarah having offered to grab some of my clothes and personal effects, while I was escorted to the hospital.

Being accompanied by an LAPD officer had its perks, as one of the ER doctors saw me immediately. I answered some basic questions to rule out a concussion and received a bandage on the cut near my eyebrow that had required only three stitches. A nurse applied some ointment to the cuts on my wrists and wrapped them with gauze secured by tape. I received an ice pack, ibuprofen, antibacterial ointment, and in half an hour was transported by my police escort to meet with the OIS investigation team.

After our interviews, I debriefed Ashby on my investigation. It was easy enough to have Morrison taken into custody. I was willing to stay as long and do whatever was necessary to make that happen quickly, but Ashby sent me on my way. With evidence they'd gathered from the gunman's phone, home, and bank accounts connecting him to Morrison on the Perkins murder, Morrison's arrest was imminent. Once convicted, he would be put away for a long time. With him behind bars, I wouldn't need to worry about anything happening to Sarah.

Once Sarah assembled what she thought I needed from my apartment, she waited for me at the station for hours and finally drove me to the hotel after the OIS investigators released me. During the drive over, she said she'd called Ashby right after I left her house and told him I was in danger. Sarah had immediately hatched a plan to try to save me. She wanted to make herself a target by pretending she knew something she didn't. Based on my attempt to get a photograph of Morrison and her overhearing my conversation with the realtor asking her to identify someone, she put two and two together and assumed Morrison was up to no good.

She'd been tipped off by a comment her father had made to Morrison shortly before his death: that Luke (via the Foundation) would be taking on Ashby's niece as a favor to his old friend—an odd statement since Sarah knew Ashby didn't have any nieces. So Sarah had insisted that I, the "niece," be hired just as her father had wished before he died. Though she'd considered asking, she knew Ashby well enough not to press him for information since he wouldn't have acknowledged the existence of an active investigation. And I hadn't divulged any information either. Not until today had she known why her father brought me on board, but she trusted him implicitly. She pieced together what she thought I must have been assigned to do.

She hadn't said it, but her comment about unconditionally trusting her father underscored that she couldn't say the same for me. Soon enough I'd revisit and obsess over it, but at the moment, I was grateful she'd fought her doubts and distrust of me, instead following her father's lead and believing I hadn't come to the Foundation to do it harm.

Because Ashby had been instrumental in getting me installed at the Foundation, they were able to save time when Sarah called him, since he knew exactly who I was and why I was involved. His invocation of Section ninety-two had already alerted him to the possibility of something going amiss. He didn't want to rely on a civilian for any police work, but acquiesced when Sarah suggested she go to my apartment so she could be the voice at the other end of the intercom. They both knew the plan had a chance to succeed only if the man believed Sarah had arrived.

Their plan was risky, since the man could have shot me as soon as he pulled into the parking lot or right after I let him into my apartment. But they believed the man wanted me to return to my apartment for a specific reason, and they planned accordingly. They didn't have time to come up with an alternative, so Ashby moved swiftly. In under fifteen minutes from Sarah's frantic call, nearby units had been positioned in the parking lot and in the buildings facing mine to ensure any other perpetrators were accounted for. My chances of survival would have decreased precipitously if the man hadn't been working alone.

Sarah checked me in at the front desk and rolled along the overnight bag she must have found in my closet. She was extremely considerate of my weary state. I was emotionally and physically drained, and my head and shoulder were still killing me even though the ibuprofen had dialed back the intensity of the pain. But as soon as we reached the suite, instead of collapsing into bed, I pushed the door closed and rested against it, watching Sarah. I'd heard the story during the car ride of how she wasted no time to contact Ashby after I'd left her house, and I was not a little thankful for her keen intellect, having been so quickly able to not only ascertain that I was in trouble but also figure out a way to help me.

Yet something didn't add up. It didn't make any sense that she could have realized so immediately that something was wrong. I needed to know what I should have done differently. She put herself in potential danger to try to save me, and while I was beyond grateful at how things turned out, on some level it bothered me she needed to take any risk at all. I should have been able to say something to keep her at her house.

To complicate matters, now that we were alone and safe, I felt ironically vulnerable. I'd said a lot of deeply personal things to Sarah and hadn't received any clarity from her about where she stood—where we stood. I tried to gather my thoughts as she rolled my suitcase into the bedroom. A few moments later, she emerged with a plastic bag full of toiletries from my apartment. She placed them on the bathroom counter and walked a few feet in my direction before stopping and assessing me with her hands on her hips.

"Sarah—"

"Cazz, you need to rest."

"Sarah, please. I need to know…" I shook my head, unsure how to put into words exactly what I was asking. "I need to know how you knew I needed help."

She paused for a moment, her gaze thoughtful. "You might not be forthcoming with information, which can be irritating, but you don't lie," she said. "Or, at least, you suck at it," she said in a teasing manner.

I thought about my job. I'd certainly said my fair share of half-truths during my many LAPD investigations. I'd gone to work for various businesses under false pretenses. I'd woven many tall tales trying to extract information from people. In fact, I did lie. Frequently. I needed to set the record straight.

"But, Sarah, I—"

"To me." She stepped in front of me and brushed aside the hair from my forehead before moving her hand across my cheek in a soft caress. "You never lie to me. I don't need to know the rest."

I tilted my head, giving her a dubious look. If she was telling me I didn't lie, or that she could tell when I did, then she was also saying she believed me when I'd told her how I felt about her. A sick feeling suffused me as I realized the implications of what I'd said at her house.

Yet she hadn't run away. She was here with me. More than that, she was taking care of me. What did that mean? But I was so tired, my head was pounding, and I wasn't sure I could stand on my feet much longer, let alone stomach a heart-to-heart during which we'd probably rehash things already said. I was glad to have the door to lean on. My eyes felt as heavy as my heart.

"Cazz," Sarah said, looking at me tenderly. "Come here." She pulled me to the couch and pushed me gently down to sit. Squatting, she lifted one of my legs and extended it to rest on the coffee table. She followed suit with the other. Then she lifted my right foot and tugged the sandal off, starting at the heel. After doing the same with the other, she set my sandals under the coffee table. Scouting around briefly, she grabbed a small pillow from one end of the couch and laid it behind my head before softly brushing my cheek with the back of her hand. "Stay."

I closed my eyes and covered them with one arm as I tilted my head back to rest more comfortably against the pillow. Moments later, I heard Sarah set some objects onto the bathroom counter and start to run a bath. Shortly thereafter, her footsteps disappeared into the bedroom.

I started at the sound of her voice close by, unsure how long I'd drifted off.

"Cazz." She extended a hand. "Come." She jiggled her fingers in my direction. I took her hand and she pulled me up and into the bathroom. She bent down over the tub and turned off the water, then grabbed small metal scissors from the counter. Taking turns with each wrist, she cut off the tape and gauze the hospital staff had put on a few hours ago, then held my wrists up between us. "It's going to sting when you first get in."

She spoke as she pointed to a tube of antibacterial ointment, a package of Band-Aids, and the bandage covering my stitches. "Pat that on when you're done, cover up with some of those, and try not to touch that." Partially closing the bathroom door, she nodded to a plush white hotel robe hanging on the back. "Put that on when you get out. I'm ordering room service." She closed the door behind her and left me to my bath.

By the time I finally finished, the hot water had turned lukewarm. I'd washed my hair and found my own hairbrush waiting for me on the counter. I brushed back my wet hair and donned the luxurious robe. Pushing back its sleeves, I lightly dabbed some ointment on my wrists where the skin had been sliced, then covered the worst spots with a few bandages. I felt almost human again, but the heat of the bath and the steam in the air, combined with my ordeal and what I suspected was a very late hour, nearly put me into a catatonic state.

When I opened the bathroom door, Sarah was sitting on the couch, a glass of wine in her hand, two clean plates in front of her, and various round silver dishes covering what I assumed was food. She'd been thumbing through a magazine and looked up expectantly.

"Better?" she asked.

"Tired." I noticed the half-full wineglass waiting for me. "I'll fall asleep in your lap if I have any of that."

She smiled. "Worse things could happen." She patted the empty seat cushion next to her, but I remained standing.

"Sarah…" I didn't know what I wanted to say.

"Cazz, you need to eat."

I closed my eyes and took a deep breath. *You don't know what I need.* "I'm not hungry." I practically whined, praying she wouldn't argue. I didn't have the energy for another tussle with her about feelings: mine or hers. The sound of her getting off the leather couch prompted me to open my eyes.

She stood in front of me and took both my hands, lightly rubbing the backs of them with her thumbs. She searched my eyes for a few moments before softly responding. "Okay."

Slipping her fingers farther into my left hand, she turned and tugged me gently toward the bedroom. Once she pulled the covers and sheets down from one side of the bed, she kissed my cheek sweetly. "Get some rest." She walked to the doorway, flipped the light switch, and closed the door behind her.

I tossed the robe to the other side of the bed, pulled the sheet and covers around me, and fell asleep instantly.

❖

I woke up disoriented, finding myself in an unfamiliar room. Groggily, I sat up on my elbows and let my eyes adjust to the dim light peeking in through the curtains and under the door. The robe on the bed reminded me I was in a hotel room. I rubbed my face, got out of bed, laced my arms into the sleeves of the robe, pulled it on, and opened the door. Propelled by my insistent bladder, I went straight to the adjoining bathroom before washing my hands, popping two ibuprofen pills, and walking into the suite.

I stopped short when I heard Sarah's voice. "Sleeping Beauty awakes. Or should I call you Belle?" She was lying on the couch, propped up on an elbow with her legs tucked under a blanket and a magazine in front of her. She smiled radiantly and my knees weakened as I stared at her.

"You stayed?" I asked stupidly, caught off guard by her presence and her beauty.

She sat up and scanned me from head to toe. "How are you feeling?"

"Starving." It felt like forever since my last meal. She reached in front of her to the coffee table, on which I now noticed two silver serving trays similar to those of the night before. Lifting off each cover, she offered its contents.

"Bagel? Fruit?" She tapped a stainless carafe. "Coffee?"

"God, yes." I sat on the chair adjacent to the couch and snatched a bagel, tearing into it with my teeth.

"We have toppings, you know," Sarah said, poking fun at my ravaging. I reached for the knife, slapped some cream cheese onto the rest of the bagel, and continued chewing my monstrous bite. She poured a cup of coffee from the carafe. "Cream, sugar, or both?"

"Eem pweese," I replied with my mouth full, though she understood what I'd said because she poured some cream into my mug. I finally swallowed my bite of bagel and doused it with a swig of coffee. I didn't have a chance to filter what came out of my mouth next. "You're a godsend."

She sat back and watched me, her eyes full of pleasure. "We can order something hot if you'd rather. Eggs or potatoes or something." The something hot was sitting next to me, looking ravishing in a pair of my old navy-blue Columbia sweats and a faded, formerly red now pinkish Redskins T-shirt I recognized. She must have borrowed some of my things when she packed the overnight bag for me.

"Nice outfit," I said. How anyone could look so good in ratty old clothes was beyond me.

"Hope you don't mind?"

I shook my head.

"They're comfy."

"They're worn and bleached and would look like hell on anyone but you, but they are comfy." I took another bite of bagel.

Sarah cupped her coffee mug with both hands and watched me take a few more bites. "You're good at what you do." She waited for a reaction.

I swallowed my bite, wondering if I was ready for whatever confrontation this might turn into.

"Uncle Jim says you're one of his best, and he's not the kind to dole out praise."

"Uncle Jim?"

"Ashby. Though, as I said, he's not really my uncle."

"Oh, right." I remembered our conversation in the car and how she said she'd known Commander Ashby since birth, which is why she had his cell-phone number—a small fact that probably saved my life.

"Do you like it? Being an investigator?" She sipped her coffee.

I reached for mine. "Until yesterday," I replied, cupping my mug between my hands, too.

"Would you stop doing it if someone asked you to?"

I shifted my gaze from my coffee to her face, searching for, but failing to find, the underlying meaning behind her question, though I understood when she said "someone" she meant "someone special."

"It's not usually dangerous."

She returned my gaze. "That wasn't the question."

"Sarah…" I turned away, biting my lip and wondering where this was going. Feeling her hand on my arm, I met her eyes.

"Please." Her eyes implored me to respond.

Caught in a web, I didn't want to say anything that might drive her away, but I'd been too honest with her about my feelings to lie to her now, not counting my nod—made under duress—at her house.

"No, I don't think I could. I'm good at it, and I help people. Yesterday was an anomaly. You have to believe me." I was desperate for her to do so on the off chance she could be the "someone" who might ask it of me.

She removed her hand from my arm. "I do. I couldn't either."

I eyed her in confusion.

She sipped her coffee. "I'm good at what I do, too, Cazz. The Kindle Hope Foundation does exactly that: it gives people hope. Second chances. What I do helps people, lots of them, and I couldn't imagine doing anything else. I could never give it up, even if someone asked me to."

"I know." That was all I could say. I understood how much her work meant to her; I'd known since high school when she would exude happiness at mentioning her father's work and anything associated with the Foundation. I had no idea where this was coming from or why she was telling me this. Then suddenly I had a hunch.

"Someone asked you to?"

She nodded. "My fiancé."

My eyebrows shot upward, which slightly tugged at my bandage and made me wince.

"Former fiancé."

I'd hit brick walls with Sarah before, and recently, so I wasn't sure she was ready to divulge any more. "Sarah, you don't owe me any explanations."

She laid a hand on my arm again. "I do. If you'll let me."

I searched her eyes, which were searching mine, and saw nothing but sincerity. I nodded.

Setting her coffee down, she sat cross-legged on the couch and laid her hands in her lap, studying them. "He was an investment banker. Still is, I imagine. The son of one of our most loyal donors. We met at a fund-raiser three years ago and were inseparable after that. Eight months later, we were engaged." She looked up at me. "His parents come from old money, so I should have expected his traditionalism." Returning her attention to her lap, she rubbed the base of her fingers with the thumb of her other hand. "He wanted me to stay home and take care of our children. He didn't like the hours I put in for the Foundation. The early mornings, the late nights, the weekend events. He said I didn't need to do it anymore." She raised her eyes again. "I thought he knew it was never a matter of need. It was what I wanted to do. He said any wife of his was going to put his children first, and that once I had kids, I'd understand. So I broke it off." She shifted the blanket in her lap and her gaze to the window. "I know what you're thinking. That we could have figured it out. Hired nannies for the kids, hired more help at the Foundation. Something." She flicked her eyes back to me. "But Cazz, I can't do it half-assed. It has to come first. And I know that's too much to ask of anyone."

Rewrapping my robe around me, I walked over to and leaned back against the desk, gathering my thoughts. It was all starting to make sense: Sarah's unwillingness to get involved with someone, her irritability on the subject of children, her distrust. She had believed this guy understood her devotion to her father's foundation, and ultimately he had belittled it.

"So," I said, "you don't ask it." I focused on the wall opposite from me, trying not to fall into the pit of hopelessness suddenly surrounding me. She was telling me I had no chance.

"I haven't been willing to."

I shook my head as I listened. She was playing judge and jury, without bothering to find out if anyone was willing to accept her conditions; she was taking the decision away from anyone else. As if I would ever want her to give up the most meaningful thing in her life in order to be with me, when her passion for her work was one of the most beautiful and attractive things about her.

Noise from the couch cushion caught my attention, and I watched as she rose and came over to me. She took my hands, looked down at them and bit her lip. Then she met my eyes.

"Until now," she said.

I narrowed my eyes, trying to follow what she was saying. "Until now...what?"

"I'm asking."

I blinked. Maybe the smack I'd taken to the head was a harder blow than I realized. There was no way I could have heard her correctly. It was only as I searched her eyes and saw the unguarded appeal, the sincerity, the desire for connection that it all clicked into place. My eyebrows leapt up in astonishment, and this time I was numb to the tug on my bandage.

She caressed the back of my hands with her thumbs. "I know I shouldn't."

I fought to keep my jaw attached since it wanted to drop to the floor. I was momentarily incapable of speech, such was the rush of hope and relief that filled me.

"I know it's not a very appealing offer." She again lowered her gaze to where she held my hands.

I was beside myself with joy.

When I found my voice, it was low and playful. "Well, maybe you should ratchet up the appeal factor." I gave her a look of challenge.

She stopped her hand caresses and regarded me. Her left eyebrow went up and she tilted her head slightly as she considered my response. "I should, should I?" she asked, as a tiny smile pulled at the corners of her mouth.

I nodded and gave her a mischievous grin. "Might help land you a favorable reply." I briefly dropped my gaze to her lips and back.

She searched my eyes for a moment before she lightly brushed my lips with hers as she spoke, her breath hot against my mouth. "You think so?"

"Mm-hmm." I was nearly swooning with anticipation.

Reaching for the lapels of my thick cotton robe, she grabbed each side in her fists and yanked me toward her, crushing my mouth with hers. Our lips and tongues danced, and I gathered her closer by wrapping my arms around her waist.

After several glorious minutes, Sarah pulled away slightly. "Is this helping your decision?"

"Uh." I had trouble focusing since the blood in my head had moved swiftly south. "I'm on the fence," I couldn't help but grin again at my patently false statement.

The smile she gave me nearly knocked me off my feet, as it contained a heady mix of lust and seduction. I was her clay to be molded as she pleased. She reached up and lightly traced a finger over my bandage.

"How's your head? Am I hurting you?"

I shook my head. It could have been stuck in a vise and I wouldn't have wanted Sarah to cease her attentions.

With her eyes still on mine, she moved her hands to my waist, where she tugged at my belt and sent my robe falling open to my sides. She slid her hands inside my robe, gently moved them along my stomach and under my breasts, and placed wet, open-mouthed kisses along my neck and collarbone. She was sending me into sensory overload, as every touch and every kiss made me shiver with a combination of delight and desire. As she moved her face in front of mine, her thumbs brushed my nipples, making them hard with arousal.

She looked deeply into my eyes. "You're so beautiful, Cazz." An instant later, she was claiming my mouth with hers. She rolled one of my nipples between the thumb and forefinger of one hand and trailed the other down my body until it lightly grazed the coarse hair below. I moaned with pleasure, wet between my legs. "I'd like to take you to bed," she said.

"A distraction?" I briefly sucked her lower lip into my mouth before letting her respond.

"You're definitely distracting, but no. I'd like to take you to bed now,"—she traced my upper lip with her tongue—"tonight,"—she teased the tip of my tongue with hers—"tomorrow night,"—she licked my lower lip—"and the night after that, if you'll let me." She kissed me soundly.

"You're sure?" I murmured through a haze of desire.

"I trust you. I want you," she said, as I kissed her neck. "I'm willing to see where this goes." She took my hand and delivered long, wet kisses along my index and middle fingers, pulling each into her mouth and sucking them slowly and thoroughly. "And where these go." Grasping my hand, she placed my fingers between her legs, delivering an incredible kiss as she did so. Far too soon, she removed her lips from mine, leaving me breathless and aching with desire. "Are you?"

"Definitely." I tasted her mouth again. After several moments, Sarah broke the kiss, smiled deliciously, and walked me into the bedroom.

EPILOGUE

I couldn't help but smile when I caught sight of the way Caitlin was welcoming me from across the ballroom. She was wearing a floor-length, violet strapless sweetheart dress with a decorated bodice that showed off her figure. Apparently the older couple she was speaking with didn't hold her interest enough that she couldn't give me a tantalizing smile, clearly undressing me with her eyes as her gaze slowly traveled from my head to my heels and back up again. The black-tie affair was well attended, and it took me a good ten minutes to make my way past the various guests that stood between us, as I had to talk to some of those I passed and stay for a few introductions along the way. The older couple was gone by the time I reached her.

"Hello, Caitlin." I leaned down to kiss her cheek. "You look ravishing, as always." I'd gotten to know her from attending a few Foundation events over the past couple months. I appreciated her sense of humor and the ego boost she never failed to deliver.

A glass of wine in one hand, she held the other out in front of her, palm up, and swept it down, gesturing at my outfit. "And you, my dear, look positively edible." Her grin was lascivious.

"Now, now. You wouldn't be trying to get me into any sort of trouble, would you?"

"Mm-mm-mm," she responded, making a sound like she was eating something delicious, her eyes never leaving my body. "You know what they say. While the cat's away." She waggled her eyebrows at me and I laughed. I stopped a passing waiter and grabbed a glass of champagne off his tray, nodding to him. He nodded back and moved on. The idea of Sarah as a cat intrigued me: a long, lean, powerful creature it was hard to tear my gaze from.

My thoughts traveled back to the idyllic morning Sarah and I had spent at her house, one of many we'd shared over the past few months since the night of the shooting. As usual, I'd awoken after she had. She was a morning person and we were definitely on different schedules where that was concerned. The phrase "rise and shine" never applied to me. I usually needed at least two cups of coffee and an hour to come to, but for Sarah, it was apropos.

I tended to wake up using my ears and limbs first instead of my eyes, which meant listening for her breathing or reaching out to feel her next to me. I'd quickly learned to channel my disappointment at realizing neither of those most mornings by focusing on the already brewed coffee waiting for me. Far better yet, I could often focus on the fresh soapy scent of her already showered body as she gently pestered me further awake. The latter did more to turn me into a morning person than I ever thought possible, since a simple touch or mischievous look from Sarah could instantly stir me awake in more ways than one.

That morning, after I'd reached out to find her spot empty, I was quickly covered by a warm heaviness that meant she'd been sitting in the nearby armchair awaiting signs of life from me, pouncing once she'd spotted them. I felt her crawl up my legs and over my back, trailing kisses as she did so. When she reached my head, she pulled my earlobe into her mouth, then traced her tongue along the inside ridges of my ear, sending wondrous tingles up my spine and forcing an involuntary shudder from me. I could feel her smile against the tender skin beneath my ear as she whispered.

"Morning, beautiful."

Since I was practically pinned, I reached my chin toward her. "Morning, sweetheart."

Sarah met my lips with hers for a brief kiss. She climbed off me and moved onto her side, resting her head on her hand while leaning on her elbow. She studied me with a smile as she caressed my hip. I turned onto my side to face her, rolled onto my shoulder, and greeted her with a lazy grin.

"Been up long?" I asked, gently tracing her lips with my thumb.

"What do you think?" She kissed me sweetly.

"Of course you have. Be right back." I gave her a peck, then jumped out of bed and made my way to the bathroom. After relieving my bladder and washing my hands, I opened the door. As I grabbed my toothbrush and squeezed some toothpaste onto the bristles, I looked back at Sarah while she appraised me from the bed.

"So, are we still on for tonight?" I asked before brushing my teeth.

"You mean dividing and conquering? Absolutely."

After a few moments, I spat some toothpaste into the sink. "Good. Because I shouldn't even be on the board if I can't relieve you of some of your fraternization duties." I watched Sarah through the mirror as she flopped down onto her back, releasing a dramatic sigh.

"When are you going to get it through your thick skull that you have as much expertise to serve on the Foundation's board of directors as any of us, maybe even more, given your SEC background? It's hardly just about having you fill in for me occasionally," she said to the ceiling. Then she lifted her head to look at me. "You make me crazy when you say things like that." She caught sight of my grin and saw I'd been teasing. I winked at her in the mirror and finished rinsing my mouth, which I quickly dried with a towel.

"Such is my intention." I flung myself onto the bed and straddled her, holding my weight on my hands and knees, peering down at her from above.

"Making me crazy? I didn't mean it as a compliment." She placed her hands around my waist and gave me a look of mock indignation.

I removed her hands and pushed them out to her sides, placing her in a cross position. Weaving my fingers with hers, I pressed our palms together and let my body weight pin her hands to the bed. Leaning down, I delicately traced her upper lip with my tongue, then followed suit with the lower one. "How crazy?" I murmured. As she surged up to kiss my mouth, I pulled back just out of reach. With a little mewling sound in protest, she dropped back onto the bed and her eyes began to burn with desire. I cocked an eyebrow and slowly lowered myself until I was barely touching her lips with mine.

"How crazy?" I asked again with my mouth hot against hers. I briefly shifted to my left leg and moved my right thigh between her legs before balancing my weight again. Moving my mouth to one of her ears, I caressed it slowly with my tongue. Her breathing turned ragged and her head moved slightly away from my lips as she struggled to handle the pleasing assault on her sensitive skin.

"You're killing me," Sarah said, before I claimed her mouth with mine and pushed into her with my thigh.

Her thigh-length, dark-blue satin robe was sexy as hell, given the expanse of tanned leg it revealed, but unwarranted for what I had in mind. I pulled my mouth away and tugged her hands, moving them, still trapped in mine, beneath her lovely ass.

"Do me a favor," I said as I used my teeth to pull on the satin belt that held her robe together, easily untying the simple knot.

"Mm-hmm?"

I used my nose to push each side of her robe off her body, exposing her completely. I trailed my tongue and lips across her flat stomach, then moved higher. As I circled a nipple with my tongue, Sarah arched toward me, begging for more contact.

"Keep your hands where they are," I said, before capturing a breast with my mouth. She inhaled sharply and her legs writhed beneath me. She tried to wriggle her hands away, but I continued to hold them beneath her.

"You've…you've got to be kidding."

I sucked and nipped and teased the one breast before shifting my attention to the other. "Unh-uh."

"You really are trying to kill me. I have to touch you."

"Later."

I pulled my hands from under Sarah and let them roam her masterful body: an intoxicating blend of muscle and softness, angle and curve, femininity and athleticism. I moved higher, leaving a path of lingering, wet kisses, and lost myself in the warmth of her neck before I had to have her luscious mouth again. Alternating between teasing and passionate, my kisses continued for a luxuriously long time as my wandering hand grazed coarse hair before moving lower to briefly trace the delicate folds hidden beneath.

"You're amazing." I kissed her deeply. When she moaned, the combination of sound and vibration that rumbled through her made me throb with desire, and I was soaked.

I shifted my mouth to her chin and across her neck, letting my hands rove along her stomach, shoulders, hips, thighs, and breasts, in no particular order. I trailed my lips across her stomach, licking along the tiny swell above her triangle. When my fingers returned to their earlier exquisite destination, another moan from her undid me, and at that moment, I had to taste her. I pushed her parted legs further astride of me and tongued the length of her. Sarah didn't usually orgasm without being simultaneously touched inside and out, but she liked to be taken to the brink with direct clitoral contact, and I was pleased for the opportunity to send her there.

As I stroked and sucked, her hands slid into my hair and I smiled at her inability to keep them beneath her. While continuing my ministrations, I reached up and curled my fingers in hers, and she tightened her grip on me as I brought her closer to the edge. Untangling my right hand from hers, I found her slick entrance and slid one finger easily inside. I slowly removed it and added another, before ever so gradually picking up the pace. Sarah began to buck against me with each penetrating stroke, encouraging my momentum. Soon she was moaning, and it didn't take long for her muscles to clench repeatedly and her hips to rise off the bed as I shattered her and she cried out in pleasure.

Some sated moments later, Sarah said, a little breathlessly, "Unbelievable. Come here, you." I crawled back up her body, planting little kisses along the way. Still sweating, I hovered above her on my elbows, gazing down upon her in wonder. I couldn't help but marvel at the many things that made up this incomparable woman: her beauty, her intellect, the vulnerability I wanted to believe she entrusted only to me.

She brushed some hair from my forehead and smiled at me affectionately, holding my face in her hands. "My hardworking gal," she said. Then she grinned devilishly, and this time when she surged up to meet my lips, I didn't pull away. She moved out from underneath me and quickly crawled atop my back, leaving me facedown on the bed. Settling her legs between mine, she used a knee to raise my leg past my hips and keep it there.

She purred into my ear. "My turn." Her voice was a low rumble that set my pulse racing. She kissed the sides and back of my neck. Then, without preamble, she inserted her right arm past my waist between my pelvis and the bed, coating her fingers in my wet center before circling my clit adroitly. Her mouth continued to cover my neck, back, and shoulders with warm, sensual kisses, and she used my body weight to increase the pressure where I needed her.

Suddenly she changed positions, mirroring with her left arm what she'd been doing with the right. From behind and underneath me with her right hand, she found me open and ready and entered me smoothly. She was no longer kissing me, needing to coordinate her movements to heighten my pleasure, but I wouldn't have been able to concentrate on enjoying it if she had been. As it was, I wasn't going to last much longer. I was pushing hard against her and couldn't get enough of her fingers thrusting into me.

I opened my legs still wider, and Sarah took advantage of the invitation. My body was humming with excitement. What she was doing to me felt incredible and I didn't want her to stop. And yet, with Sarah sending me into ecstasy, I couldn't hold out for much more. I was panting and moaning, and with one final shove of her hand, I tumbled over into orgasm, arching my back before dropping helplessly into the sheets.

Sarah crawled over me again and trailed her fingers along my back and shoulders, as she leaned into me and whispered. "God, I love making love to you." She kissed my ear and snuggled up next to me. I turned onto my side to face her, still pulsing from the after-effects of my climax.

"Lucky me," I said, kissing her mouth.

"Mmm. It's a massive turn-on."

"Is it?"

She raised her left eyebrow and nodded. "Mm-hmm."

I rolled onto my back and pulled her on top of me, kissing her thoroughly.

Then Sarah sat up, straddled my hips, and started caressing my breasts. "I've been neglectful." She rubbed her palms across my nipples before taking one into her mouth.

"Jesus." I was in awe of the sensations this woman could elicit in me. She teased and sucked and gently nibbled my aroused peaks until I was practically senseless. I wanted her mouth on me, but more than that, I wanted to be inside her again. Pushing up on my hands, I forced her up until she was kneeling on either side of me. I lightly tapped her right knee and said "lift" as I slid my left leg to the outside.

"What do you need, beautiful?" she asked as her fingers deftly took a deliciously familiar path along the inside of my thighs.

"I need…" I held myself up with one hand and brought my mouth to Sarah's for another dizzying kiss.

"Tell me." She stilled her movement but kept her hand where it was.

I moved my hand to her core and flicked my thumb across her clit. "I need to be inside you." I continued stroking with my thumb as I dipped my fingers into her wetness.

"And?" she asked breathlessly, her eyes fighting to stay open as she melted into my touch, lowering herself to give me better access. Her fingers restarted their movement. There hadn't been an "and," yet with her hand where it was, I knew what she wanted to hear. Obliging her in this small way was one of my favorite pastimes.

"I need you inside me." I was instantly filled by skillful fingers that made it extremely difficult for me to concentrate on my own duties. I brought our mouths together again as we both worked diligently to give the other what she needed.

Sarah broke away. "Harder. Take me harder, Cazz." I was nearly regretting our positions because I couldn't quite get the force I wanted, but it was difficult to be too upset given the incredible things she was doing to me. As I responded to the command, she, too, ratcheted up the pressure until we were both groaning and grinding together.

"You're making it…I can't…concentrate," I said.

"I'm…so close."

"Um-hmm." Suddenly my body clenched in the telltale signs of my impending climax, just as Sarah jerked against my hand. We both shuddered and fell onto the bed together, me on my back and Sarah on her stomach, partially lying on top of me.

"My God, you're incredible," she said, still working to catch her breath.

"I can't keep up with you."

"You just did." She gave me a wink, then rested her face in the crook of my neck.

"You're so beautiful." I kissed her head and pulled her closer.

"You're so biased."

"Just because I'm biased doesn't mean it's not true." I scooted down next to her, gently stroking her cheek, conveying my sincerity with my eyes.

"Well, I'm perfectly content to have that be your delusion, instead of, say, you seeing little green men or being told by God that you're the Second Coming."

"I may be delusional, but I'm quite sure the second coming I just experienced is altogether different than the one you're referring to."

She grew wide-eyed and smacked me on the shoulder. "You're horrible!"

"I am. In fact, I'm surprised you're not going to chaperone me this evening, given my propensity for bad behavior."

Sarah gathered me into her arms and kissed me. "You know full well you hold your own at those events, though I'm sorry I won't get to see how hot you look in that new dress of yours."

I was thinking she could see me in that dress if she invited me to stay over tonight, but kept it to myself. She'd already told me she wasn't sure how late she'd be out, and with my long night at the Foundation fund-raiser, it made perfect sense that this would be one of the nights we'd spend apart, she at her house and me at my apartment.

It was an ongoing internal struggle to not show disappointment when it came to wanting more of her time, especially time she spent working. I couldn't allow her to misinterpret that disappointment as my being upset or unhappy about time she dedicated to the Foundation. I also didn't want to scare her off. It wasn't hard to miss the fact that the few times I'd told Sarah I loved her, she hadn't reciprocated. I hadn't asked her how she felt, hadn't wanted to put her on the spot. I'd simply told her what I was feeling. But I often found myself clamping down on those words, avoiding their utterance, so Sarah wouldn't run from what was developing between us.

She'd already changed by agreeing to see me on a relatively consistent basis and by allowing herself to open up to me to the extent she had. I wasn't exactly content to move forward at her pace, but understood I needed to be patient if we were going to have any chance at a future together.

And I'd do anything for a future with Sarah.

"As for your propensity for bad behavior," Sarah said as she gently bit my lower lip, tugging it slightly before releasing me, "maybe you could enlighten me with further examples."

"Aren't you hungry?"

"Not for food," Sarah said with a glimmer in her eye.

Like I said, I wasn't a morning person, but somehow I was coping.

After my vivid memory flashed through my mind, I responded to Caitlin. "It's true that the cat is off trying to woo the CEO of Pipeline Technologies," with whatever means necessary, I thought unflatteringly, with a pang of jealousy. Although Sarah had unassailable integrity when it came to the Foundation and would never purposefully scope out a personal *distraction* while entertaining a potential donor, she'd met her former fiancé at a Foundation fund-raiser. It wasn't out of the realm of possibility—hell, it might even be probable—that while working, without any intention on her part, she could meet someone else who intrigued her as much as her fiancé once had. She spent a significant amount of time at fancy country clubs, dining at fine restaurants, and entertaining at various cultural events. In these travels, she was bound to stumble upon one eligible bachelor after another, many of whom could offer her any number of things I'd never be able to: wealth, celebrity, connections.

Though I knew she was working tonight, I still experienced an occasional proprietorial flare-up, however inappropriate, when thinking about the company she kept. I certainly had no claim to stake. After all, Sarah and I never talked about any kind of future together and never broached the subject of monogamy. We spent much of our non-working time together and communicated well enough. But certain aspects of my job required secrecy, and, likewise, I assumed Sarah didn't tell me everything. I was happy to get whatever time with her I could, and my acceptance onto the Foundation's board freed her up more nights because I could stand in for her at functions like these, allowing her to concurrently court prospective donors instead of taking extra nights to do so.

"So you're stuck with me," I said to Caitlin.

She delivered a mock sigh. "I'll suffer through."

"Excuse me a second," I told her before gently grabbing the arm of a middle-aged man passing by with his female companion. "Mr. Crawford."

The man turned to me with a practiced semi-smile.

"I wanted to introduce myself." I held out my hand. "Cassidy Warner."

His face relaxed as recognition dawned, and he shook my hand. "Ah, Miss Warner, I thought that might be you. It's so good to finally meet you. I'm sorry I wasn't able to attend the last board meeting in person. I'm very pleased you've decided to join us."

"Please, call me Cassidy."

"And you must call me Alan." He nodded to the attractive redhead on his arm. "This is my wife, Marianne. Marianne, this is Cassidy Warner, our newest board member."

His wife extended her hand and I took it, both of us exchanging pleasantries. I turned to Caitlin, prompting her to move forward. "And this is Caitlin Winters, one of our—"

"Hello, darling," Marianne kissed Caitlin on the cheek. "We know very well who this is," she said with amusement as her husband gave Caitlin the same greeting. Marianne delivered a mock warning to me with her index finger. "Be careful with that one."

Caitlin touched her fingers to her own chest and offered a feigned "*moi?*" gesture.

"Seems you have something of a reputation," I said to Caitlin, pretending I didn't know she was a shark amid chummy waters.

She smiled. "I'm happy to let you find out for yourself whether it's deserved."

"She likes to keep all the pretty, unattached women to herself," Alan said teasingly while pulling Marianne a little closer.

Caitlin scowled, which I wasn't sure related to his statement or to his keeping her away from his wife.

"Without Sarah in attendance, I appreciate you stepping up to play hostess. I've been noticing you for the past hour and you seem pretty comfortable with this rather unofficial aspect of your board duties," Alan said.

"Thank you. I'm certainly not as adept at it as Sarah, and definitely not as charming, but I'm trying."

"Well, we've been fortunate to have her with us since she was a teenager. She's grown up in this environment and has had lots more practice."

"The Foundation's just as fortunate to have one of our nation's most notable philanthropists on our board," I said, indicating Alan with an upturned palm. "You and your wife are an inspiration for children's hospital foundations around the world, and it's an honor to meet you both. I'm very much looking forward to working together."

"Ah, and you've done your homework, too." Alan grinned. "I'm impressed."

Marianne threaded her arm through his elbow and smiled at Caitlin and me. "Before my husband's head swells to the size of

Sacramento, we're going to continue to mingle. So nice to meet you, Cassidy. Great to see you again as always, Caitlin."

I turned back to Caitlin after the Crawfords were out of earshot. Her normally flirtatious smile had dissolved into a slight frown.

"Don't they know you're together?" Caitlin asked.

"Who?"

"You and Sarah."

The question confused and surprised me. I pondered it a few moments, unsure how to answer. Caitlin had been one of the first people Sarah told that we were seeing each other, but I was pretty sure Sarah had merely wanted to keep Caitlin's hands off me rather than make some sort of declaration that we were a couple. Of course, no woman, spoken for or single, gay or straight, was off limits in Caitlin's mind, but she held a certain respect for Sarah. Despite her unrelenting flirtation, she would probably never take her overtures with me to another level.

"Well, first of all, it's not at all relevant to my duties as a board member. And second, I'm not sure we're quite at that level," I said honestly.

"You're not sure you and I are quite at the level of talking about you and Sarah, or you're not sure you and Sarah are together?"

"The latter." Then I thought about it a little more. "Both, I guess, because she and I don't even have those conversations. But I'd be thrilled if you were right."

"Trust me, honey. I've never seen her regard anyone as possessively as she does you. You are definitely off the market, which I personally find greatly annoying." Caitlin arched an eyebrow before grinning widely.

Before I could respond, Caitlin's eyes flicked past my shoulder to the ballroom doors and widened. When I saw what had captured her attention, the wolf whistle she let fly could have just as easily come from me. I was in wholehearted agreement.

"Holy good God," I think I said aloud, without meaning to.

Sarah entered the room, commanding the attention of nearly everyone in the immediate vicinity. She wore a stunning number that balanced elegance and sophistication with dazzling sensuality.

It was a black, one-shoulder satin dress pulled in over her right hip, its fabric cinched up to highlight her curves, the cinch affixed with a rhinestone brooch matching the one on her shoulder. A thigh-high slit cut toward the brooch exposed the toned, sun-kissed leg beneath, and her wavy auburn hair fell loose behind her shoulders. But what put her outfit over the top, almost literally, were the five-inch heels that made her tower over nearly everyone in the room.

Everyone except her date.

Sarah was linking elbows with an incredibly attractive man in his mid-thirties. He was impeccably dressed in a black tuxedo. Instead of a bow tie, he wore a dark-gray patterned tie with matching vest and handkerchief. Classy. He had thick dark hair that seemed made for a woman to run her fingers through. His blue eyes were a few shades darker than Sarah's, and he was tall, at least six-five. He was gorgeous. And seeing him walk in with Sarah disrupted my heartbeat. She wasn't supposed to be here tonight, yet here she was with a black-haired version of Captain friggin' America.

But damn it all, when my eyes refocused on Sarah seconds later, I couldn't help but smile. No wonder she'd decided to show up. Would any man or woman be able to deny her if she asked whether he or she might consider contributing to the Foundation's latest efforts? It seemed doubtful that Mr. tall, dark, and handsome would be able to. They were both beaming with delight—the picture-perfect couple that may as well have just been joined in holy matrimony and turned to walk down the aisle as husband and wife.

"I thought she wasn't coming tonight," Caitlin said.

I blinked several times before pulling my gaze from the pretty couple. "Guess she got an offer she couldn't refuse." I regretted the comment instantly. I had a job to do, which didn't include speculating about Sarah's unexpected arrival. After gulping, rather than sipping, my beverage, I affected a serenity I wasn't feeling and returned to the safer ground of Foundation business. "That is, I'm sure whatever brought her here must mean good news." By practicing with Caitlin, maybe I could believe it myself.

At that moment, a man in a gray suit walked up to me. "Pardon me. It's Miss Warner, isn't it?"

I nodded, noting his MANAGER lapel pin. "Is there a problem?"

The man seemed hesitant to respond, as if he didn't know precisely what to say. "Not exactly, ma'am, but I was told to contact you in case any, uh, issues arose with the guest accommodations." It took me several seconds to understand he was referring to the block of rooms the Foundation had booked for out-of-town guests wishing to stay overnight. "Would you follow me, please?" he asked.

"Sure," I said, with more confidence than I felt. What did I know about it? And how could I fix anything better than this gentleman could?

"Right this way." He offered Caitlin an apology. "I'm sorry to interrupt, ma'am."

I shrugged to Caitlin and handed her my glass. "See you soon," I told her, and followed the manager.

As we walked toward the elevators, the man introduced himself as Henry Beldon and issued more apologies for hijacking my evening. During our ride up to the 53rd floor, the second from the top, he vaguely explained he was in an unusual situation and needed to sort things out with a Foundation representative. He said he typically dealt with Miss Perkins on such matters, but she had informed him to contact me in her absence. Having noticed her, I thought briefly about telling him he could take the matter up with her, but silenced myself. After all, I'd offered to be here and expected to take the reins from Sarah tonight, and it shouldn't matter that she'd changed her plans. Only if it turned out I couldn't handle the situation would I have Henry contact her.

I followed him to one of the few-and-far-between doors, thinking the suites on this floor must be huge, having noticed the brass placard indicating suites 5301 and 5302 to the left, 5303 and 5304 to the right. Once he used the key card to suite 5303, he pushed the door open and held it for me. As I walked into the spacious, beautifully appointed room, he flipped a switch that lit up the wall sconces. I took in the large living room, full bar and media section. I peered into the bedroom and stood amazed by the dark, rich wood with a highly intricate pattern on the king-size bed frame and nightstands. Next to the bed, a small rolling cart held a champagne bucket with a bottle of Dom Perignon. Was this how the Foundation would be greeting all its overnight guests tonight? I walked to the floor-to-ceiling windows and gazed down at the city lights below. Considering there was apparently some kind of trouble I had to deal with, I was surprised by Henry's silence. I faced him and shook my head.

"Henry, this is spectacular. What could possibly be the trouble?" My confusion grew as he backed out of the suite.

"I'm sorry, Miss Warner." He gave me a slight bow once he reached the door. "If you will allow me a few moments, it will all be clear soon enough. I promise. Stay, please." Then he departed and the door clicked shut behind him.

This is so bizarre. It felt strange to be suddenly standing in an expensive hotel suite, waiting to discover some major problem. Was it the plumbing? Had one of our guests been caught smoking in a non-smoking room? Had the Foundation reserved too few rooms and it would fall to me to inform the unlucky folks and find them accommodations elsewhere? Wasn't Henry experienced in handling such matters?

I wandered back to the bedroom to peek into the adjacent bathroom. I flipped on the lights and stared at the large Jacuzzi tub, double sinks, and eight-showerheads shower. Nice.

As I eyed the numerous massage spray settings, an image of a naked Sarah and her dark-haired companion lathering one another with soapy caresses—their lower bodies masked behind a Captain America shield painted onto the glass shower door—abruptly popped into my head and made me flinch in horror.

I swiftly turned off the lights and returned to the living room. Normally imperceptible, my uncertainties regarding my relationship with Sarah were suddenly conspicuous and manifesting themselves in bizarre ways. I needed to get a grip. I rid myself of the unsettling vision by wondering what Henry was up to.

Hearing a soft knock at the door, I called out, "Come in," appreciating Henry's courtesy in not simply using his master key again. Moments passed without any sound. There was another soft knock. I walked to the door and opened it, catching my breath at the sight of Sarah, all ten feet of her (or so it seemed), standing in the doorway, smiling shyly down at me. In reality, with my own heels, the height difference was only a few inches, but her bared leg somehow accentuated it.

"Hi," she said. "Can I come in?"

"I…uh, hi. I don't know. I don't know if I'm supposed to let anyone in. I don't even know what I'm doing here," I said dumbly with my hand on the doorknob.

She raised an eyebrow in amusement.

Then it struck me to ask, "What are you doing here?"

She smiled, more broadly this time. "I heard you were here. I think it's okay if I come in. The Foundation does a ton of business with this hotel, so they know me around here." She winked.

I moved out of the way to let her in and she brushed by me, taking a few steps into the living room before turning around. I closed the door and stood facing her. Gawking at her, really. Just because my imagination was running wild didn't mean I couldn't admire this very real, glorious woman. I licked my lips and shook my head slightly.

"You look…" I couldn't think of words adequate to describe her magnificence. "Wow," I said, displaying astounding command of the language.

Her gaze unhurriedly roamed my body. "Wow, yourself. Definitely digging the new dress." She took a step toward me.

"Wait." I held up my hand, continuing to appreciate the loveliness before me. Compliments still didn't come easily to me, but if ever one was called for, it was now. "Wow doesn't do you justice. You're the most breathtakingly beautiful woman I've ever seen. I'm…I'm completely blown away by you right now." It was the truth.

Sarah looked down at her dress and back to me a little sheepishly. "Thank you, sweetheart. I thought you might like it."

The term of endearment thrilled me. She'd used others, like "beautiful" or "sunshine," but none quite so intimate. It made me want to tell her I loved her, but once again I held back, trying to keep things light, mindful not to force the issue or make her feel obliged to respond.

Instead, I eyed her shoes. "And I see you're wearing my favorite designer: Nine-one-one. Which is who you'd be dialing if I tried to wear those."

Sarah chuckled, encircled my waist, and pulled me to her.

"Before you kiss me, I should confess I'm expecting a man named Henry to come into this room at any minute, which I'm going to find difficult to explain," I said, putting my arms around her shoulders and enjoying her strange height.

"I know." Sarah made me weak in the knees with the way she kissed me then. When she stopped, she regarded me with incredible tenderness. "I asked him to ask you up here. I was hoping we might have something to celebrate tonight," she said before again claiming my mouth with hers, causing delightful fluttering in my abdomen. She pulled back and scrutinized me. "What's wrong? You look…" She cocked her head slightly. "You look wary. Are you okay?"

I nodded. "Just happy."

"That's happy?" Sarah studied my face.

It was highly unnerving how well she could read me. She was right: what with the disheartening imaginings besetting me, happy was probably overstating it.

"I'm happy you're here," *and not with Captain America or anyone else.* I was trying to focus on the fact that Sarah was indeed here with me—*me*—and had even roped in an accomplice to arrange it. And I'd spoken in earnest. No matter my brain's conjurings, I was happiest when I was with Sarah. Time spent in her company was easily my favorite.

Changing subjects to avoid further examination, I asked, "What are we celebrating?"

She took my hand and led me to the bedroom. "Depends. Ah, good, it's here." Dropping my hand, she removed the champagne from the ice water and wiped it with the towel that lay atop the cart.

"Depends?" I asked as Sarah started to open the Dom Perignon. "I would hope it's something a little more definitive if you're going to open *that*."

"Oh, we're definitely celebrating. The question is whether we're celebrating one thing or two." She jimmied out the cork, causing the delightful popping sound that foretold the delicious bubbly action we were about to enjoy.

"Okay. I'll bite. What's the thing we know we're celebrating?" I asked as she began to pour.

She finished filling the glasses, grabbed both flutes, and handed one to me. She took my other hand and gently tugged me toward the window so we could take in the city lights. After several moments of silence, she drew a deep breath and spoke quietly toward the window.

"The Kindle Hope Foundation is officially going to be one of only three organizations that Pipeline Technologies will support next year as part of its one-percent-of-profits giving program. And unless their program charter changes, we can expect the relationship to last well into the future." She turned to me with an expression of satisfaction and gratitude.

It took me several seconds to digest what she'd said, but as I recognized the pride on her face, it hit me. "Wait a minute. Pipeline's profit was something like six *billion* last year. That would mean…" I did some quick math. "That would mean, Jesus, twenty million dollars to the Foundation annually!"

She nodded and smiled.

"Oh. My. God! No way!" I nearly jumped up and down.

"Way."

I threw my free arm around her for a hug, trying not to spill our champagne. "Oh, sweetie, I'm so proud of you. My God. I can't believe it." I pulled back and beamed at her, holding out my glass. "Your accomplishment calls for a hell of a lot more than a toast, but for now, cheers to the most impressive woman on the planet."

She gave me a dubious look but clinked glasses. After a couple sips of champagne she said, "I was so excited by the news, I couldn't wait until tomorrow to tell you. So I called Henry while we were en route and asked him to put some champagne in one of the rooms and figure out a way to get you up here." Her eyes gleamed with mischief.

"We?"

"Oh. Philip and I." She could tell I wasn't connecting the dots. "Philip as in Philip and Donna Landrey. Philip's the CEO of Pipeline and Donna's his wife. After we sealed the deal with a handshake over dinner, I asked if they had any interest in getting gussied up and joining me here, since I wanted them to meet some of the Foundation staff and board members and get to know us better. Donna has an early morning tomorrow, but Philip said yes, and an hour later, here we are. I had just enough time to introduce him to the Crawfords before I ducked out to come find you."

My relief about Captain Philip was probably palpable, but I tried to feign nonchalance. "We should go back downstairs so you can introduce us. You should be entertaining him, not here with me."

"Don't be silly. I'm sure he's had enough of my company tonight, and since he's here without Donna, I have a feeling he'll be more than happy to pretend he's available for the evening. Even though he's very much in love with his wife, I'm sure he'll enjoy a little attention. You should see him." She rolled her eyes. "You should see both of them. They're the most ravishing couple ever. Like they both stepped off the runway at a Madrid fashion show."

I sipped my champagne, annoyed with myself for having thought Sarah could show up with a date at an event she knew I'd be attending. As if she didn't have class or tact. Iago was right: jealousy was indeed a green-eyed monster. Enough about Philip.

"Not that anything could come close to topping your news about Pipeline Technologies, but you did mention there might be another thing to celebrate."

"I don't know. I think Pipeline could pale in comparison." Sarah kept her eyes on mine while she tossed back the remaining liquid in her glass. She refilled it and set it down, regarding me with an uncertain expression that was unusual for her. Biting her bottom lip, she surveyed the room. "Hmm." She walked to the entryway between the bedroom and living room, scanning both areas.

"What are you looking for?" I asked after a few seconds. She wasn't much of a drinker but she'd finished her champagne quickly. Was she gathering the courage to say something I didn't want to hear?

She eyed me for several moments, crossed the room in a few elegant strides, and set my glass down. Pulling me to sit next to her on the edge of the bed, she held my hands.

"I don't know how to say this, or where, but I do know what I'm looking for," Sarah said as she studied our hands and rubbed my fingers and knuckles with her thumbs.

My delight at the Pipeline news quickly dissipated. I wasn't her girlfriend, so she couldn't break up with me, exactly, but was she trying to find an easy way to let me down? That didn't seem likely, did it? We'd shared a brilliant morning together and hadn't had any sort of argument since. Not that we ever did. And I was the first person she elected to share the Pipeline news with. Plus there was supposed to be something else to be celebrating, wasn't there? It wouldn't be like her to break out some seriously nice champagne moments before ending our relationship.

I ceased my internal inquiries. Whatever was on her mind, good or bad, I had to let her know she could talk to me. She already had my heart, so it wasn't as if she could hurt me any less simply because I might not want to hear what was on her mind. I refused to let my insecurities about what we were to each other—no, what I was to her—prevent me from having the fortitude to listen openly to whatever she had to say.

I gently placed my hand under her chin, tilting it up to get her to look at me. "Sweetheart, whatever it is, you can tell me." She still wouldn't meet my eyes, which troubled me, but I didn't want to press. Opting to let her tell me when she was ready, I caressed her cheek for several moments before taking her hands again.

When she finally brought her eyes to mine, they were moist and full of emotion. She gave me a small smile but her lips were trembling. "I…I wanted to thank you for being so patient with me," she said in a quiet voice. "You haven't pushed me into something I wasn't ready for, you haven't asked me to define our relationship, you haven't once made me feel guilty for any of the time I've spent working, and you've been more supportive of me than I deserve. By not telling you how I feel, I haven't made it easy for you to be with me, and I'm sorry."

Was she crazy? I had to immediately quash her ridiculous notion that she made it hard to be with her. There was no place I'd rather be. "Sarah, being with you is the easiest, most natural thing in the—"

She pressed a finger to my lips. "You know I'm right."

I had to concede that wondering how she felt about me wasn't supremely reassuring, so perhaps her notion wasn't completely crazy. But thanking me and apologizing was starting to sound like good-bye, making whether she was right or not moot. I redoubled my efforts to gather courage to hear her out and simply nodded.

She walked to the window, which seemed like a bad sign.

"You were right," she said. "What you said a few months ago. I *have* been afraid to love again. But it's more than that." She faced me, protectively wrapping her arms around her waist. "I've been afraid to love *you* again. You, specifically. I fell for you in high school, but like you, back then I didn't realize it for what it was. All I knew was you were who I wanted to spend time with, and when you left and never contacted me…I felt some part of me had died. I know you've explained it to me and I understand why you did what you did. What I'm trying to say is that you terrify me because I feel…" Sarah's voice cracked. "I've been down this path."

It dawned on me for the very first time that I had hurt Sarah. Deeply. I couldn't believe I'd been so blind. She'd felt the connection we'd shared at Claiborne every bit as much as I had. No wonder, once I started working at the Foundation, she'd tried to distance herself from me after our first dinner at her house. No wonder, after delivering her searing kisses in the hotel room, she'd shut down emotionally after I told her I wouldn't hurt her. No wonder she'd seemed so sad when I'd ascertained how much more she cared about grant-making than fund-raising, because while I knew her better than anyone else—the real Sarah, not the one-dimensional trophy others found attractive—she wasn't about to let me hurt her again. No wonder she'd had difficulty trusting me, even when she'd had some hint as to the reasons I hadn't come clean about my role at the Foundation. It made perfect sense. She'd been conflicted about letting me back into her life.

And she'd been letting me in anyway.

Not for the first time, I was completely in awe of this woman. Here I'd been thinking she'd made some strides by letting me in as much as she had. But I'd underestimated her. Sarah hadn't only made strides: she'd moved mountains. If I'd hurt her like her former fiancé had, she shouldn't even be speaking to me, let alone dating me. She'd been giving me a chance—a second chance—and all I'd been doing was feeling grateful for getting what I'd uncharitably thought were mere bits and pieces of her: pieces that were nice to see and hold, but ultimately not vital. Now I'd learned I was responsible for inflicting onto Sarah some of the very scars I'd been trying to pry back open.

How could she ever forgive me?

Maybe she couldn't. Maybe that's what she was alluding to. Maybe she couldn't go down this path again.

Please, love. We've come so far. Please don't walk away now.

I couldn't bear the distance between us and met Sarah at the window. She didn't seem ready for me to touch her, but I stood before her and reached out a hand, hoping she'd take it. She did, and when she continued speaking, it was barely above a whisper.

"I saw it another way, too, back then. When I was with you, a whole other part of me was alive. That part of me is alive again, and I don't want to lose it. I keep thinking…" She swallowed hard. "I keep thinking if I don't tell you how I feel about you, I won't risk my heart again. But not only is that unfair to you, it's untrue. You already have it."

A tear rolled down her cheek, and tears started to well up in my eyes, too. Sarah continued. "I'm hopelessly in love with you, Cazz. I can't stand the thought that I might lose you because I never summoned the courage to tell you how I feel." She wiped a tear with her finger. "I don't want to be with anyone else," she whispered. And then, so quietly I almost didn't hear her, Sarah said, "Please tell me you feel the same."

I stepped to her and wrapped her in my arms. I didn't know whether I was crying from relief or joy, but my throat was so tight I could barely swallow, let alone talk. This amazing woman was risking her heart in the worst way: she was willing to believe once more in someone who had previously disappointed her. She was forgiving me and trusting me. Loving me.

"Yes. Yes. Yes. Of course I love you, sweetheart. Always you. Only you." I felt her staggered intakes of breath and wasn't sure if she was crying from relief or leftover anxiety. I'd never seen Sarah more vulnerable. I pivoted onto the balls of my feet and gently kissed her lips. Having been there myself, I knew how hard it had been for her to tell me how she felt. I was overwhelmed by gratitude and humbled by love. I wiped a tear from my eye and brushed one falling down Sarah's cheek.

I pulled her tightly to me once again. "I love you so much, Sarah. Thank you for telling me." We kissed sweetly, and when we pulled apart, we both sighed, our hearts full. "One last thing." I dashed to the table for our champagne, then quickly offered her flute to her. Once she took it, I held my drink in one hand and her hand in the other.

"You're right." I beamed. "As special as the Pipeline deal is, it's small compared to the other thing we're celebrating." I held up my glass, but since it had been Sarah's idea, I let her do the honors.

Smiling, she squeezed my hand and raised her flute to mine. "To us."

Who would believe that a two-letter word could instill so much joy in a person?

"To us," I said, as I clinked my glass to Sarah's and linked my heart with hers forever.

About the Author

Heather Blackmore works in finance and accounting for technology startups, where she puts in her two cents then counts them. In a seemingly counterintuitive move, she got her MSA and CPA with the goal of one day being able to work part-time so she could write. She's finally living her dream, thankful for however long it lasts. *Like Jazz* is her first novel.

Heather is married and lives in California. She spends much of her leisure time reading and writing, interspersed with an occasional burst of exercise. She enjoys theater, traveling, hiking, and trying new vegetarian recipes. When she's home, a four-legged friend is always nearby.

Visit www.heatherblackmore.com or drop her a line at heather @heatherblackmore.com.

Books Available from Bold Strokes Books

Love and Devotion by Jove Belle. KC Hall trips her way through life, stumbling into an affair with a married bombshell twice her age. Thankfully, her best friend, Emma Reynolds, is there to show her the true meaning of Love and Devotion. (978-1-60282-965-7)

Rush by Carsen Taite. Murder, secrets, and romance combine to create the ultimate rush. (978-1-60282-966-4)

The Shoal of Time by J.M. Redmann. It sounded too easy. Micky Knight is reluctant to take the case because the easy ones often turn into the hard ones, and the hard ones turn into the dangerous ones. In this one, easy turns hard without warning. (978-1-60282-967-1)

In Between by Jane Hoppen. At the age of 14, Sophie Schmidt discovers that she was born an intersexual baby and sets off on a journey to find her place in a world that denies her true existence. (978-1-60282-968-8)

Secret Lies by Amy Dunne. While fleeing from her abuser, Nicola Jackson bumps into Jenny O'Connor, and their unlikely friendship quickly develops into a blossoming romance—but when it comes down to a matter of life or death, are they both willing to face their fears? (978-1-60282-970-1)

Under Her Spell by Maggie Morton. The magic of love brought Terra and Athene together, but now a magical quest stands between them—a quest for Athene's hand in marriage. Will their passion keep them together, or will stronger magic tear them apart? (978-1-60282-973-2)

Homestead by Radclyffe. R. Clayton Sutter figures getting NorthAm Fuel's newest refinery operational on a rolling tract of land in Upstate New York should take a month or two, but then, she hadn't counted on local resistance in the form of vandalism, petitions, and one furious farmer named Tess Rogers. (978-1-60282-956-5)

Battle of Forces: Sera Toujours by Ali Vali. Kendal and Piper return to New Orleans to start the rest of eternity together, but the return of an old enemy makes their peaceful reunion short-lived, especially when they join forces with the new queen of the vampires. (978-1-60282-957-2)

How Sweet It Is by Melissa Brayden. Some things are better than chocolate. Molly O'Brien enjoys her quiet life running the bakeshop in a small town. When the beautiful Jordan Tuscana returns home, Molly can't deny the attraction—or the stirrings of something more. (978-1-60282-958-9)

The Missing Juliet: A Fisher Key Adventure by Sam Cameron. A teenage detective and her friends search for a kidnapped Hollywood star in the Florida Keys. (978-1-60282-959-6)

Amor and More: Love Everafter edited by Radclyffe and Stacia Seaman. Rediscover favorite couples as Bold Strokes Books authors reveal glimpses of life and love beyond the honeymoon in short stories featuring main characters from favorite BSB novels. (978-1-60282-963-3)

First Love by CJ Harte. Finding true love is hard enough, but for Jordan Thompson, daughter of a conservative president, it's challenging, especially when that love is a female rodeo cowgirl. (978-1-60282-949-7)

Pale Wings Protecting by Lesley Davis. Posing as a couple to investigate the abduction of infants, Special Agent Blythe Kent and Detective Daryl Chandler find themselves drawn into a battle over the innocents, with demons on one side and the unlikeliest of protectors on the other. (978-1-60282-964-0)

Mounting Danger by Karis Walsh. Sergeant Rachel Bryce, an outcast on the police force, is put in charge of the department's newly formed mounted division. Can she and polo champion Callan Lanford resist their growing attraction as they struggle to safeguard the disaster-prone unit? (978-1-60282-951-0)

Meeting Chance by Jennifer Lavoie. When man's best friend turns on Aaron Cassidy, the teen keeps his distance until fate puts Chance in his hands. (978-1-60282-952-7)

At Her Feet by Rebekah Weatherspoon. Digital marketing producer Suzanne Kim knows she has found the perfect love in her new mistress Pilar, but before they can make the ultimate commitment, Suzanne's professional life threatens to disrupt their perfectly balanced bliss. (978-1-60282-948-0)

Show of Force by AJ Quinn. A chance meeting between navy pilot Evan Kane and correspondent Tate McKenna takes them on a roller-coaster ride where the stakes are high, but the reward is higher: a chance at love. (978-1-60282-942-8)

Clean Slate by Andrea Bramhall. Can Erin and Morgan work through their individual demons to rediscover their love for each other, or are the unexplainable wounds too deep to heal? (978-1-60282-943-5)

Hold Me Forever by D. Jackson Leigh. An investigation into illegal cloning in the quarter horse racing industry threatens to destroy the growing attraction between Georgia debutante Mae St. John and Louisiana horse trainer Whit Casey. (978-1-60282-944-2)

Trusting Tomorrow by PJ Trebelhorn. Funeral director Logan Swift thinks she's perfectly happy with her solitary life devoted to helping others cope with loss until Brooke Collier moves in next door to care for her elderly grandparents. (978-1-60282-891-9)

Forsaking All Others by Kathleen Knowles. What if what you think you want is the opposite of what makes you happy? (978-1-60282-892-6)

Exit Wounds by VK Powell. When Officer Loane Landry falls in love with ATF informant Abigail Mancuso, she realizes that nothing is as it seems—not the case, not her lover, not even the dead. (978-1-60282-893-3)

Dirty Power by Ashley Bartlett. Cooper's been through hell and back, and she's still broke and on the run. But at least she found the twins. They'll keep her alive. Right? (978-1-60282-896-4)

The Rarest Rose by I. Beacham. After a decade of living in her beloved house, Ele disturbs its past and finds her life being haunted by the presence of a ghost who will show her that true love never dies. (978-1-60282-884-1)

Code of Honor by Radclyffe. The face of terror is hard to recognize—especially when it's homegrown. The next book in the Honor series. (978-1-60282-885-8)

Does She Love You? by Rachel Spangler. When Annabelle and Davis find out they are both in a relationship with the same woman, it leaves them facing life-altering questions about trust, redemption, and the possibility of finding love in the wake of betrayal. (978-1-60282-886-5)

The Road to Her by KE Payne. Sparks fly when actress Holly Croft, star of UK soap Portobello Road, meets her new on-screen love interest, the enigmatic and sexy Elise Manford. (978-1-60282-887-2)

Shadows of Something Real by Sophia Kell Hagin. Trying to escape flashbacks and nightmares, ex-POW Jamie Gwynmorgan stumbles into the heart of former Red Cross worker Adele Sabellius and uncovers a deadly conspiracy against everything and everyone she loves. (978-1-60282-889-6)

Date with Destiny by Mason Dixon. When sophisticated bank executive Rashida Ivey meets unemployed blue collar worker Destiny Jackson, will her life ever be the same? (978-1-60282-878-0)

The Devil's Orchard by Ali Vali. Cain and Emma plan a wedding before the birth of their third child while Juan Luis is still lurking, and as Cain plans for his death, an unexpected visitor arrives and challenges her belief in her father, Dalton Casey. (978-1-60282-879-7)

Secrets and Shadows by L.T. Marie. A bodyguard and the woman she protects run from a madman and into each other's arms. (978-1-60282-880-3)

Change Horizons: Three Novellas by Gun Brooke. Three stories of courageous women who dare to love as they fight to claim a future in a hostile universe. (978-1-60282-881-0)

Scarlet Thirst by Crin Claxton. When hot, feisty Rani meets cool, vampire Rob, one lifetime isn't enough, and the road from human to vampire is shorter than you think… (978-1-60282-856-8)

Battle Axe by Carsen Taite. How close is too close? Bounty hunter Luca Bennett will soon find out. (978-1-60282-871-1)

Improvisation by Karis Walsh. High school geometry teacher Jan Carroll thinks she's figured out the shape of her life and her future, until graphic artist and fiddle player Tina Nelson comes along and teaches her to improvise. (978-1-60282-872-8)

For Want of a Fiend by Barbara Ann Wright. Without her Fiendish power, can Princess Katya and her consort Starbride stop a magic-wielding madman from sparking an uprising in the kingdom of Farraday? (978-1-60282-873-5)

Broken in Soft Places by Fiona Zedde. The instant Sara Chambers meets the seductive and sinful Merille Thompson, she falls hard, but knowing the difference between love and a dangerous, all-consuming desire is just one of the lessons Sara must learn before it's too late. (978-1-60282-876-6)

Healing Hearts by Donna K. Ford. Running from tragedy, the women of Willow Springs find that with friendship, there is hope, and with love, there is everything. (978-1-60282-877-3)